Ashes

Ashes

Matthew Crow

Legend Press

Independent Book Publisher

Legend Press Ltd, 2 London Wall Buildings,
London EC2M 5UU
info@legend-paperbooks.co.uk
www.legendpress.co.uk

British Library Cataloguing in Publication Data available.

ISBN 978-1-9065582-0-8

Set in Times
Printed by JF Print Ltd., Sparkford.

Cover designed by Gudrun Jobst
www.yotedesign.com

Legend Press
Independent Book Publisher

To my Dad

Acknowledgements

Dad, Annie, Nigel, Sophie, Luke, Jess, Jenny, and all at
Legend Press. With a special thanks to Broo Doherty.

Chapter One

It ran out of sight.

"Get it!" Jimmy squealed at Bobby, tottering across the curb towards their prey. A small, shabby cat with a grey streak above its right eye ran forwards and snuck through a torn wire fence. The boys pushed through the same gap, widening it with their bodies, pressing their stomachs and limbs against the jagged mesh. Nylon snags of their clothes caught and clicked on some of the sharper spokes. The concrete posts scratched white marks into the soft palms of their hands.

The fence was tall and frail but imposing – the sort of barrier that could physically be crossed yet seldom was. It separated the back end of the estate from the rest of the world. From civilisation, snider neighbours would say. The wire was gapped and broken and the concrete crumbling and vandalised, swimming in a sea of litter and broken glass. On a tattered car bonnet that rested against the fence the words 'Fucking Filth' had been sprayed in neon pink paint. A vague representation of a policeman spewing non-specific fluids accompanied the text. For all their fragility the pillars stood tall, meaning that whatever the weather there were always shadows cast upon these streets.

They ran on across muddy grasslands away from the estate. They had not planned their attack; it was simply a spur of the moment decision – shared intuition on seeing the creature;

something to do. The greenery itself had turned a dank, brutish yellow that led from the estate like dinner in reverse after a heavy night out. The air of another grey September made the whole expanse wither and sag. Sporadic onyx-patched sparkled throughout the field, remnants from a bonfire or car burnout, and glistened in the silvery light like false promises.

"Come on, there it is... under the brown one." Jimmy's vowels hardened and swapped around one another, making his prepubescent voice sound sweet and unthreatening.

A ginger cat sprang to its feet and darted in front of them, away form the allotment and out of sight, leaving its friend to fend for himself. Jimmy picked up a stone from the floor.

"Do it then!" Bobby shouted.

"What you gonna do about it if I don't?" Again his vowels stretched and rearranged themselves effortlessly. The 'o' of 'Do' became a long, syrupy 'eee' and the usually soft, rounded ending to 'about' climaxed into a jagged crescendo. 'Ooooot' it said. Word endings stopped short and the beginnings and middles remained unformed; half words, spirits of sounds, as though Jimmy's tongue had been paralysed. This was not an affliction specific to Jimmy, however, but the Geordie tongue in all its glory.

"I'll give you a tab if your finish it off." He said taking three cigarettes from his top pocket "Nicked them off me mam last night. She reckons it was Aunty Alison."

"Yeah right!"

"I will!"

"Fucking right!"

The allotments had been all but abandoned save for the occasional squatter or when used as a hiding place by some of the local pharmaceutical experts. And enthusiasm for maintaining vegetable patches had dipped somewhat among the residents themselves, meaning the once vibrant plot had been left to shrivel and rot.

Jimmy looked beneath the shed; the cat cowered behind a narrow patch of grass. He made a barking sound. The cat jumped in shock and sprang forward. They followed it stealthily, its sleek body winding in and out of daylight, seeking survival amid the dark shade of the delicate wooden structures. They reached the end of the line and the cat stopped still beneath the last shed, a particularly unwelcoming, tar black square with just one small window encased in dirt and mould. Bobby took a step back while Jimmy gripped his stone tighter and ducked so that his head was beneath the shed. The cat looked directly into his eyes, struggling to gain some empathy between hunter and hunted. Jimmy paused for a moment, locked in the black gaze of a helpless creature.

"Psss, psss, psss," he beckoned, stretching out the hand which held the stone, teasing his fingers together to endear the creature further. The cat stirred, curious as to its change in prospects. Slowly but cautiously it edged forward, first just a nose, then a head, then its neck, followed by a small, smooth, ripple of a step in Jimmy's direction.

He flicked his arm, jolting his wrist, and allowed the stone to curl towards the cat at great speed. The hard, jagged surface hit the creature and sent its head flying back with a painful screech. Bobby laughed in the background. The cat limped unsurely towards the back of the shed, injured and bleeding. They followed it quietly as it shuffled back into the shock of daylight. As it limped forward its feet trailed along the wet dirt and its head hung low, solemnly and unhealthily.

"Finish it off then," said Bobby, taking another step back. Jimmy picked up a second stone.

In the distance a woman's voice could be heard, loud and coarse. "Jimmy, back in this fucking house. *Now!*"

"Shit. It's my mam. I've got to go."

Bobby made a chicken noise that Jimmy ignored while running past him back to the torn rear entrance to the estate.

"Here," he said, passing back through the wire, "What about my tab?"

"You never finished it off, did you?"

Outside of the estate two pleasant rows of houses stare at one another like disapproving neighbours, their eyes whispering truths their lips daren't. Trees even in the autumn dark flourish and grow tall. Halfway through one street, beneath two unassuming if small homes, lies a gap. Most streets contain a gap; however this one is different. This is the gap that leads to another world. Behind it lays a labyrinth of homes, some boarded up, almost all vandalised. Sprayed messages warn off visitors and glass carpets the pavements along with cigarette ends and crushed bottles. It has been this way for so long that any good that once was has been forgotten; the carcass of the estate has been left to rot in the sun. Assumed that it would pick away at itself, decay through time, until eventually there would be no trace of it left.

If these streets could talk they would do so through broken teeth, through stubbled jaws and the salty sting of held-back tears. They would talk of beautiful industries and proud homelands; of safe environments and well-maintained estates; of socialist dreams and community pride. In fact, if these streets could talk they would probably prefer not to; sometimes it's easier to remain silent than to accept what you once had. And sometimes its better to break something fast than let it fade and die slowly. Behind this gap lies the Meadow Well Estate.

The fuzz of the radio stuttered static belches into the smoke-filled interior of the car.

It made him feel like he was on the television. His first fortnight on the job had been bliss, if slightly more monotonous than he would have liked. But, nonetheless, his enthusiasm overtook even the most objectionable aspects of the job – primarily his newly assigned partner, Constable Charlie Bowers. A large man with a face like fallen velvet whose bald head thinly encased the most cynical thoughts Billie Morgan had ever experienced. He was the sort of man, thought Billie, to whom no words were ever required. When Charlie Bowers was confronted with a scenario his opinion seemed to pop and burst straight from his head like cartoon bubbles. A naturally suspicious man, the only quality that surpassed his cruelty was his own laziness. Billie found this annoying on a personal level, yet enjoyed the prospects it presented; next to Constable Charlie Bowers it was difficult not to seem like the better man.

'...*We have reports of an incident in the Job Centre of the Meadow Well Estate, two males believed to be violent, over.*' The voice ended as abruptly as it had begun with an artificial beep. Morgan, for all his wide-eyed enthusiasm for the job, looked sceptically at Bowers.

"The Ridges," muttered Bowers, exhaling smoke through his nose in two almost perfect arrows, "You'll be lucky love."

"Now now," Billie said, eager to persuade his partner to change his views, but equally keen to keep on his good side, "It's The Meadow Well now, remember? Rebranding they called it... Running water, the lot."

Bowers rolled his eyes suspiciously and sped up towards the gap where the entrance to the Meadow Well Estate lay.

"They can toss it out among themselves. They made their bed, they can fucking well die in it."

He drove straight past the entrance, marking their passing only by forming his hand into the shape of a gun, which he shot directly into the centre of the two trees. 'Boom' he mouthed silently, the smoke of their exhaust pipe lingering momentarily in the chilly afternoon air.

Chapter Two

A gang of children passed by Shirley's front gate heading towards the burnt out car at the centre of the estate – a regal vantage point, from the top of which you could see the entire area; from the entrance out towards the small row of shops and pubs; the back exit; and the criss-cross of boarded-up houses that formed the main body of the Meadow Well. In the distance the doctor's surgery was just visible. The brick-red of the newly built community centre roof glimmered brightly like a star. Graffiti adorning the vandalised bus stops shone like a slick sentence in a bad novel.

Shirley's house was as feeble as the rest – a tangled, thorny, dying garden led to a front door that had chipped and tarnished over time. Small, self-scrubbed patches of window glinted like peepholes through the dirt and litter from the street blew into the garden and caught on the spokes of the gate and the jagged bricks of the wall. The inside, however, had been well-maintained. Small time pleasantries was how she thought of her trinkets and ornaments, her comfortable furniture and clean surfaces, patterned wallpaper and pathologically vacuumed carpets. Life may be one long hard slog, but so long as it was slogged from a pleasant and well-kept home then you had nothing to complain about.

The coffee table and expertly placed photographs created a beating heart inside of the withered corpse. A colour television on loan from a local delivery truck was the focal point of the front room and, accordingly, every chair pointed towards it. On top of the flickering plastic box stood Shirley's prized possession – Jack's one and only school photograph. There he sat, every day and every night, where she could keep an eye on him, still just a boy, trapped in innocence and nylon.

Shirley's one time prettiness had been held hostage inside the shell of her circumstance, her twinkling eyes framed by the worry lines and liver spots. A deep line from the time her husband had left her, eight months pregnant and without so much as a pot to piss in. One circle around each eye from the night her window had been smashed during a brawl that had gotten out of hand. A piece of glass had gotten into Jack's cot and when she couldn't locate it she had rushed him to hospital, frantic at the thought that he might have swallowed it. Cheeks hung heavy like overfull shopping bags, drooping from the sleepless nights she had experienced since Jack had been away. A short enough sentence and barely even a crime, but enough to make his mother worry and her face to fall. Her forehead hung low, her cheeks mourned beneath their natural resting point, dipping towards her mouth.

However Shirley's was a mouth with just the faintest trace of a smile, today at least. A smile at the prospect of a son's return. Twenty-two and back where he belonged – in his mother's arms, in the house he grew up in.

She sat on the living room floor. Her ornaments had been placed with a killer's exactitude around her bent legs so she could polish the uncluttered face of the coffee table. She scrubbed hard though carelessly, with no pattern to her movements.

"He's been learning a trade too, you know?" she said while facing the window. In the kitchen Bob's radio played a familiar tune. He stood on a ladder, eyes to the heavens, penetrating a light socket with his screwdriver. "Joining, I think he said it was," Shirley continued, upbeat. "And with skills like that he'll walk straight into a job. We'll see though... *Here*!" she was taken aback with her own sudden idea. "He might even be able to start his own business. Get a run around, work to his own hours and that."

"Yep," Bob's voice drifted through from the kitchen, "Let's just walk before we start sprinting, eh love?"

"But its not half bad though is it?" Shirley stubbed out her cigarette and placed her ornaments back on the coffee table as she stood up. "Free food and board for a couple of months and he gets trained for a job while he's at it. Who needs uni, eh?"

"Shirley love, he's not been to Pontin's for a fortnight, he's been in the bloody nick – and it's no holiday camp I can tell you."

"How the hell can you tell me?" Shirley said, walking into the kitchen. "You don't even watch *The Bill*."

"No, but I hear things. Bad things. Down the pub, from the lads."

Bob loved Shirley the way most men love their wives. However the thrill of their affair – illicit only because they made it that way – was part of the appeal to both of them. Both single save for one another they had been enjoying each other's company for the past six months. Bob had high hopes that one day he could make an honest woman of Shirley. She on the other hand lived in desperate hope that Bob would never change their arrangement by making any rash demonstrations of love. Her love for him was undeniable and unflinching but marriage had ruined the only good relationship she had ever had.

Once she and Jack's father became official he turned almost overnight into a man who talked with his fists and kissed with his forehead. A man that never asked. By the time he left it was not his company that she would miss. But then again it was not his company that she was hoping would provide for her and his child over the following two decades. Afterwards her superstitious streak had frightened her into believing in some sort of jinx. It wasn't, she had concluded, financial troubles, or whiskey, or casual domestic violence that had ruined her time with Him. It was marriage. As such it was something she was keen to avoid, lest her humble happiness with Bob ever fade.

"And don't you be raining on my parade, either," she said, gently nipping the hanging denim at the back of his jeans, causing him to jump slightly on the ladder.

"Hinny, man! You'll have 'us over the bloody edge if you're not careful. Here, pass 'us that spanner will you?"

On the stove a pan of specially boiling soup began to bubble and hiss in the pot. Flecks of liquid formed into oily balls and popped at the rim, splattering the surface of the hob. The pan began to vibrate on the gas rung but neither Shirley nor Bob noticed. She passed him the spanner and lent gently against the table, stroking his leg.

"*You bloody love it*. Anyway, I just want him back, here, where I can keep an eye on him. He's not bad you know Bob?"

"Aye."

"Misdirected intelligence – that's what the social said when he got kicked out of St. Cuthbert's the second time."

"Always was a clever 'un."

"Yeah." Shirley thought back to her boy. One of the few good ones around. Stupid, but never nasty. That was the difference. Stupidity could be cured; nastiness went all the way to the bone. "Still doesn't stop him acting thick as pig shit sometimes though." Bob placed his spanner back on the kitchen table.

"Well," said Shirley, poised for a defence. "Nah," she gave in, ultimately aware of Jack's ability to drop common sense on a whim. "But it was only a glitch; we'll soon have him on the straight and narrow. So long as her over there keeps her miserable trap shut."

"Who?"

"*You know*." Shirley looked at Bob conspirationally though this left him none the wiser.

"I don't know or I wouldn't have asked."

"*...Bangladeshi Mary!*" Shirley spat through pursed, angry lips. "Nosy cow. In The Comet the other night she comes up to 'us and tries it on like." "

What did she say?"

"She says she hears my Jack is coming out of prison and that it means we've all to pray for safety with one more menace on the streets. I said 'what bloody God would that be to then?' You know she's going to church now?"

"*Mary?*" Bob asked in disbelief. A first generation Pakistani immigrant, Mary was the owner of three shops in and around the estate. A local empire as far as most were concerned and a force only a brave few had the courage to confront.

"Oh aye," Shirley continued without taking breath. "She's still one of them, but I cornered her Sayeed the other day outside the shop, reckons it's so she can get tanked up on the communion wine before the pub. Tight cow!"

"What did you say?"

"I told him it's a waste of her time; they've been using Vimto since Adam was a lad."

"No man," said Bob, attaching the new light to the ceiling with one final screw "*about Jack*."

"Oh," Shirley rolled her eyes, "I said my Jack's never hurt a soul in his life, couldn't even if he wanted to. He's soft as you like once he stops growling. *And he's only in for breaking and entering and petty theft.* But he said he never even nicked the wallet; he just picked the wrong one up on the way out. Anyway, I said if he ever did want to go inside for something more serious then I'd make sure he handed out a bit of GBH. And do you know what she said?" She looked up at Bob in complete disbelief at the words that were about to leave her lips.

"What?"

"She said she blamed the parents." Shirley's face clouded and stormed.

"Oh Shir, you didn't batter her did you?"

"Bob McGregor! I'm a woman of certain repute and I'd like you to bear that in mind at all times!"

He looked sceptically at her, all too aware of Shirley's tendency to resolve things as quickly and brutally as need be. The mother who claimed that Jack her been responsible for the nit outbreak during his third year at school ended up having her arm reset in two places. And the inspector whose report lead to Jack's ultimate expulsion was unable to believe that one person had had both the time and inclination to collect such an abundance of dog shit in the space of just one afternoon, a collection that Shirley had deposited through the smashed window of his new car.

Bob still didn't know what exactly became of the sister of the woman Shirley's husband had run away with after she goading the jilted, expectant mother one night in the pub. All he knew was that hushed tones were used on the rare occasion that her name materialised.

"What did you do?" he asked again, firmly but not entirely seriously. Shirley looked petulant, like a child forced to recite a silly incident in the head teacher's office.

"I had young Sean piss in her Pernod and black while she was in the loos."

Bob screwed his face up like a damp tea towel ready for the wash. "Oh Shir, you didn't?"

"Well!" Shirley sprang to her own defence. "She shouldn't be so bloody interfering. And everyone thought she deserved it – else they'd have tried to stop it."

Both Bob and Shirley knew that this wasn't entirely the case. "And besides, if alcohol's kosher then a bit of pale ale won't do her no harm."

The pan on the stove began to boil more rapidly. The heat pushed gaps of air between the hob and the pan, which was skittering slowly forward like its feet had been tied and it were trying to escape. The liquid spat angrily in graceful arches over the rim and landed in splotches.

Shirley bit the top of Bob's leg as he put the finishing touches to the light. He climbed down, steadying himself on the unfamiliar terra firma of the kitchen floor and took Shirley's face in his hands as he kissed her on the forehead

Her whole being lightened as he did this; the attention, the softness of touch from such a hard man, all of it made her life seem that little bit easier if only for a moment.

"Light's fixed."

"Cheers, *stud*." she slowly prized herself from his embrace, kissing him once more on the lips.

The pan was boiling with a white, angry heat, spitting its content onto the flames below and almost extinguishing the fire in the process. As Shirley hugged Bob the click of the metal finally caught her attention and she noticed the large metal drum teetering uncomfortably on the hob.

"My soup!" she cried as she ran to the stove and with a damp tea towel picked up the throbbing metal. The heat from the handle seared through the wet cloth and stung her fingers, but Shirley had become accustomed to blocking out pain of all varieties. That, she felt, was the key to everything in life. If you stop feeling it, it can't hurt.

"*Shit!*" She threw an empty bowl into the sink and carefully started pouring the liquid into it, expertly allowing the meat chunks to fall through with the softened barley and leek pieces, all the while ensuring that every blackened fleck that had formed on the pan's base didn't tip in. Smoke billowed out as the scolding waterfall poured gently from one receptacle to another. The steam wrapped itself around her shoulders and made her seem ghostly and fragile, disappearing before Bob's eyes.

"Bloody hell man," she said to no-one in particular, focusing instead on the task at hand. "It's turned to bloody coal at the bottom."

"The hob," Bob added, arranging his tools onto his belt.

"What?"

"Turn your hob off."

"Oh." Shirley placed the half-full pan of soup on the bench and for once did as she was told. She turned back to the soup and hung her head, as though in shame.

"It's turned to fucking coal on the bottom," she said again, solemnly "How the hell is Jack expected to do anything with his life when I can't even make a pan of bloody soup without messing it up?"

Bob moved towards her and kissed her neck. "I'm sure it'll still be smashing," he said softly, the warmth of his breath causing her neck to prickle and rise.

"It's his favourite." She paused for a moment. The half empty pan dribbling with burnt liquid caused a carousel of memories to jump and turn in her mind; fragmented images and sepia reels flashed behind her eyes like the stuttered snapshots of information that come with the worst kind of hangover.

"Well, I suppose if I'm careful to scrape the good bits from the shite on the bottom it'll be alright. Won't it?"

"Aye," Bob said, leaning on the surround of the kitchen door. "I'll see you hinny. Send my love to your Jack, tell him there's a pint on me when he's ready to come down the pub."

"I will," Shirley said, "mind, he doesn't know his Mam's getting a good seeing to yet. So don't you be saying nothing; as far as he's concerned you're still just my odd job man."

A filthy smile etched across Bob's life-worn face. He looked at his watch with the enthusiasm of a pantomime bit-player and snaked back across the kitchen, grabbing Shirley from behind. She screamed in protest but could do little to conceal her own grin. The attention made her feel so happy she was almost frightened that it would lead to a hangover.

"Thinking about it," Bob grabbed her waist and nipped her in areas that made her jump and squeal, "I couldn't half go for a quick odd job myself."

Shirley turned herself around so that she was facing Bob once more and grabbed him between the legs.

"Go on Shir', finish 'us off – call it payment for the light-bulb."

She dug harder into his groin and he flinched back. "Get off 'us you filthy git! You'll get a name for yourself round here." She kissed him and he kissed her back twice as hard.

"I've already got myself a name – one for each of my odd job girls."

"I'll smash their faces in." Shirley took his balls in her hands and this time squeezed tightly. "And make bloody sure you never dip your nib for the rest of your days, *mush*." She let go of him and turned back to the soup. Bob flicked his palm across the back of her tracksuit bottoms which caused her to jump. He kissed her neck lovingly and walked to the door.

"Ta for the light love," Shirley said without turning to say goodbye.

"Any time hinny," Bob said, leaving her alone in the kitchen, pouring her soup. Specks of unavoidable black tumbled into the good bowl, but Shirley was past caring; she had her boy and her man. For the first time in a long time she felt as though her life was starting to fit again.

Chapter Three

The sky ached beneath its own monochrome. Various gangs littered the estate reeking of violence, Impulse and Lynx. They fizzed not just with the usual hormones of youth but with an anger that had been instilled from birth, wound up and eager to charge. The girls' hair framed their beautiful faces and sad eyes like helmets – scraped back and polished like fibreglass, ready for war. Boys' tracksuit bottoms tucked into their socks – all the better for legging it – and branded jackets imported from the Far East. A group of younger schoolchildren took up residence around the burnt out car in the central grass verge, sipping cider from plastic bottles and passing one soggy cigarette around their group in no particular order, all sucking hard with pursed, wiped-dry lips through fear of duck arsing the filter.

"Save 'us the letters," instructed Dean, one of the older boys, as he stood up with Sean, kicking their football to the exposed wall of an end house. The ball pinged as it hit the concrete, bouncing back to the slap of the side of their foot. Without speaking they initiated a game where Dean would kick the ball twice against the wall and then allow Sean to do the same. The object was not clear; it was simply a means of momentarily evading boredom.

They soon become hypnotised by their own rhythm, their bodies moving on instinct, their legs and feet stopped feeling.

They simply followed movement like machines or prehistoric beasts, endeared to the simplistic, easily replicated pattern of their actions.

The green bar of the volume rose on the television once more as she exhaled through flared nostrils like a bull ready to charge. Above the din from outside the chatting presenters started to shout their magazine cut-out segments to Agnes '... *and following our interview with the latest bad boy to hit Coronation Street we will be taking an in-depth look at inner city violence among youths from nine-thirty until nine-thirty-five, before our daily competition and your chance to win a whopping five hundred pounds. If you want to get your hands on the jackpot then answer the following question...*'

She leaned forward and paused as the a's, b's and c's tiled onto the screen.

"B," said Agnes, narrowing her tired eyes and nodding in concurrence with her own answer. She smiled, a rarity in itself – a smug bracket that passed as quickly and un-memorably as a roadside accident – as she imagined herself winning the cash. She'd stick her job, for a start. They never thanked her for it anyway, so fuck 'em. Then there'd be a holiday without question. It made her body tingle to think of the fun she could have when the money arrived, failing to realise that five hundred pounds would barely cover Craig's outstanding fines and perhaps more importantly that the chances of winning were almost nil. Same as they had been yesterday. And the day before that. On the back of a takeaway leaflet she scribbled down the telephone number and her final answer.

Boing. The ball hit the side of the house. With the noise still echoing in her ears she heard him stir in his sleep; harrumphing snores interrupted only by the creaking of the cheap bedding as he turned over awkwardly to the sound of life outside.

That bed was a nuisance, and an embarrassment. Thank God she was married; she'd be far too embarrassed to invite anyone round to see it. Two boys with thick eyebrows and no teeth had accosted her one afternoon in an unmarked white van.

"Here missus, lovely bed we've got for you here – straight from the shop. Double like. Call it a hundred."

"Call it a bloody cheek," she'd said. "Quiet day round the caravan site was it you little shysters? Get off my street before I call the police."

Eventually she had managed to haggle them down to sixty quid and a few bottles of no-brand vodka for their troubles. They'd fled before she'd realised that it had been left in eight different pieces.

Boing. It hit the wall again and she stood up. Ash from her cigarette snowed onto her freshly washed tabard.

"Stupid little bastards!" she yelled through the wall, trying to pick the white specks from her front before they smudged and blurred into a more questionable looking stain. Her slippers were looking tired too; the fluffy pink outsides had turned grey and flaky like a week old corpse. They were new the day she'd been on the telly. The regionals had been round doing a section on the locals' response after they'd scrapped *The Ridges* in favour of the softer, less intimidating *Meadow Well Estate*. A council committee had decided that an inspirational name would instil pride among the residents. 'New name, new start' read the leaflet.

"We don't want better clothes hinny," she'd frowned into the camera as the bonny lass with the big shoulders and small bust thrust the microphone into her face. "We want better bodies. Do you understand what I'm saying?" Her fifteen seconds had been captured on a borrowed video recorder. That was for keeps. Unfortunately for her so were the slippers.

From upstairs he called her name. "Coming," she yelled back up, extinguishing her cigarette into a cup of almost cold tea.

Fully naked save for his socks the blankets only just protected his dignity. Craig looked the way he acted – square and miserable with a chronically grey outlook. Picking one of his cigarettes from the emergency bedside packet she lit it and inhaled deeply as reward from having manoeuvred the stairs so selflessly before work.

"That bloody ball," he said groggily, still exhausted from last night's shift. "I can't get a moment's bloody –"

"I've got to be going soon." She severed his sentence badly like a war surgeon with blunt tools. "There's some dinner for you in the oven. We've nowt in 'til pay day so it's last night's scraps and a bit of bread. There's a couple of cans an' all for you if you feel the need so you're not to be going down The Comet for a sly one."

"Get them to shut up out there will you our Ag?" he asked pitifully from his bed.

"Aye."

"While you're here hop back in for a minute," he pulled on the deep blue of her tabard, "I may as well do something useful if I can't sleep."

"Not on your life kid." She pulled the scratchy cloth from his hands and smoothed herself down. "I've just had this through another hand wash and I'll not be rumpling my clothes for anything, especially not *that*."

Rolling over in disappointment the bed squawked angrily like a disgruntled beast.

"And we'll be getting a new bed soon as the provvy man comes back round," she huffed.

He didn't respond until she was halfway down the stairs. "Stop them banging that fucking ball!"

"Heard who's back today?" Dean asked, eyes remaining firmly on the game.

"Who?"

26

"Jack."

"It hasn't been that long already."

"Well aye it has."

"Is that all you get for theft?"

"Yeah, long as you don't do anyone in or owt."

"Mint."

A door opened with a bang. Their trance was broken yet still they managed to retain their game as Agnes emerged from the house in her ruffled work clothes and pink slippers. Two rollers still stuck to the back of her head like a sly 'kick me' sign and the long, king-size cigarette which she gripped between chipped crimson nails was now heavy with ash; the slightest movement would have knocked off the entire tip.

"Gonna drop your cherry if you're not careful," said Dean, glancing at her briefly before returning to the ball. She was standing behind the gate, hanging the top half of her body over the side, facing the boys.

"What have I told yous about that bloody ball?"

"Fuck off man Agnes," said Jimmy, without looking up at her but kicking the ball more gently than he had before. "My Mam said I could play wherever I wanted."

"Well your Mam doesn't own my bloody house!"

"Neither do you," he retorted.

"You cheeky little twat! He's been on nights all week. If he's got to come down he'll play war with you. Clear off."

"We're only messing around man." Despite his objections Dean picked up his ball from the ground and cradled it beneath his arm like a baby being burped.

"I mean it, piss off, the lot of you!"

Agness shooed the group away with her hand, brandishing her cigarette in the air. The children began to chant. Nothing particularly audible – no point made – just a growing mutter through which only the occasional obscenity could be distinguished.

"Go on!" shouted Agness after them, determined to claim the last word as well as make sure they did as they were told. "If I catch any of yous back here I'll tan your hides and go and see all your fathers!"

One boy turned and spat in the direction of her house as they left to find a less troublesome spot. Nathalie watched from her front room window, shaking her head. She held the curtain lightly, only allowing a crack of the window to remain exposed. She was a beautiful and dark haired, the sort of girl over whom most schoolboys had burst into crunching socks on the bedroom floor after the long process of pressure against desks. Barely no longer a girl herself, she had waved goodbye to her teens just over a year ago and four months later had given birth to her own beauty, Nicole.

She held the baby in her arms as she gently pulled at the curtain, each inch to mark the further passing of the particularly loutish looking gang. Nicole stared up at her mother with hungry eyes, her mouth just learning the art of smiling. She had a wise face for a baby so young. Older, but not old, as though she was already aware of the effect her beauty would have on the world.

Nathalie pulled the curtains halfway open and a blast of light filled the room. "We could have a swing, eh sweetheart?" she said to the baby, playing her favourite game. "And we could put a proper three-piece suite in, right in front of the telly. We'll have tea together there every night. And... and what else? Maybe we could have a sandpit, eh? A sandpit when it's cold and a paddling pool when it's warm." She kissed Nicole's head and moved her further towards the window. "– And hanging baskets, how about that? Hanging baskets so you could smell flowers every time you came to your house."

She paused. A tough girl by nature she swallowed her sadness for the sake of her daughter. She had read in the torn lifestyle supplement at the doctor's surgery that babies could sense sadness, particularly within their mothers. Nathalie was adamant that her daughter would never know sadness.

"I've got big plans for you and me kid. Big plans."

She took Nicole to the settee and clipped a shiny red lady-bird clip into her single tuft of cereal blond hair the colour of the paper crowns she used to hand out at Burger King. Nathalie was pleased that she had inherited this from her father – tight, golden curls that Anthony insisted on straight-ening and darkening with masses of cheap, luminous hair gel. Blond on lads wasn't right, he said. Puffs, ponces, and south-erners was his theory. One and the same, Nathalie thought. Girls with light hair were perfect though. Blondes have more fun, everyone knows that. But they're also dirty easier, as Nathalie's mother had reminded her.

"There you go," Nathalie said, returning Nicole back to the window, "Let that world see what a real angel looks like. You'll be the bonniest baby no bother, you already are to your Daddy and me. You've just got to show them you've got the goods... yes you have! And as soon as you've won and your silly Daddy gets back, we'll run away and never come back."

She looked out of the window once more at the crumbling streets that locked in and around one another like a spider's legs trapping its prey. To the left of her house, in the blurred distance, a figure approached, tall and stoic. It moved slowly but determinedly. The walk of someone with their head held high out of knowledge rather than arrogance. It was a familiar walk and a face that became all the more recognisable as it approached.

The figure was older than her but only by a year or so – almost exactly the same age as her husband and one of his best friends to boot. They were known among their area as the voices of reason; the boys who could, and would, sort it out if need be. They were seldom required to however; their public displeasure at a situation was enough nine times out of ten to stop it entirely. It was their kindness rather than their brawn that made them both so popular, and with her husband away the knowledge that his friend was back made Nathalie feel safer somehow, partially protected.

The boy she saw approaching the estate carried a large black bin bag and had his hair cropped shorter than it was when she last saw him. Haircuts always make men look vulnerable and childlike, Nathalie thought. But this boy didn't walk like a child. He walked like a man and one that had learned his lesson.

Jack stood outside of his gate for a moment. Not for too long as the pressure building in his bladder had gone past the stage whereby it could be ignored and was approaching desperate on-the-spot relief. But long enough to take in the surroundings. The air felt just as thick as he remembered it. Prison was no fun, Jack knew, and he would do everything he could to avoid returning. However, the simplicity of it was the only aspect that he could bring himself to enjoy. Doors were locked, regimes were set and enforced, authorities and civilians would treat you like a second grade citizen because you had done something wrong. Life, thought Jack, was crueller than prison. Life to him felt like it came with a padlock, a regime, a bulleted set of instructions and activities that he must obey, yet lacked the luxury of a cast iron release date.

He scanned the street. Two boys sat outside of the boarded up launderette, drinking from cans. A blue bag waited next to them full of unopened drinks; skittles ready to be knocked down. One of the boys raised his head from the patterns of the cracked concrete that seemed to be entrancing the pair so thoroughly. He clocked Jack and nodded once, tribally, to mark the occasion of his return. Jack nodded back. He recognised the boy though not by name. He remembered him being particularly eager to fight, the sort of person to whom it's an activity, rather than a necessary action.

Jack looked up at his bedroom window and breathed in deeply.

"What's this our Jack?" Agnes asked briskly on her way to the bus stop, pointing at the bag he held in his hand. "You working on the bins now?" Before he had a chance to answer she was gone, hot footing it for the 363 into town, her shoulders moving more than her legs as she walked, like twin machine guns firing at any obstruction that dared cross her path. He thought for a moment to call after her and alert her to the curlers in her hair, but decided against it – karma for the bin-man jibe.

He opened the front door. The familiarity of the routine – leaving the lock off the latch only when visitors were expected – made him smile for a moment as he felt it click and lock behind him.

Shirley sat bolt upright as she heard the door open and close. She exhaled heavily to clear her mouth and lungs of smoke, and she stubbed out the cigarette gently so that it could be relit. Her hands dragged quickly through the air in front of her to clear the white, bitter smelling streaks, eager to make her son's return as unspoilt as could be. It was as though the reality of the situation was temperamental – like it was an old video that if jogged ever so slightly would snap and disappear. Shirley had almost convinced herself that she had imagined Jack's return and if she thought too hard about it then it wouldn't really happen. A shadow appeared in the living room.

"Well well well, look what the cat dragged in. I only sent you for a pint of milk."

The room's atmosphere was frozen. They were on pause, neither daring to make the first move. To anyone observing their encounter it would seem a cold, harsh introduction. Jack and Shirley understood one another though; they had their own secret codes and symbols for the words that other families were too eager to throw around. Love. I love you. They were words almost never uttered by the pair. Not because it wasn't true, but because it was a fact so ingrained that neither felt the need to waste time saying it.

Shirley broke into a smile; uncontrollable and wild it burst like a Catherine Wheel, wrapping around her entire face. She stood up and rushed over to Jack, suddenly finding herself having to wipe tears from her eyes. Jack smiled too but let his mother come to him. She flung her arms around his neck and gripped him tighter than she had intended, desperate to absorb ever moment and every sensation – she was a drunk sucking on her last drops of Special Brew.

"My bairn! My bairn!" she repeated, pressing her face into his neck. Jack held his arms around her back, frightened that if he let go Shirley would topple over with excitement. "How are you my son? Let's have a look at you."

She pushed herself from Jack and held his face in her hands. Light stubble prickled her fingers. Jack was unable to grow the soft, easy beginning of a moustache the way most boys his age were. Instead he was left with prickly pinheads of black and grey, like those of a teenager before being given their first razor as a suggestive Christmas present.

"You've had yourself a haircut, what's the matter – you get a girlfriend when in there or something?" She ruffled his short crop with her right hand, pulling away when the grease of his brylcreem slobbered over her palm.

"Aye," Jack replied. "Big Steve. Canny lad, said he'd come round for tea if he ever gets out. You'd like him."

"And the comedian's back!" Shirley slapped him gently in the stomach and kissed him again on the cheek.

"I missed you Mam." The bluntness of the sentence hit her like a train pulling to an emergency stop. She wanted to never let go of him. She wanted to weep.

"You're telling me" she said, quieter than she had been before. "Don't leave 'us again, eh Jack?"

"Mam!"

"I'm not kidding Jack. Worst time of my life wondering what the hell they were doing to you in there. I haven't slept a wink, I've been off my food." Jack ducked and looked jokingly around Shirley's hips. She slapped him playfully again. "You little shite. Here, do you want some soup? I made you some soup. I messed up a bit towards the end but it'll be better than the clarts they shoved into you in that place."

"Aye, just let 'us get a slash first. I'm busting. The bus was half an hour late."

"Could you not have just gone round the back of the bus stop? I always do."

"Oh aye," Jack laughed "And get done straight away again for indecent exposure. Canny plan Mam."

"Fair enough. I was saving up you know, to come and get you in a taxi, but the leccy was due and I thought what's the point in being chauffer-driven back to a shithole with no heating and not so much as a bit of telly to keep you going with."

"Don't worry about it, I'm here, aren't I?"

"Yeah, canny eh? That's all that matters. Anyway – go on my son, you piss like there's no tomorrow! I'll heat the soup up for you while you sort yourself out. I tidied your room –"

At this Jack's mind raced immediately the way every man's does when faced with the prospect of a loved one having sifted through their belongings. He ran through his mind the objects that he would least like his mother to have seen. Porn ranked highly, ditto condoms. Moisturiser doubly so. But worst of all would be the secret items he kept, the ones that held emotional gravitas. The sole birthday card his Dad had sent him. The ink-stained jumper from school that he said he'd burned sacrificially after his last day. Illiterate messages – 'C U Soon Jak' and 'Luv Y M8' – scrawled across the grey fabric along with the requisite cocks and tits dotted about the torso.

"And I threw a few bits and pieces out."

"*Mam Man!*"

"There's no way you'll be needing roaches and weed now. You're on the straight and narrow my son. *For good*."

"You didn't." He went along with his role of the mortified son. He had forgotten he had even bought the weed.

"I most certainly did. And don't be looking at me like that – *I didn't flush it!* I'm not thick you know. I flogged it down the Comet. Tidy little profit I made too if I may say so myself. Padded it out with some veggie cuppa-soup. I left the money on your bed. Go and buy yourself a canny shirt or something."

"Cheers Mam."

"Go on," she chivvied him forward, "bugger off while I sort this lot out." She picked up his bin bag from the floor – an entire life wrapped in a throwaway plastic bag, the sort people use to dispose of the most disgusting and unwanted aspects of their life, to disappear and never be acknowledged again.

Upstairs the toilet settled and refilled as Jack stood in front of the mirror. The cold room swamped with steam from the small amount of hot water he had run into the sink. Soap from the side of the basin slipped on its newly lubricated surface and dropped into the water with a rewarding plop. Jack picked it out and placed it back where it belonged, but the suds had already begun to cloud the clear water, turning it a murky, opaque shade of off-white.

He stared at himself in the mirror, his shirtless chest now only slightly bruised. He had found prison to be easier than he'd thought. The violence didn't worry him the way it did most; it was a language in which he was fluent. Jack knew the unspoken practices. He knew when a fight was brewing. He knew when to look and when to avoid eye contact. He felt as though he could initiate a fight in a room without so much as speaking, simply by selectively raising his eyebrows, narrowing his gaze between two inmates. It was a skill he had developed during his recreational hours. A glance at one inmate, nod his head towards another. Eyes widened, develop a link. Then drop his glance, look over at another inmate and replay the routine. If all went to plan he would – like some bastardised matchmaker – have the pair staring anxiously at one another within minutes. And in the pressure cooker of Her Majesty's Travel Lodge this was all it would take. Four times he had managed this trick; the wordless power he yielded throughout the halls.

It was only on the fifth occasion that his ability had failed him and a particularly gruesome lifer had imagined Jack was trying to initiate another type of physical exertion. He had accosted Jack in the showers the next morning. A bar of soap wrapped in a damp sock had done the majority of the damage. It was the perfect prison fix; maximum impact yet no chance of bones broken. With fists it was too easy to get carried away – forget the plight of the victim beneath your hands and just hit out at the way your life had ended up. Jack had seen one man die this way; gently liquefying beneath the fists of a tattooed father of three. The victim looked acceptant and peaceful as he slid towards stillness; his killer looked vacant throughout the attack – his eyes ahead of him, glassy and cold, his fists raining punches without him even realising anymore. Eventually he stopped and looked down. A single, juicy tear rolled down his face and landed on the forehead of the still body beneath him.

Jack stopped thinking. It hurt. He sprayed a single streak of Shirley's neutral Right Guard beneath each arm and looked at himself in the mirror once more, straightening his hair and running both hands across the smooth lines of his face. He smiled without realising it and with his finger traced the route of his smile across the foggy mirror. The pattern held for a second before the beady drops of condensation began drag-ging the shape downwards towards the windowsill, making it appear more sinister than Jack had intended. He heard a siren in the distance and a raining patter of feet flutter past their house.

Chapter Four

Jack slurped his soup slowly. He wasn't really hungry having bought and eaten a bag of crisps on his walk from the bus stop. But he was aware of the effort that had gone into the slight feast and so ate out of honour rather than necessity. Shirley stood by the stove, smoking a cigarette and warming her back against the cooling hob. She was pleased nothing had changed. Most people she knew said that their sons or daughters had returned form prison a different person, the same but different somehow. Jack was normal though. This was testament to her longstanding belief that Jack was one of the few children of the Meadow Well that wouldn't benefit from changing. A truth defined by the way in which his given name had become an adjective in itself. When asked of his wellbeing she always had and always would respond by saying that "Jack's Jack". And this, the majority of the time, sufficed.

She talked non-stop while he ate, not to fill in awkward silences but to make up for lost time, pleased to back in an environment with permanent company. Shirley was a tree falling in the forest – she felt as though she only really existed when there were people around to experience her.

"And you want to see the size of her?" She was telling Jack about baby Nicole, whom Jack was largely expected to be made Godfather of on Anthony's return.

"Yeah?"

"Oh she's a smasher – Nathalie's got her in for Boots' Bonniest Bairn. She could win an' all."

"I bet?" He tried to hide his grimace as a burnt speck crawled to the back of his throat. The taste marred his entire mouthful; a bad smell in a small lift. He chewed hard on the bread to try and neutralise the sensation but this only stretched the taste over a larger surface area. Shirley didn't notice his displeasure.

"Their Anthony's still away on the rigs, reckon we'll have him back for a bit within the month."

"Anthony's coming back?" Jack's mood lifted.

"Yeah, that'll be nice for you?"

"What else has been happening since I've been away?"

"Nothing much. Oh I got the light fixed, look." Shirley moved to over the switch and flicked the light on and off, over and over again. The room sprung to life and died over and over again; it hurt Jack's eyes.

"Alright mam, give it a rest will you?"

Shirley eventually stopped and sat down in front of Jack, adopting a more serious tone. "We've been having more bother though Jack"

"Like what?" he knew exactly what she meant. Bother was a codeword – an all-encompassing description of the state in which they lived. Bother meant theft, vandalism, crime. It meant residents tearing up their own homes, glass smashed, cars stolen and burned. It meant shouting and swearing, people frightened in the streets, gangs snarling at one another over imaginary boundaries. "Oh, the usual. Fighting and that. Almost every night now. I think it's with them all being laid off, though they've nowt to be ashamed of. It's happening to them all. But they've nowt else to do, just wind one another up, beat their chests and frighten the life out of everyone else. Kenny Walker had to have his ear stitched back on."

"Fucking hell!"

"You know…" Shirley stood up and stared out of the window as an empty bottle cascaded over the fence and into their yard, fizzing the remainder of its contents onto the dead lawn before settling peacefully, "… they called the police when they were brawling, said they were kicking seven shades out of one another, said one of them'd end up dead if they didn't hurry. Do you know what time they turned up?" She paused but left no time for any real attempt at an answer. "*Half ten!*"

"That's not that bad."

"*The next bloody morning!*" Though not particularly surprising, this made Jack's heart sink. "Janet in The Comet said what bloody use is that? Young Jimmy'd found his Dad's ear by then. Useless sacks of shite. How's the soup?" She switched subjects as abruptly as she had flicked the light switch, bored with life's more serious issues.

"Nice. Where did you get the ham?"

"There is no ham," Shirley smiled menacingly at Jack, "I didn't say they found all of Kenny's ear, did I now?"

"Fuck off man!" Jack dropped his spoon in disgust.

Shirley laughed at her own joke and tossed her tea towel at Jack. "Oh eat it up you soft shite. There'll be nowt but the best for my boy." The clatter of the front door interrupted their banter.

"Who's that?" Jack asked.

"I don't bloody know, do I?" Shirley went to open the door leaving Jack alone in the kitchen. "If it's the catalogue," she said from the front room, tossing Jack's few remaining clothes behind the settee, "then they can piss right off because the skirt wasn't a size fourteen and the boots had a scuff on them." Peering through the window she recognised the visitor. "Oh."

"What?" Jack called from the kitchen. There was no response but he could hear her greeting their guest.

"Alright Shir'?"

"Hiya Darren flower, how you keeping?"

"Not too bad, where is he?" Jack sat up, excited for this reunion at least.

"He's in the kitchen, go on through." The front door shut and Darren entered the kitchen, followed by a smiling Shirley. Darren was a tall boy, an inch short of Jack's mighty height, but skinny with it. His face was drawn out into a sharp point made all the more severe by his cropped hair and prominent teeth; the sort of face that had from day one drawn unfavourable comparisons to rodents. Because of this, as well as a number of other behavioural ticks, Darren had been bullied at school; a situation which changed when he became acquainted with Jack. To Darren he and Jack were best friends. Jack felt similarly, though saw Darren as a different calibre of friend to Anthony. A boy can have two types of friends. One is the kind that you can go months without seeing and, on reinstating contact, carry on like nothing had ever changed. And one with whom you shared life's day-to-day quirks, their constant presence breaking up the lengthy inertia of everyday life. Darren was the second type.

Darren extended his hand to Jack, who accepted it gracefully. On the second shake though Darren used the force of their clutch to drag himself down to where Jack sat, half-hugging him in an awkwardly blokey embrace.

"Alright Jack the lad?" Darren stood up and joined Shirley leaning next to the hob.

Jack remained seated. "Alright Darren, how you keeping?"

"Not so bad mate, not so bad. Free man eh? What was it like?"

Shirley moved over to the table and began fussing around the condiments, rearranging the salt-shaker and ketchup bottle like she was planning a battle strategy. Suddenly she felt overly sensitive to Jack's misdemeanours and his recent brush with prison, as though it were a physical mark on both of them, something everyone would see and comment on. Gossip was a force that had never affected Shirley in the past, however now she feared that endless streams of inquisitions and congratulations might confuse situations, encourage him back into that direction, red-carpet the path that went backwards.

He had a strong head on his shoulders, of that she was sure, but Jack – as shy as he could seem – felt a tug for the glitz of the limelight. A broken leg had been the result of his friend's applause as Jack leapt from the top of the climbing frame at school. Eager to replicate the buzz of an ecstatic audience his second trick had been a similar feat from the edge of the art-block roof. A dinner lady had found him while on her cigarette break, his leg bent painfully beneath his body. There were a million other such injuries: the scar above his eyebrow from running into barbed wire as they fled the wrath of a local farmer (cow tipping); two tear-shaped purple marks just beneath his shoulder blade (pellet gun); an eternal bald patch on his right arm (aerosol /lighter). His body was a rich tapestry of raised red and purple marks on which each and every one of Jack's glory moments could be traced.

There were other scars, too. The sort that even antiseptic cream and bandages couldn't fix. Even his bravado couldn't hide the flush of his cheeks at the prospect of open water after he had decided to attempt the walk to St. Mary's Lighthouse as the tide came in. Halfway through a kind gentleman on the promenade had driven to the nearest call box and alerted the authorities. Jack had to be air-lifted to safety. It had happened the day after his thirteenth birthday, the day on which Jack for the first time saw physical evidence of a father; the scrawled, spidery lettering of the sparse Birthday message in his cheap card. Sometimes she thought that Jack was daring life, testing its seriousness. He was renowned as a child for being the unbeaten master at Chicken – a Morris Miner once flipped onto its roof due to Jack's concrete stance in the centre of the road.

"Nowt to tell" Jack responded unenthusiastically "Properly boring. It was wank really."

"No shower time horror stories then?"

"Fuck off!" Jack swallowed his last triangle of bread and passed his plate to Shirley who dropped it into the frothy waters of the basin.

"Lend us a tab Shir', I'm busting." She was the only person he knew that would never dispute sharing her cigarettes, asking was merely a formality. Shirley would always say yes.

"Don't give him one!" Jack shot back indignantly.

Shirley rolled her eyes to Jack and passed Darren a cigarette from her open packet, pleased that the subject of prison seemed to be over before it had really begun.

"Here you are flower," she said as she passed it to him. He inhaled the heat of the hob deeply but carefully, anxious not to singe his eyebrows which tingled so close to the pressing heat.

"Cheers Shir'." He winked at her and then turned his attentions back to Jack. "Good to have you back though mate, thing's have been getting worse."

"I was telling him."

"Not now you're here though Jackie? Eh? You can sort them out."

"No, he bloody well can not!" Shirley interrupted loudly and suddenly. "You're not getting involved in none of that. And you, Darren Pearson –" she slapped Darren across the back of the head, gentle enough to be construed as a joke but with enough force to show that she was serious " –should know better. He's keeping his head down and his hands clean from not on. *It's the new us.* Isn't that right son?"

Jack at that moment did have his head down and it remained there, though his eyes raised to the dispute between mother and friend like two suns lazily rising in the desert, scanning the horizon. Something about the discussion made him feel uneasy. Jack felt unconvinced. Though he wasn't sure as to whether it was Darren's presumption or his mother's optimism that rang less true.

"*For now!*" Darren smirked at Shirley who slapped him again.

"I don't know why I even bother, yous never were exactly the Batman and Robin of the Ridges, where you? More like the bloody Del Boy and Rodney."

"Piss off mam!" Jack snapped back "*We were sorted!*" He was pleased that they had stopped discussing him seriously, as though they knew or had any sort of control over his actions. His new life was his to play with as and when he felt like it.

"Aye Shirley, what you on about? Remember that brawl down The Social? We sorted that out."

"Yous bloody well started it!" There was a brief pause. Jack looked down at the crumbs on the placemat and pushed them in towards one another with his finger, forming a blurred star shape where his bowl had sat.

"I'd be Del Boy though," he said eventually.

"Fuck off!" Jack had the ability, common among friends with a distinct gap in intelligence, to wind Darren up over a subject he had almost no care for whatsoever.

"You're Rodney every time," Jack said with a lazy smile.

"Eeeeh – *Darren... Del!* It's obvious, and my Uncle Tommy used to work down the markets,"

"Like you'd be Del Boy. You're Rodney. Everyone knows that, you skinny twat."

Outside, the light settled from a filthy grey to the dank indigo of an early autumn evening. The urgent orange bars of the fire shone an intense but localised heat next to where Shirley's feet rested, but Darren and Jack remained chilled on the settee. Jack clutched his cup of tea and curled his body around the steam, trying to absorb some of the warmth. Darren held his beer can with a hand shrouded in the stretched fabric of his jacket, allowing no skin from the neck down to be exposed to the chilly night air. Shouts could already be heard from outside; sirens wept in the distance. They sat quietly in the living room, comfortable enough with one another's company to avoid forced small talk. Eventually Darren stirred from his daydream as though he had been asked a question, remembering one of the objectives of his visit.

"Here, look. My mam was clearing out our Joy's room and she found this photo." Without unwrapping his hand from his sleeve, Darren pulled a picture from the unzipped pocked of his tracksuit bottoms, handing it to Jack.

"Has your Joy moved out?" Shirley asked, surprised at the prospect of Joy having developed any sort of independence. Joy, Darren's sister, frequented the dentist more often than she frequented school; though this is not to say she had a particular interest in oral hygiene. She attended only when the relevant governing bodies sent enforcement officers on a home visit and threatened her with grim alternatives such as the special needs course at college – Maths with Mongs as it was more commonly dubbed – or residential opportunities at a young offenders' institute. She had virtually fallen through the cracks by fourteen, getting by on a monthly visit and a promise that she was really, really going to apply herself from now on. She worked nights at a local chip shop and since the age of eight had been a part-time arsonist and a full-time psychopath.

"Juvie," Darren said. "Went at her education officer with a compass."

"Oh."

"Look." He handed Jack the picture. Jack laughed; his eyes scanned the image warmly, his fingers teasing the corners that tore like lightning bolts into the otherwise sunny image.

"State of them two!" Jack said. "I remember that day though."

"Give me a look then!" Shirley leant over and took the photograph. It showed Jack and Darren smiling and linked to one another on the tumbling greenery outside of Spanish City. The lights of the funfair battled with the intensity of the sunshine that bounced off the sea as the two boys held their arms in the air, so close they were touching. Stripes from their identical football shirts pressed together so that you couldn't tell where one ended and the other began. They stretched their faces into enthusiastic, childish poses; Darren's ear was still red from his first piercing and Jack had keenly positioned his arm so that his new sovereign ring was proudly visible. Still too big for his bald, child's hand it looked like an elaborate weight he was being forced to carry as punishment. The picture had been taken by Darren's other, more functioning sister who had accompanied them on a summer jaunt to mark the final days of their school holidays.

"Do you really remember it?" Darren asked.

"Course I do." Jack took the picture back from Shirley. "First sip of cider I ever took and my first tab."

"It better bloody not have been!" Shirley shrieked, though she knew this was probably the truth and, secretly, she found the idea funny. "Yous were only twelve!"

"It was funny though," said Darren

"Yeah." Jack looked at it again but with a sadder smile.

"Well I think it's dead canny, back when yous were bairns. Can we keep it?"

"Yeah, we'll not miss it. Mam's doing Joy's room out for a lodger – wants as much of the shite cleared out as she can get."

"Cheers love."

Darren stood up and drained the final dregs of flat lager from his can. "I best be off anyway. Are yous coming down the Comet tonight?"

"I reckon," said Jack, without looking up. He was gently

trying to smooth out the creases in the photograph without adding to the scratches that were beginning to widen into tears.

"What about you Shir'?"

"Well, I migh pop down for a sly one. Don't worry though – I'll not embarrass yous."

"See you later on then, cheers for the cans, and the tab."

"Bye love." Shirley stood up as Darren left.

"In a bit mate." said Jack.

"Funny, eh?" Shirley stood the photograph on the mantelpiece, resting it against the carriage clock.

"We were tossers back then. I do though, remember it."

"So you should – it was no time at all, really, since you were a bairn."

"Suppose." Jack fell quiet for a moment. He didn't want to approach the subject he was about to, as in some way he felt it was easiest for his mother to pretend that the previous two months had never happened. All talk of prison had ended abruptly after their initial reunion and this, he knew, was how she wanted it to stay. But facts were facts and certain technicalities could not be avoided.

"We'll be getting a visitor tomorrow," he said. Shirley sat back down. "Probation officer. Keeping track and all that. HE's got to come round every day for a week; it's part of this new scheme to monitor my progress and, like, I dunno really... help 'us on my voyage or some shit."

Words stumbled on purpose as they left his mouth; reluctant children being traipsed to school. He knew exactly that it was to evaluate his release and assist in his reformation. However, Jack imagined that by articulating it with any sort of care he might somehow cosmically heighten the severity of the situation.

Shirley smiled, but her eyes became full. The words tangled

in her hair and on her skin. *Probation Officer*. It felt filthy. It reminded her that Jack was not yet free, that the last few months weren't over. More so, it reminded her that Jack was, and to a certain extent always would be, a marked man.

"It'll be no bother," she said, overly cheerfully. "I'll make sure we've got some milk and tea in." There was a silence. Jack knew he had upset her but didn't know how to begin mending the problem without first making it worse. "Now come on, you'll be wanting a bath if you're going out tonight. I've had the hot water on all day," she said before he managed to respond.

"Are you going to come tonight?" he asked.

"We'll see. Maybe just for a bit. Go and get yourself sorted, eh kid?"

"Is my stuff done?"

"I'll iron it while you're in the bath, leave it on your bed for you."

"Nice one Mam, honestly."

Chapter Five

Noise from The Comet drifted like smoke into the night and merged with the sound of the world – engines humming in the distance; shouting behind slammed doors; unseen groups rustling like dead leaves throughout the darkened streets. Outside the pub a single, tattered armchair sat staunchly in its place. Originally a royal blue but now the colour of autumn, duct tape secured the gaps where the acrylic filling tried to burst through the tears. Two empty bottles of brown ale lay on the floor rolling noisily in the breeze and a bottle of an almost empty spirit was clutched in the hands of Willie Telford, teeth black from woodbines, body sore from the cold. The redness of his eyes was so ingrained that no amount of rehabilitation would change his physical state, not that this concerned him. He savoured the night air through his crumpled face – he was a rusting scrapyard, disorganised and tarnished – and took another sip from his bottle. Spirits for his soul, he would inform those that passed him on the way into the pub. Half-cut already his face felt foreign to his body, tongue light but lazy in his mouth. As his head fell back against the soft damp chair the faintest murmur of *Danny Boy* danced on his breath.

Inside the pub was packed. It looked like any other low-rate, unkempt pub. In fact it was so much like every such pub that it could easily have been the blueprint, the mould from which all other dodgy boozers would later be crafted. Metal chairs with burgundy fabric covers circled each of the Formica tables. The once cream walls streaked with brown that oozed as though freshly bled – thick tar that trickled from the auburn clouded ceiling to the sticky floor. When treading from seat to bar the carpets squelched and the wood crunched beneath your feet. By the pool table, which stood in front of the fruit machine, men lined up to bet their last pennies; as much about the power kick as the financial incentive. Though the money didn't hurt.

Shirley stood at the bar with Bob and another couple. Jack sat with Darren and Thomas around a large table towards the back of the room. A bigger group of friends surrounded them – using Jack's return as an excuse to celebrate. Jack's lack of drink was noticeable. His friends held pints and halves depending on income; girls sipped shorts or soft drinks topped up with the quarter bottles of spirits hidden in their handbags. However abstinence was his new mission. If he wanted to stay on the straight and narrow then he had to have a clear head at all times. Feeling vulnerable without a glass to sip from he filled the void by smoking constantly throughout the night, lighting each new fag with the still-lit end of the last one and inhaling as deeply as his lungs would let him.

Janet, the landlady, approached their table with a smile and a tray on which she carried three pints of anaemic-looking ale. She was attractive but hard and robust; a traditional model, she would tell customers. This was accurate, Jack thought, was the model in question a Ford Sierra. Her brawn was partly the inadvertent effect of over three decades' access to fizzy beverages and salted snacks, but also a conscious development: a slight lass would make little impact during the now regular brawls. And so Janet consoled herself on occasion that her size was in fact as much a business venture as anything else.

"Here you go lads," she said, parking the tray onto the table in front of them. "On the House. Welcome back Jack, my son – nice to see you home in once piece. You've certainly made your Mam a happy woman. You should go away more often!" She nipped Jack's shoulder affectionately and his friends laughed. Jack looked over to the bar where Shirley was downing a cider and black, holding court with a group her own age. Jack left his pint on the tray.

"Cheers Janet, I'm not drinking though. Got to sort myself out, you know..."

"Teetotal! You fucking puff!" Darren shouted through mouthfuls of beer, hurrying the complimentary beverage before Janet changed her mind.

"Piss off," Jack said, beginning to blush. "Plenty of people don't drink."

"Aye," said Thomas, philosophically. "*Puffs*."

"Piss off man." Jack could feel himself getting more and more heated. He had always been known as the quiet type. This wasn't due to embarrassment; he simply preferred to say nothing than to have to explain himself. Hassle made him uneasy.

"Go on!" Darren egged him on.

"I'm not drinking."

"Ah go on," Janet began "You'll have to be inside for best part of my life to see another free pint in this place. Make the most of it while you can love."

"Nah Janet, cheers and all though. Give it to Willie Telford or something; tell him it's Christmas again."

Through the window Willie was standing in front of his chair, shrouded in the amber glow of the streetlight, swaying to a tune that only he could hear. The larger group around Jack began to jeer and chant, egging him on, encouraging him to take just one sip of the pint as though it were some sort of necessary initiation. He sat, reddening, shaking his head, widening his eyes at Darren – desperate for him to stop them. Janet shook his shoulders from behind like he was a boxer about to enter the ring.

Jack looked around. The growing noise of the crowd was beginning to attract the attention of the whole pub. He picked up his pint reluctantly, eager to stop the fuss, and took one sip. The chants turned into light cheers and then dipped as a steady clapping sound filled the pub. Jack felt his insides shift. He no longer felt bad about drinking, he felt obliged. He took the pint and downed it in one awkward, spluttering manoeuvre that resulted in much of it dribbling onto his shirt and the floor around him. The first sips of beer tasted metallic and wrong. Alcohol was in short supply in prison, maybe a smuggled whiskey miniature here and there, but Jack always pawned them for cigarette money. Within seconds though it became familiar. It felt organic. The glass hit the table with a thud. There was more cheering momentarily and then the whole crowd turned; normal business resumed. Jack felt slightly let down, anticlimactic.

"Nice to have you back mate!" Darren slapped him on the back, which cheered Jack cheer slightly.

"Ah man," Jack said, puling his damp shirt away form his body. "Look what you made me do! And in front of the missus an' all."

Janet wrapped her arm around Jack's neck. "Now come on," she said, "I've watched Shirley wipe caked shite from your arse plenty of times before now. A few drops of ale down your civvy's going to make no difference. You'll always be bloody gorgeous to me." She pinched his cheeks and he pulled his face away as Darren and Thomas laughed. Janet stepped away from the table, back to the waiting queue at the bar where the struggling new girl was fighting with the temperamental beer pumps and the advances of the more lecherous locals. "Just go canny, eh? Tough as old boots that one –" she said, nodding at Shirley " – but she's soft as shite when it comes down to it. Just watch yourself, eh Jack? For her sake as well as yours."

"Cheers Janet."

"Any time hinny. And you lot are paying for the rest, you tight bastards."

Jack was negotiating a round of pints at the furthest end of the bar. He smiled across the room at Shirley and she returned the favour as she continued to chat to another old couple whose son Jack had once been close to. John stood next to Jack waiting for his chance to be served, still clutching the pool cue in one hand. Having already welcomed Jack's return he had quickly become aware of a lack of conversational prompts and so stood eagerly waiting for Jack to make the first move.

"So what you been up to then?" asked Jack, grudgingly, waiting for the head to settle on the final pint.

"This and that," said John.

"Shit, eh?" said Jack

"Yeah."

Already Jack was bored. From across the large main room of the pub a woman's shrill laugh caught his attention. Mark had whispered something into Tina's ear as they stared over at Jack and John, which she had seemed to find amusing.

"So you back with Tina then?" Jack asked.

"Aye, canny lass," he said. "Don't know why we finished in the first place."

Jack considered reminding him of the sawn-off shotgun incident but it would have been too easy.

"She's nice. She's always been close to that Mark though, hasn't she?" Jack asked, balancing the three pints carefully in his grasp. "Go back a long way. Weren't they seeing each other at one point?"

John coughed slightly behind him and edged further

towards the bar, gently nudging Jack out of the way.

"Yeah, well..." he began to mumble as his face drained its usual milky pallor and refilled with a gentle crimson. "Their fathers were inside at the same time and all that. Nothing like that though. Nowt funny going on or owt..." He said unsurely.

"Oh no mate, she's a good lass. Nowt funny I don't reckon," Jack said as he turned his back on the bar, still balancing his drinks carefully. "I'd trust her with my life – she's been a good mate to our Nathalie my Mam told 'us. Mark's just a bit of a funny 'un if you ask me, gets a bit close and that. I'd just keep an eye out if it was me. That's all. She's a good girl, worth fighting for..."

John looked over to where they sat. Mark whispered another joke in Tina's ear. Less funny than last time it still caused her to giggle and blush, slapping him playfully with the back of her hand as he skipped backwards towards the pool table, before simulating cartoon sex with his pool cue.

Jack didn't turn around to see John redden further. He heard him exhale sharply, like the blast of air that propels the bullet. He couldn't help but smile.

"...best give 'us a chaser too Janet," Jack heard him say just before he had wandered out of earshot. "Make it a double."

"Must be nice though," Peggy said to Shirley as she pocketed her change at the bar, taking a sip from her brown ale.

"Oh it is, he's going to get a job as well," Shirley said as she followed Jack's route back to his friends' table like a sniper "– straight away he said. And he wants to start paying board by next week; I said he didn't have to but he's desperate to." Shirley beamed with a mother's pride and only the slightest hint of superiority. Peggy's son was one of the many wasters throughout the estate. The type of boy that couldn't even be bothered robbing to earn his own keep. Thieves and scallys were not considered particularly insulting terms because they implied at least some degree of initiative. Dosser was the most cutting insult and Tommy was the king of them all.

"Well, that's more than our Tommy ever did," she said coldly, having the good grace to at least acknowledge her own son's shortcomings.

"Your Jack never was a bad lad," added Tom, Peggy's other half – a small man whose wife had always added the extra inches he lacked. Those signs that would become inexplicably popular – *Sod The Dog, Beware Of The Wife* – seemed to have been invented with Peggy in mind. Even her most affectionate words were barked.

"None of them are," said Shirley "They're not angels, I'll tell you that for nothing, but they're not devils either. I just wish..." she paused and looked around at the boys, "I just wish that they didn't all have to hit rock bottom these days before they started clawing their way back towards the top, you know? They all think it has to get worse before it can get better." She took another drink and the sweetness lifted her a little.

"Not to worry though, eh?" Peggy said. "He's back now. Send him our love. We've just got to pop over there and see young Jimmy about fixing our back fence."

Shirley nodded as they left to go to the other end of the bar. Bob then moved in close, staring secret eyes at Shirley who turned away, keen to deter any public displays of affection but also quietly enjoying the power she had over him. Bob moved closer still. The music in the background grew louder over the din of the drinkers.

"...Howay," he nudged her with his knee.

"Eh?" She turned to face him.

"Howay, hinny." He gently took her hand beneath the bar and nodded towards the door.

"What have I told you?" she snatched her hand back and wrapped it around her drink. "Bloody one track you are."

"Oh come on love," said Bob with a desperate, canine look in his eyes. "Just a quick one – I'm busting over here. If it gets much worse I'm going to have to cut a hole in my mattress."

She finished her drink in one go, tipping the glass back to get her money's worth. Her bare, extended neck made Bob's jeans spring once and then settle achingly off kilter. Eyeing Jack's table she clocked him, Darren and Thomas, oblivious to her whereabouts, and then checked once more that the brief walk to the side entrance was unobstructed.

"Oh come on you filthy get. Quick, mind, round the back."

"Must be my lucky night!" whispered Bob, finishing his pint and stubbing out his cigarette.

"Round the back of the pub, you bloody nonce! Quick as well; I mean it – no funny business. Just in and out, that's your lot."

"Whatever you say my flower." They walked out of the pub with their heads held low, close enough for their hands to be touching, but not close enough to hold. The thrill of their homemade secret made even Shirley eager for release.

Jack didn't notice his mother leaving. Nor was he particularly engaged in the conversation that was happening at his table. His mind was somewhere else, processing the information and providing appropriate answers, but still not engaged.

"So there were no birds in there at all then?" asked Thomas, nudging Darren.

"No."

"And you didn't, like, start fancying other blokes?"

"No, but it can be done you know? I was only in there for the month."

"Just over," Thomas added

"Aye, whatever. I'm out now. That's all that matters. I'm getting a job you know?" Jack turned to Darren.

"Aye?"

"Straight up. Probation officer's coming round tomorrow. He'll be fuck all use, but I'll sort something out. I don't need telling by some twat with a clipboard."

Darren looked anxiously from side to side before leaning in closer to Jack. "Look, mate, I wouldn't normally ask you this, but –"

"Darren man!" Jack interrupted. "I've got nothing, I can't lend you owt until –"

"No." Darren leant further forward and scanned the area suspiciously. "I've got a way."

"What?"

"A way to help you out. Get a bit of cash to start yourself off with. Just help us out tomorrow."

Jack felt nervous immediately, like he had been given bad news. "What yous up to?"

Thomas broke into a proud smile. The music dipped to a slower, more sombre song as curls of smoke from Jack's cigarette wound around his body like tentacles.

"Me and Thomas here," said Darren. "Have got a little plan."

"What?"

"We've sorted everything out –" Thomas's speech was slurred and gluey through unfortunate genetics rather than alcohol intake. He always spoke like his words were battling through treacle. " – but Darren reckons if you help out we can split the profits three ways," he said with a slight tinge of resentment.

"What are yous up to?" Jack asked sceptically. He, Thomas and Darren used to arrange a job once a month. Bigger houses, shops, cars on occasion but that was beginning to prove too risky. Always for profit and never if there was a

direct victim. Jack felt that a robbery could only be successful if you were honourable about your intentions – taking
from an innocent person that might have a family to provide
for was bad. Entering a house where children may be sleeping was wrong. But taking from a man whom you knew to
both live alone and deserved everything he got, well that was
a different matter. Most of their initial plans had revolved
around teachers and ex-teachers from school. Occasionally
social workers, the odd policeman, a shop that had unfairly
barred them. But this was in the past. To return felt both
impossible and pointless; like growing your virginity back.

"You know St Cuthbert's has just had its roof done?" His
voice was hushed and intense as much to create a sense of
spectacle over their ingenious plan as it was to keep it strictly
on a needs-must basis.

"Yeah."

"It's so easy mate." Darren laughed. "We nick a motor
tomorrow night, right?"

"Right."

"Drive round school when it's dark, yeah?"

"Just get on with it mate," Jack said as his knee began jerking through a mixture of impatience and anxiety.

"Strip the roof when no-one can see. Bomb down south,
sell the lead on. I've been in touch already; they reckon a
couple of grand easy for that amount of gear. Fucking perfect! What do you say?" He sat back up, having laid his plan
and awaiting his praise and gratitude.

Jack remained still for a moment. The money was undeniable and the risk minimal. Back in the day, he thought, this
would have been the perfect scam.

"No," Jack eventually said. Darren's face fell.

"I said he wouldn't." Thomas smirked, pleased to have
retained a third of his profit.

"Jack, mate, it's watertight."

"Why not just sell the motor?"

"Come on Jack the lad – you've not been out of the loop for that long. You know that's a dying art, more trouble than it's worth."

"Nah man, cheers and everything. But no. I can't be doing with it anymore. We're not kids."

"Jack –" Darren grabbed his arm as he spoke, eager to involve him in the plan. To him the money was second to Jack's company on their mission. Darren was a perpetual deputy and he preferred it this way. With just himself and Thomas he became Sheriff and this, as well as being less fun, would lead to far greater risks. The first time Darren had been arrested it was because he had left his wallet in the victim's bathroom after taking a piss. He knew he was not the stuff criminal masterminds were made of. " – Don't think of it as stealing. We're just shopping in other people's lives."

Jack laughed. There was no way Darren had invented that on his own but he still found it funny. "Think about it–" Darren went on " – few hundred quid each way, no invest-ment, canny trip down south. We can pull a few spins, have a burnout when we get back. It'll be like a reunion, welcome young Jacky back to the hood! We can have a fag on the roof at St. Cuthbert's, like old times."

Jack nodded solemnly. He knew it was important to Darren but that he couldn't change his mind. "Here," Darren went on, "Imagine Stape's face when he realises his roof's gone." He pushed his chair back and threw his hands in the air, pulling his face into that of a shocked, doddery old teacher. Stape was the last of the old-style teachers at St Cuthbert's, which meant he struggled all the more with the new-style youths who marched through his classroom each and every day. The stony boys with arms bigger than their intellects and criminal records by year ten; expectant moth-ers that had yet to learn trigonometry. They were a different breed of people. Born angry. Born bad. Born so far down that the top was invisible, so why bother trying? Their moods combined with a teacher's ever decreasing ability to enforce the rules meant that to him any sort of breakthrough was futile, and so he just did all he could to remain sane. He became cold and hard – harder than them, harder than stone – and he became closed, allowing them to do what they liked when they decided to turn up so long as it didn't interfere with his safety.

Despite this, he was one of the few teachers who would, on occasions of extreme pressure, allow himself to physically interfere with the children. A back-hander to one boy that had thrown a chair at him during a particularly heated Oxbow Lake discussion, or pinning the occasional spotty thug against a wall to highlight the seriousness of a frenzied hacksaw attack. Stape's car was the only vehicle that Jack, Darren, and Thomas had taken not for profit but for malice. It floated for a moment after they pushed it into the quayside. Swirling on the dark waters optimistically as though someone may have taken heart and would pull it back out it didn't take long for it to realise the futility of its hope. And as it plunged down with a series of rewarding, belching bubbles on the water's surface they had laughed before realising that their dramatic conclusion meant they would be walking home in the rain once more.

"Yous do it," said Jack eventually. "I'm definitely out."

"Come on mate," Darren pleaded

"Just leave him," said Thomas. "We can do it on our own. It'll be alright, if he doesn't want to then you can't force him."

"I can't," Jack said. "I would, but it could ruin everything. You know what it's like Darren. It's my first probation meeting tomorrow. I'm getting a job. I'm getting sorted. Don't worry about it though, I won't say nothing."

"I know you won't say anything mate. It's just free money, that's all. Where's the risk?"

In the background the pub suddenly began to move more vigorously. Mark and John scuffled by the pool table, veins in their bald heads writhed like worms coming up for air. People around them began to move towards a safer corner of the bar. It was no surprise and there was no confusion. The commotion caused Jack to look up above the empty glass that he had been focusing on throughout Darren's proposal. He wanted to smile at the scene unfolding but stopped himself.

They started pushing one another, hands pressed into their chests with loud thuds, necks arched and heads pointed forward like deer in a mating ritual. They pushed one another so hard that they both flew backwards but remained standing. John walked to where his girlfriend sat holding his drink and handed her his jacket, turning his back to the fight. Mark grabbed a snooker cue and swung it to the side. The thin stick sliced through air and landed flatly across the side of John's head. He fell to the floor, his hand clutched to his ear. The impact was more shocking than it was severe, yet it cut through the atmosphere of the pub and everything fell quiet, then noisy with mutters of disapproval at the attacker's cowardice

"Take it outside!" Janet yelled from behind the bar. Mark left, followed by an anxious crowd. John raised himself up from the floor, livid and red. He started screaming and shouting, swearing promises of death and disfigurement.

"Outside, now!" Janet shouted again. John removed his bracelet gently despite his rage – a present from his daughter – and handed it to his girlfriend. He flew through the crowds and out of the double doors that swung behind him like bridesmaids at a wedding flapping over a creased train. Tina ran to the bar so quickly that by the time she got there she was still bent over in the shape that she had been while sitting down.

"Call the police Janet, please, he'll fucking kill him, please Janet I can't be doing with all that again!" She clung to the bar like she was drowning, tears forming in her eyes.

"There's no bloody use sweetheart. They'll never come round here, especially not this time of night. Let them beat it out of one another – they'll be back inside to pop the black before your tab's gone out."

"*Shit!*" Tina ran on the spot before pushing herself from the bar and rushing outside to join the braying mob.

"You're sure then?" said Darren, standing up, still clinging to the possibility of Jack's company on the job.

"Sure. Cheers anyway though."

"Alright then," he said flatly. "No worries, eh?"

"No worries."

"Fancy a bit of boxing?" Darren nodded towards the door. Through the window the crowd was visible but Mark and John were out of sight. Willie Telford had taken to standing on his chair, balanced dangerously and clapping uncertainly over the heads of the swarm.

"Come on then," said Jack, joining Darren.

"Welcome back mate!" he said again, excitedly, pushing Jack gently as they walked towards the door. Thomas followed behind.

A ring of spectators had formed that the boys pushed their way towards the front of. Bedroom lights began to flick on throughout the street as though the houses themselves were waking up, stirring at the commotion. The men circled one another like animals; their anger was no longer human. The fight itself had become more important than the sentiment. The spilled beer or crude remark about one man's family was long forgotten. It never mattered that much in the first place. "Think you're fucking hard, do you?" John screamed. His head flew forward with a choreographed grace. The crack of his skull against Mark's nose made Jack silently retch. It was a sound you could only appreciate had you been on the wrong end of it yourself at some point in your life. He felt his gag reflex kick in at the thought of it, the sound of your own bones crumbling into your face. He remembered that it hurt, more than anything, and this made him nauseous. Yet the sensation itself was something he could not call to mind; pain is the only thing you can never remember.

"Cunt!" Mark spat as he stepped backwards, holding his face in his hand. John moved towards him cautiously, calculating his next move. He reached down and pulled him into an upright position with one hand, swinging his other like a sword into the side of his head. Mark's neck bent wrongly and he pushed himself towards him, allowing no space for his fists to gain momentum. They began a more even fight: tearing their arms around in the air, landing erratic bruises onto one another's bodies, their thrashing shape swaying towards different ends of the crowd.

Shirley and Bob emerged from behind the small row of shops that adjoined The Comet. Shirley pulled her skirt downwards and checked to make sure their emergence wasn't noticed by Jack. She straitened her shirt and coat around her breasts, covering her exposed bra. Bob's smirk was not so easy to conceal.

"Do you think we should sort it out?" Jack asked Darren reluctantly.

Shirley pushed herself to the front of the crowd and grabbed Jack by the arm. "Don't you bloody dare," she said. "Let someone else get their hands dirty. Stupid bastards. I never trusted that Mark anyway, deserves a good kicking if you ask me. *Filthy gyppo*. Rule in life son – never trust a man whose eyebrows are that close together, because you can bet your last provvy cheque he'll have been paddling in the wrong end of the gene pool."

"Rule number two," said Bob, pressing himself softly against Shirley as he watched the fight. "Never lend them a fiver if their house is on wheels."

They continued to brawl, their fists working furiously into their tender bodies, exhausting one another, each blow softer than the last. More lights throughout the estate flicked on, curtains twitched as frightened residents peered out at another night's damage. An elderly man stepped out of his front door, his wife watching from the darkened bedroom window. He looked tired but unsurprised by the incident. In his hand he clutched a baseball bat, the only object that he had slept with more than his wife. Other residents came to their doors, bleary-eyed and curious as to the specific cause of tonight's upset. Women in nighties smoking cigarettes, turning back to warn their children into the safety of their beds; men stomping to their front gates angrily, clutching bats and crowbars; in the warmth of the doorway their children stood like their fathers' phantoms. They watched them fighting in the burn of the streetlamps, blasting the commotion in a circle of fiery orange.

The enthusiasm of the crowd had tumbled from encouragement to concern as blood began spilling from the fighters more constantly, dripping to the floor and spreading with the damp of the ground. Exhausted, Mark swung one hand sharply into John's eye and his vision clouded; patches of diamond the colour of oil began to merge in his right eye as he tottered backwards. Looking to regain the upper hand he rushed at Mark, grabbing him by the face. He pushed him through the crowds backwards, holding his throat in a lion's clutch. With one final thrust he pushed him back through the air. Mark's feet left the ground and his body cascaded through the long plate of glass at the front of the betting shop. He fell through with a smash, falling gently to the floor as glass tinkled around his body like Christmas bells, chiming sharply as they hit the concrete of the floor before spewing out of the shop like bile.

Mark lay still on the floor, his sporadic steams of breath the only sign that he was still alive. Glass continued to fall gently around him, crunching and biting hard into the ground. A jagged lip of teeth hovered dangerously above his sleeping body. John stared at him for a moment, fuming, his red face pounding to the beat of his heart. Blood that seeped between his teeth tasted unsatisfying. He felt hungry for more – teased but ultimately unfulfilled. He spat once in Mark's direction and then walked back into the pub. Mark didn't move. The crowd began to make way back inside, narrowing eyes at him as they passed.

"Do you fancy another one before we head off then?" asked Shirley, stamping her feet on the spot to keep her shivering legs warm.

"You buying?" asked Jack. "Because I'm skint"

"One night only. After this you're on your own kid."

"Fair enough." She linked his arm and together they walked back into the pub, followed by Darren, Thomas and Bob. Beneath the shattered glass Mark murmured a broken sentence that no-one heard. The words fell from his mouth and hit the ground like a dead animal. He turned on his side and looked around at the empty streets.

"You stopping out for a bit?" Shirley had asked Jack as Bob dragged her towards the door. Bob was an alright sort of bloke. Canny, Jack would have said, if pushed for an adjective. He wasn't perfect but he was comfortable enough and had been used as a sort of in-case-of-emergency stand-in, like the cracked plate you never get round to sending to the charity shop. But Jack wasn't stupid and their secret romance was more for their sake than his. It hadn't been a subject he'd ever broached with Shirley – the way your mother's reproductive action seldom was – but he knew that Bob had been having her for months now. They'd even nicked one of his condoms while he'd been away. Either that or a desperate and concise burglar had raided his room in a frenzy before washing and ironing his bedding and placing a welcome home card on his pillow containing just one kiss.

Jack let them get on with it. "Yeah, I am, not for long or owt like that."

"Hmmm, be good," she mumbled with her eyes squinting through two black postboxes, slurred herself though she'd never admit it. Kissing him on the cheek she felt his face warm up.

"Mam man!" he pushed her away and she looked mock-shocked at his friends who laughed and cheered her on.

"Go on you tight git, one more for your poor, poor Mam." Jack shook his head and allowed himself to be drawn to her ample bosom. As her damp lips pressed into his cheeks he smelt the chalky, tobacco-infused scent of borrowed makeup and chained fags that always made him think of Shirley. "I'll leave the key in the nearest pot to the door," she whispered in his ear. "No-one back to the house mind, or you'll wish you were back inside."

"Right. Whatever. I'll not be long."

"Mind," she shook her finger and pursed her lips, signalling all sorts of warnings. "You young 'uns watch how yous are going. And don't do anything I wouldn't do."

"That doesn't leave much!" Darren shouted.

"Darren Robinson you watch that mouth of yours 'else I'll bend you over my knee and really give you something to smirk about."

"Promises Shirley, promises!" Thomas and his friends laughed as Jack shot them what may best be described as an old-fashioned look. Bob lead Shirley to the door as she took one breast in each hand and shook them playfully at the group.

"Maybe once you've got your pubes in, eh lads?" Shirley yelled across the emptying room as the door closed behind her to the sound of boos and wolf-whistles.

"You going to talk to him then?" Clare asked. Rachel sat poised for success: legs crossed, skirt hitched, cleavage padded to within an inch of its life. Soft, caramel, cupid bow lips had been drawn on over the course of the evening to compensate for her naturally puckered oral garniture. Directly opposite her Jack kept glancing in her direction; magnetised by her convex assets he snuck peeks between the filtering locals as they stumbled through his line of view towards the main exit. Tectonic thighs grazed knowingly against one another. Her caramel skin was as sweet as the dib-dab perfume she doused behind her ears and knees before a night out. Grown up scent was beyond her; Rachel's appeal was that she always had, and always would, smell like a gorgeous girl. It suited her. She had the fast, flash beauty that exploded so fast in youth that adulthood never would be able to keep up. She'd be completely extinguished by the time she hit twenty-five and she felt it her duty to make the most of it while she could. She was a firework. Clare however was a different kettle of fish. The ugly best friend and everything it entails. Even when made up to within an inch of her life she looked like a Christmas tree in January and permanently held a vinegary, resentful sort of look.

"Dunno. Do you think he'll remember 'us?" Rachel asked nervously as she stared at his angular body – uncomfortable and anxious as though waiting for something. In the dim light of last orders Jack looked like a question.

"Who cares? Come on." Clare dragged Rachel up by the arm. Linked like jewellery they walked across to the group who were chatting in a low, synchronised patter.

"Oi-oi, everyone hide it's Clare in the community!" Darren yelled and moved one seat across to accommodate the pair. "Here, Clare, suck 'us off and I'll mend your Mam's back fence."

"Fuck of Darren," she said, sitting down next to him. Rachel smiled at Jack and he moved his feet from the stool on which they rested and watched her carefully as she sat down.

"Wouldn't need fixing if your Alex hadn't gone off on one with our Kirstie. Who the fuck brings a sledgehammer to a christening?"

"Who the fuck has a christening and doesn't invite the father?"

"Whatever Darren, I can't be arsed with it to tell you the truth," Claire said as she placed her bag on the seat beside her. "Alright Jack –" she turned her attention from Darren who snooped his eyebrows to try and catch a glimpse of her carefully manufactured cleavage "– how you been?"

"*In prison*," he shot back drolly. Clare was a hard girl to like. Maybe she'd been given an unfair disadvantage. Jack had always found Clare to be a hard name to like in itself and couldn't think of one that he'd gotten on with entirely. It felt like a name that tried too hard. Saying it felt like tea with too many sugars in. Rachel laughed and rolled her eyes secretly at Jack. "Alright Rachel."

"Now then Jack," she said looking up at him through playful eyes. "How's life?"

"Short and shit." He downed the remainder of his pint. "You need another drink?"

"No point is there – last orders already gone. You going down the squat tonight?"

"Dunno – might not be a wise move with my recent track record."

"We're going."

"Maybe for a bit then."

"Canny." She took a stray pint glass from the centre of the table and finished the flat leftovers in one gulp. Jack felt himself stiffen and tense. Sex wasn't something you thought about in prison. Or rather it was something you thought about all the time but told yourself you shouldn't. Over excitement inside was like having a cocked pistol and no target; only bad things could ensue.

His arm curled around her twisting waste as they walked through the streets. Darren and Thomas walked ahead clutching smuggled pint glasses which they necked and smashed off the pathways in a rewarding explosion of glass and sound.

"Can't believe you've got us going back to this shithole," he whispered to Rachel as they crossed the battered threshold.

Two buildings that even the council couldn't fill formed the body of the squat – adjoining semis that had been knocked through by teenagers desperate for an after school hiding place. It had become a sort of community centre; a derelict crumble of rotting architecture and swollen damp patches in which the local youngsters could find solace to do as they pleased beneath a skeletal roof. The brickwork between the two houses had been hastily deconstructed one summer's evening when Jack and some of his friends had gathered tools to place their mark on the landmark. Like lions they started by christening the walls with streams of their own savoured piss before tearing a through passage to create one large living space between two unsteady staircases leading to the bedrooms. In the long stretch between ten and sixteen – when halves seem more significant in years than inches – you weren't worth mentioning had you not experienced a first in The Squat. Most of Jack's firsts had been in the squat. His kiss was at twelve as his glutinous, lethargic tongue edged its way to the back of Tina Outhwaite's throat. Gagging at the sudden insertion she had dug her nails into his sides in an attempt to stop herself from throwing up, an act which he mistook for amorous advances. Shortly after which he had experienced his first proper slap. Two tabs of e had been dropped on his fourteenth birthday as a treat from Darren via one of his pharmaceutically inclined cousins, shortly before his first joint of tac to bring his jittering limbs back into the conscience of his own nervous system. Jack's first time had been on a filthy mattress that was wetter than Jayne Armitage as she writhed uncomfortably through his grunts and gurns. Still a year from her legality it was, she had later told her classmates, like the earth had shifted, failing to mention that it had shifted into a new existence where it felt as though she had stubbed her insides sharply on a doorframe.

Like a playground after rain the whole space smelt warm and rueful despite usually registering as close to freezing as a building can get even in the summer months. Sunlight never entered because of the peephole iron boards that were nailed tight to the window frames, yet somehow streetlamps illuminated the living room at night, meaning that in the mornings the squat was engulfed in almost total darkness, but the afternoon came in a hazy, uncomfortable dim.

In the space that was once the dining room a gang of ten or so youths passed around a limp joint as they huddled to keep warm.

"Two toke pass," one of the boys said in pinched tones as a hazy wave of smoke swirled from his lips. Passing to the left each member took a hit and held their breaths tight, chests expanding under the pressure. As the joint reached the same boy for the second time they exhaled in unison and relaxed, allowing a mellow wave to engulf them warmly like a smile from a stranger.

"Now kids, who's got the gear?" Darren led Clare by the hand. She had thawed to his advances in an attempt to stop his constant jibes rather than to satisfy her own lust and had put him on a promise so long as he lay off the fat jokes and slag jokes. They sat down with Thomas and some of the others and initiated themselves into the game of smoke.

"Let's not," Rachel whispered to Jack. Her hands curled around his. He nodded and led her to the staircase – travelling first to unearth any hidden loose planks. Dean Gibson had lost his left bollock after falling drunkenly through a floorboard in the stairs of The Squat. Splintered wood and nails had supported him tightly around the upper thigh until his friends were alerted to his scream. Doctors said that if they wanted to stop the bleeding from developing they would have to operate. Dean said he'd take his chances; his mother had insisted otherwise. He was known as the Cyclops.

The first empty room they came to had just a sofa and a bedside table. Bottles rolled across the floor as Jack opened the door and were stopped suddenly by the wall at the other side of the small room. Needles from the smackheads' occasional jaunts pointed downwards into the ground, broken and empty.

"Pull up a pew," she said, sitting down on the sofa and dragging Jack down with her. He sat and for the first time since his first time felt nervous about what may ensue.

"Relax," she said, kissing his neck.

He did as instructed and took her face in his hand, kissing her hard on the mouth. Locating his tongue with hers she kissed back, sucking him further into her as she parted her knees and straddled his waist.

"I've got an idea," she said, picking something out of her bag. "Here, have one of these babe – welcome back present." The tiny white tablet looked odd between her fingers, like a giant holding a saucer. As it perched on the pink tip of her index finger he stopped himself from gulping it on instinct.

"I can't," he said painfully, as though he was missing a beer and sex festival for a dentist appointment. "I'm on the mend – getting a job, getting sorted. I've just come out of prison for fuck's sake Rach."

"God Jack, you make it sound like you were a nonce. You're just a robber. Your only mistake was getting caught. Come on, for me."

"Can't we just carry on... you know?"

"Well I'm doing one, and it would be rude to let a lass go there on her own. I need a chaperone, to keep 'us safe." Unconvinced by her rhetoric his nose scrunched and his eyes narrowed. "Come on babe." She leant forward and bit his ear. "Where's the Jack we all know and love? I want him tonight, not some tosser that can't handle a good time when it slaps him in the face..." she kissed his neck "... kisses him where it's good..." she placed her free hand between his legs and whispered an act that made his entire body levitate an extra inch.

Although reluctant, he felt himself edging towards her extended finger and dry swallowing the pill. It only took a few minutes of kissing for it to hit him. His insides were a warm lava lamp. Exempt from gravity and all bad feelings he floated through the following hours as she drained completely. Her back arched, his pressed against the mouldy couch; jerking uncontrollably his body felt like a dog returned home after days of being missing. He felt like he was being slotted back into himself. Yet even through the piquant snap of his double-ended euphoria he felt a nag. Unusually something had crawled through the beautiful tangle of the chemicals and wrapped around his brain like a fire blanket, trapping all good thoughts in its shadow. Despite his best efforts it seemed that gradually his old life was growing back upon him like dry rot in a beautiful new house. Rachel kissed him again and he forced himself not to care.

Chapter Six

Nathalie pushed the pram through the estate, the hard wheels clicking a Morse code that became more jumbled as they travelled faster and faster across the pavement towards the corner shop. She had heard the noise the night before, but preferred safety over curiosity since Nicole had arrived and so had secured the fire guard to the downstairs window, just in case, and hid upstairs with her daughter. Growing up she had been one of the girls in the pub that would encourage violence. Or rather she would be one of the girls sitting nervously with those that caused the violence, the girls that began screaming after just four drinks, who played boys off against one another and then shrieked when the sound of smashing became too much.

She was quieter though, gentler. Her looks had gotten her to the top of the food chain at school but they were at odds with her attitude. She was a mouse trapped in a giraffe's body. Her friends were the wild girls, tough lasses, hard as fuck but loyal with it. Her friends were the girls that said fuck me hard but have me home by eleven, who never tried at schoolwork but practised every night to make sure their flawed sentences were executed with perfect penmanship. They were sweet, if fiery, and to be in with them meant that the atrocities of life between five and sixteen were made just a little bit more bearable. And so she played the game, layered on her stolen makeup like a clay death mask, glossed her lips so that her words reflected in their gleam, shortened her skirt so much that she would often weep with shame in the changing room after PE. She thanked God that for her final four years of school boys spent more time staring at her tits and arse because one glance at her face would have revealed a blush that no amount of foundation could have concealed.

She bent down and stroked Nicole's soft, chalky cheek as she mounted the step to the shop. Patches of red still stained the ground next to the betting shop and a makeshift wooden board shielded the men that had already left the Job Centre disheartened. Hunched sadly over marked scraps of paper they fondled their mini-pens and stared at the grainy screens, looking past the race to a time when their days were so full the notion of home was all that got them through the day. Now it was everything they wanted to avoid.

Shirley was inside of the shop, clutching a packet of broken biscuits. Ellen stood behind the counter teasing her shock of white hair as she spoke to Shirley of another family crisis.

The bell chimed once as the door closed behind Nathalie, who harrumphed around a stack of dented tins with the pram.

"Hello love." Shirley rushed over and took the front of the pram, directing it to the shop's counter.

"Cheers Shir', hiya Ellen."

"Hello flower, how you keeping?"

"Not so bad," said Nathalie, breathing deeply to claw back some breath and alleviate the redness in her cheeks. "This one's had a bit of a cough; I hope she's alright for the competition."

Shirley took Nicole from the pram and held her to her chest, kissing the baby's chilled forehead.

"Ah, you come to see your Aunty Shirley?" She jogged the baby twice in the air and caused the most distant ripple of a smile on her lips. The maternal snap flicked back and caught Shirley like a static shock, disappearing as quickly as it had appeared. For a second she felt empty and desperate. "The bonniest bairn in the world this one Ellen."

"Oh aye."

"Aren't you? Aren't you a little jewel?" She picked up a chocolate bar with a shiny wrapper in one hand and held it front of the Nicole's face, allowing beams from the strip light to glimmer and shine in its colourful reflection. Nicole made a gurgling noise and reached for the treasure like a magpie, wowed by the beauty, oblivious to its inexpensiveness.

"Have you heard from Him recently?" Shirley asked.

"Yeah," Nathalie swooned over the small freezer cabinet, "He said he missed us."

"Bless him." Shirley and Ellen melted. "He'll be seeing you soon. He's one of the good ones."

"Yeah. Hey, I saw our Jack yesterday. Is he back for good?"

"He bloody better be." Shirley glanced at Ellen who rolled her eyes as she sparked up another cigarette.

"I'm dead pleased for you Shirley. I was thinking I might bring Nicole round later on. You know? Let him see her now she's got a bit bigger. *You'll be forgetting what your Uncle Jack looks like if he's not careful,*" Nathalie said as she teased Nicole's hand beneath her towelled gloves.

"He'd be made up flower. Thinks the world of that little 'un. And you.

"Oh, yeah – I've just come for my milk Ellen." Nathalie said still smiling. She handed her tokens over the counter which Ellen checked on instinct against the light. Shirley tutted at Nathalie who shook her head knowingly at the familiar routine.

"Help yourself love," said Ellen, convinced of the authenticity of the tokens. "We've moved the boxes – they're round by the dog food."

"Cheers Ellen." She bent down and piled the boxes of milk into the gap at the bottom of the pram before pushing it towards the door. "See you later then Shir'."

"Aye, you watch how you're going mind."

"You an' all. Bye Ellen."
"Ta-ta love."

Peter was a man who had both looked and felt anxious for most of his life. This was not a quality that he relished, yet found it almost impossible to alter. He was the sort of boy that always stepped left when he should have stepped right and jumped a disproportionate distance at the shock of the telephone's first ring. His gaunt frame looked out of place in a suit; like a girl in her mother's stilettos. This was the case with suits in general, he had found, though was made doubly obvious by the fact that the only suit he could afford was a Medium grey number reduced to half price, and so had to rely on the questionable seamstress skills of his mother to tailor it to his needs.

Peter also felt as though he was the wrong shape for life. At school he had found solace in books like most boys to whom friends and ball skills are in short supply, and his studious nature marked him as different throughout. He was the swot, the freak, the one that tried. The one whose PE kit would always go missing and turn up smelling of piss.

He was the only boy at his school to apply to university and he often felt that his acceptance had only been as some sort of remit. His accent had marked him out at first, as well as his bemusement at the student way of life. Why, he would ask, would you choose to wear ripped jeans and mess your hair up when you came from families rich enough to provide you with a lifetime's worth of new clothes and grooming products? His only friends he had made by chance when on the first day of Fresher's week he had worn a shirt and tie and a crowd whose cockney accents were at odds with their designer clothes took it to be an ironic statement. He went along with it, pleased for the company, but remained bemused at their lifestyles and the fact that they put more effort into appearing 'wacky' than they did into the courses, which they said were just an excuse to get pissed for free for a few years.

At twenty-four Peter's accent had faded already so that just the faintest trace of background could be detected. You had to listen hard to hear it and even if you did catch a lazily ignored 't' or a hardened vowel every now and again it spoke more of income than geography. Returning to his homeland had been hard, now being considered too posh to fit in. Likewise, the job he had secured with the prison service proved equally unwelcoming, being deemed too common by co-workers to be lecturing ex-cons.

He left his car parked at the top of the estate. Partly through a basic, juvenile fear that the most expensive object he had ever owned would be damaged. But also because he wanted to make the best impression, get the balance between authority and friendship that would prove his colleagues wrong. This was his first case after months of groundwork – paperwork and tea making, bullet-pointing every utterance from his boss and developing that forced 'can do' attitude that his careers advisor had told him he would have to work on. The whole performance ached.

The Meadow Well was grim but he was not frightened of it. He had grown up not on it, but amid its residents – at school or at youth club on the rare occasion he'd risk it. His estate had not been much better, of a similar ilk if not as extreme. As a result he had been particularly eager to take this case – "*Who fucking cares, he'll be Her Majesty's responsibility in a matter of weeks,*" was the office consensus. Peter protested silently, filled with a fresh enthusiasm.

In the house Jack sat in the armchair, hair gelled and freshly ironed shirt donned at the insistence of his mother, his eyes staring two holes into the wall. Shirley rose lazily to answer the door.

"Just give it a bloody go," she hissed on her way past, already disgruntled at the hangover Jack had insisted didn't exist. "They're only trying to help you, you miserable little shite."

Through the door he saw a rakish shadow, like death had come to take his mother. He smiled at this thought and then swallowed his own amusement, determined to remain stony and silent throughout. They entered the room; Jack remained seated. "Hello, um, Jack, right? Hi I'm Peter." His voice was thick but posh, Jack thought. He was timid with an almost clumsy eloquence that Jack loathed. Grow a pair, he felt like saying, but didn't. Peter extended his hand to Jack as though he were a cautious child on his first trip to a petting zoo. Jack shrugged vaguely and turned his head to face the window, the sudden blast of light hurt his eyes but he forced himself to remain staring in the opposite direction.

Peter felt his heart skip a beat. Not the way they talked about at university, the way you're supposed to when you see someone you love for the first time. His insides moved downwards, like they were trying to escape his body and slink off into the grey day. It wasn't his nervousness that was causing his discomfort – and in a way this pleased him – but the futility of his words. He could make no difference, he knew deep down. Nothing he did mattered. Abandon all hope ye who enter The Ridges. He felt hollow and only slightly like taking Jack by the neck and squeezing him until he turned blue.

"Right, um," he bumbled on. For the first time he felt like he had stepped out of himself, hearing what everyone else heard when he spoke. Even he wanted to punch himself in the face. "So, anyway, you know I'm your probation officer, yeah?"

"You can sit down love," said Shirley. Peter nodded and did as instructed, sitting alone on the wide settee. Jack stared past him from one chair; Shirley glared at Jack from the other.

"Thanks. Now, Jack." Peter began fiddling with his black file holder on his lap, making more work than was necessary to find the relevant papers. "It wasn't that serious an offence, so employment oughtn't be too difficult to sort out. Have you had any thoughts about the type of job you'd like to go for Jack?"

Peter looked up. No response. He delved back into the files, ruffling papers for authenticity.

"...Um, right, well." The words bumped clumsily and frantically into one another and then shifted direction into what Peter hoped might be a more coherent sentence like a bee trapped in a sealed glass jar. "Well, according to your reports you've been learning a trade – um, joining, was it? Right, so that could come in useful, but the way things are we've got more chance if we look perhaps in logistics, perhaps delivery work? Or with some luck we may be able to get you into the hospitality industries. Have you ever worked in the hospitality industries before Jack?..."

Still no response. No, Peter found himself thinking, you probably still can't even spell it you fucking useless oaf. He ground his thoughts to a halt and apologised mentally to Jack. "Or maybe you could go for an Earn While You Learn course? They're new. I've got some information here if you'd just like to hold on..." He rummaged in his file, this time genuinely unable to locate the correct colour-coded sheet.

"Sorry. I'm nervous. It's my first proper week after the training and that. You're my first proper case – they gave me an easy one, said you were cooperative enough, everyone was fairly positive about the whole situation... I know it's in here somewhere." Peter pulled out a handful of coloured sheets and handed them to Jack who looked at them before turning his head back to the window. Shirley took them and placed them on the coffee table.

"Right. I'll just leave them there for you to have a look at when it's convenient. That's sort of the purpose of our visit today Jack; we just need to introduce my role in your rehabilitation, establish a few ground rules that sort of thing. What I can do is present you with what we see to be your immediate options career-wise, and with regards to accommodation... I presume you'll be living at home."

"Oh yes," Shirley answered before Jack had a chance not to. "He knows where his bread's buttered."

"Of course. So, um, have you heard of a mood board Jack?" Peter felt the words stick reluctantly as they left his mouth. It was a stupid idea and the only thing worse than a stupid idea is a stupid idea with an appropriately stupid name. He pressed on like he was travelling on autopilot, touching down the facts that he was contractually obliged to recite with a view to escaping as quickly as possible. Breathing became a painfully conscious activity the more he spoke, as though it controlled him rather than the other way round. Great lungfuls of air would swoop into him midway through words. "Basically it's this new thing we're trying out where we place some realistic goals on a piece of paper – the sort of things you want to make up your new life – and together we can go about working out how we might be able to achieve them."

Jack's face moved from the window to Peter; his eyes remained stony and dead but his jaw dropped just half an inch.

"Sorry love." Shirley stood up like a lighthouse; her face was a red stop sign desperate to switch back to amber. "Would you like a cup of tea?"

"Yeah, please," Peter said, momentarily forgetting that this would leave him and Jack alone in the room. He wasn't sure but thought for a moment that he had groaned out loud and became terrified that Shirley might return to find his bruised body impaled on a rolled up Mood Board.

"I'll sort that out for you flower." She left the room and he and Jack were alone; the hiss of the kettle from next door framed the silence like a certificate, rather than piercing it as Peter would have preferred.

"So what are your immediate goals Jack? Have you thought of anything at all?" Peter tried, in no way expecting a response but eager to fill in the coloured silences that ached like elevator music. Jack remained silent. He turned his head to the interviewer and was filled with all sorts of nausea – the shiny suit, the plastic briefcase, those awkward limbs that even Jack could tell felt wrong on Peter's body. Everything about him suggested effort and if, thought Jack, he was where effort got you then perhaps there was a lot to be said for devout idleness. Jack couldn't help himself – it was the eyes that did it. Those tortured, brown pools looking up through expectant brows, as though he was going to have some sort of breakthrough. Jack knew what he was to him – a target, a mission, a chance for a plus on the end of his A that would prove everyone wrong; those that said this lot were best left to crash and burn. If the shoe fits was his philosophy.

He made eye contact with the bloke, grudgingly, and nodded once towards the window. The sound of angry steam scorched through from the kitchen, dulling Shirley's gentle hums. Peter noticed Jack's nod, but didn't recognise the significance. He widened his eyes, scanning the room. Jack nodded again. Peter caught him this time and for a moment imagined that he had broken the ice. It must be some sort of delayed introduction, a wordless greeting, two boys passing each other in the school corridors. Peter did as Jack did: widened his eyes and nodded, slightly askew, towards the door. Jack's eyes then rolled dramatically to the side. He nodded again, this time mouthing words that Peter could only just make out. 'Fuck off' were the words his lips formed, as he nodded once more to the door.

"Here you go." Shirley came into the room as though on cue and handed Peter a cup of tea, who took the sturdy mug with hands he wished weren't trembling so noticeably.

"So," she sat back down with her own cup of tea and stared a warning at Jack. "University, that must have been canny?" She felt for the lad; he was polite enough. Too polite for her but this was hardly a crime. There was something different about him though, more fight inside of him than he was letting show.

"It was OK. I'm from round here though."

"Tynemouth is it?"

"Crompton Estate. Neville Street"

"You never are!" The words shone like gold to Shirley. From his voice to his suit to his job to his manner there was no trace of the area left on him; he was a clean slate with only the faint chalk marks of a new life etched onto his surface. This, she thought, could change things.

"Neville Street and you went to uni?" It was the first time Peter had heard Jack speak. Even though each word was bleached with disbelief and disdain, that words had left his lips was more than he was expecting.

"Well, yeah." Easy does it he told himself – let him know you're one of them and he might just let you in, might just coop-erate even if only for a bit. "I got some money off the course with my grades and that, and had a couple of jobs so that I could afford digs." Nicely done, he thought to himself. He felt his mouth teasing into a premature smile of relief but quickly sipped his tea to hide any traces of smugness.

"Oh you've done alright for yourself then haven't you hinny? Are you living at home at the moment?"

"Yeah."

"Well our Irene's just round the corner. That's my sister – she's a bit of a slag but harmless enough. *You could drop her hairdryer off for 'us when you're on your way back round*"

"Um, yeah." Peter allowed himself to smile for the first time.

"Thanks, it'll save 'us having to get the bus. It's fourteen Neville Street."

"Fourteen, right. I'm twenty-eight."

"Ah, isn't that good?"

"You can tell you never went to my school." Peter tried to stop himself. He knew it could ruin his chance of promotion and broke just about every rule in the book. But what use is the book if you can't do the job? The words just jumped from his mouth like they were escaping a burning building and didn't care who or what they left behind. "I did actually."

Part of him regretted it on impact, but in for a penny was his philosophy, or would be from now on. "St Cuthbert's, I was in the year above you." He tried to claw a link between himself and Jack. They didn't exactly move in the same circles. Jack's was more of a lynch mob and Peter tended to avoid contact with them at all costs. There were no shared experiences he could distinctly remember; Jack may have been in the background at some of the fights or in the library on a lunchtime detention, but Peter was never hard enough, or fit enough, or cool enough to have been associated with him. Then he remembered.

"You started that rumour about my sister."

"Amanda Storey?" asked Jack cautiously.

"Kerry Hart." There was a moment's silence and Jack looked pained.

"... *sorry*," Jack said sheepishly. Peter felt like dancing with victory, like kissing Shirley and Jack and taking them out for a drink. The least he felt like doing was laughing but even this he refrained from.

"I wouldn't worry about it," he said instead. "Turned out to be true anyway."

"Fuck off!" Jack sat bolt upright.

"Yeah, Dad still won't speak to her."

There was a pause. Jack relaxed and looked at Shirley whose smile was as obvious as Jack's submission to the cause.

He rolled his eyes again. "Job," he said.

"Pardon?"

"Get a job. That can go on the...*mood board*. I want to get a job. Fast."

"Right, brilliant!" Peter jumped into action and began rear-ranging coloured leaves of paper "Excellent. That's exactly the sort of thing we need to be thinking about Jack."

Chapter Seven

As the darkness seeped through invisible cracks into The Meadow Well so did the estate's children, testing the newly black waters for a safe spot to lurk. They clustered like cancers around shop fronts, bus stops, dead grass patches, burnt out cars. The sound of smashing glass twinkled in their wake making popping noises throughout the estate like tribal communications. These were the warning sounds; the danger sounds; these were the sounds that said we've got our patch, approach at your own risk. They looked anxious, angry, like a bad trip – suspicious of life and eager to fight. They made the night feel thundering and doomed. They were fireworks next to an open flame and they were desperate to be lit.

Nathalie kept the lights off at night. It was a decision based as much on safety as cost. Sometimes she had to turn them on – darkness made her feel panicky and sad; it went over her loneliness in a giant neon highlighter and she would run through the house flicking every light switch, frightened that the darkness may be having the same effect on her daughter. It had only happened to her the once, when a young gang caught her looking out at their spray painting session and spent the next twenty minutes hurling obscenities and stones. Two windows were broken. Nicole didn't cry once. She hadn't told Anthony on his return. Not because she didn't want to, and not because he wouldn't help, but because she was frightened of losing him and feared what he may have done to the culprits whom Nathalie could easily have named. He was always gentle with both of them, but his love as a father and husband was ferocious; he felt that he himself was irrelevant when it came to the comfort and safety of his girls and wouldn't think twice about destroying anyone that put them in danger. Part of Nathalie liked the sense of protection; a love that would kill for her; a love that would die. But sometimes it frightened her – not his actions, rather the thought that they may result in him being taken away from her. The courts had little regard for boys of a certain age and postcode.

As she flicked the curtains to scan the area she noticed that among the most prominent gang stood Jack, taller than the rest and mightier. His face had a different look, a different type of sadness to the people that surrounded him. His eyes seemed not to be scanning the estate for targets but escape routes. The sound of a smashing bottle made Nathalie jump back and close the curtains. Nicole stirred in her pram but didn't fully wake.

"Come on sweetheart." Nathalie flicked the brakes of the wheels with her foot and steered Nicole towards the door. She gently took away the broom handle that secured it in place. The lock and catch of the door had broken the week after Anthony had last left and the council were yet to fix it. On the rare occasion she left the house she had to be careful to shut the door gently as to make it seem locked. She placed the broom handle on the stairs and pushed the baby outside, the sudden blast of fresh air gently teasing Nicole from her slumber and she sang wordless songs to alert her mother to her newfound consciousness.

"Shhh love, we'll be back inside soon." She glanced fleetingly at the gang where Jack stood, disguising her peek as a soothing roll of a stiff neck. He nodded to her and she nodded back towards Shirley's house. She closed the door once but it sprang back open; the second and third time it did the same. It was only with her fourth attempt, slowly pulling the chipped wooden board on its hinges, that the door stayed closed, giving the impression of security. Her body was almost bent double as she walked down the street, eager to protect the baby from the world, shadowing her pink body from the night. Nicole squirmed in her white cot, teasing her woolly hat with her fingers – still a relatively new discovery to her. Against the stark white of her blanket she was the last shrimp in a penny mix-up bag. Nathalie breathed deeply and heavily when she arrived at the foot of Shirley's garden.

Thomas tipped the green plastic to his lips, draining the last few drops of cheap, sickly cider from the nameless bottle. Despite the sugar it tasted strangely bitter. The crushed cans around their feet rustled in the breeze, each one trying to roll over the grass verge but couldn't because of the dents and creases in the metal from having been crushed by Darren as he'd finished each one. The third can had bent suddenly into a sharp spike that cut into his hand, drawing the tiniest drop of blood in the process. Shocked by the pain he winced but acted as though nothing had happened.

A breeze of optimism filled Jack as he caught Nathalie's eye and saw her walking towards his house. Their relationship was the closest he had ever felt to that of a sibling. He enjoyed the quiet role of protector that he got the chance to play on the long lonely stretches of time her husband spent away at sea. Thomas and Darren noticed her too, though failed to see the shared glance between her and Jack.

"Nathalie Morley. Wouldn't kick her out for crumbs," Thomas said, tossing the empty bottle onto the path where it landed with a faint, unrewarding clicking noise against the concrete.

"Too bloody right." Darren lit another cigarette as he spoke and grimaced at the stale taste of the first drag. Their banter snapped Jack out of his slight daydream and back into reality. Darren could be an idiot, but was harmless enough. Dumb, but sincere. Thomas, thought Jack, was a moron. He had no particular feelings for him and those he did have weren't entirely pleasant. Thomas's life revolved around few activities, all of them disgusting. He had been caught on several occasions masturbating in the school toilets and his porn stash was bordering on the encyclopaedic. A born wanker.

"Don't even joke," Jack snapped "You're not bothering her."

"Calm down mate, we were only having a laugh," said Thomas.

Jack found himself becoming increasingly more riled with every word, particularly 'mate.' "You know you weren't. I know you were trying it on when I was inside. Fucking prick. How do you think that helps? You'd have no chance anyway."

"Eh?" Thomas looked perturbed at Darren, who shrugged and occupied himself with the invisible activity in the damp grass beneath him.

"Down The Social," continued Jack, the sound of his voice rising with each word. His Northern accent increasing in anger. "Telling her if she needed some company while her Ant was away... you sly git!" A few of the younger gang members laughed at Thomas's embarrassment.

"Just being neighbourly," he tried as means of an explanation through the sting of a blush. He felt himself shudder gently at Jack's increasing temper. The chilly vibration throughout Thomas's body slightly shocked Jack, who forced himself to calm down. Sometimes anger was something he couldn't control, something he was unaware of; a dark cloud that snuck up behind him and was only noticeable to him through the reactions of others. He forced his mood downwards, past his belly and extinguished it as best he could.

"Out of bounds mate," Jack said, quieter than before. "Don't even talk to her. I'll tell Ant when he comes back if you go near her again. Just let her be; she doesn't need the hassle."

"Shit mate." Darren stood up and threw his beer can onto the road. "We better be off."

Thomas grudgingly stood up next to Darren and shook himself, pleased for an excuse to be leaving the group.

"Too right," he said, "didn't realise what time it was."

"Where you getting the car from?" Jack felt a niggling, anxious nausea about the pair's plan as though he were involved. It would be an easy enough job to pull off between three, but two is never a good number – two means there's no chance of anyone taking control. A pair always gets caught. Gangs are the key.

"Saw a couple round the back of the Job Lot, night shifts and all that. We're going to need plenty of space to get that much lead in, and a white van would be too fucking obvious." Jack raised his eyes, impressed with Darren's forethought, however slight. "Ah, you see Jack – not just a pretty face. Are you sure you don't want in though?"

"Na. I can't. Well, I won't. Not anymore."

Darren had clearly expected a last minute turnaround – one final glory moment in overtime. He looked crestfallen. "If you're sure. Here, I forgot to ask you – what was your probby officer like?"

"Alright. Bit of a twat I suppose. Canny though... *Uni*." A picture is supposed to paint a thousand words but to Jack and his friends sometimes one word could paint a thousand pictures. 'Uni' was one of these words and the simple, gauche noise signified everything they needed to know about a character. "Although he went to St. Cuthbert's," Jack added trying to soften the blow. It was only when asked to voice an opinion that Jack realised he actually had one to give. He ended up liking Peter, the way you sometimes like a rubbish dog with matted fur and three legs. He wouldn't particularly like him around all the time, but realised that beneath all the crap that Jack was less fond of there lay a person who was fundamentally good. There were few others he could say the same about.

"Who was he then?" Darren asked, trying to remember anyone from their school having made it to university. He had been kicked out at fourteen for selling cannabis at lunchtimes. This didn't bother him, but the indignity of having to take the short bus still irked. "You'll never guess."

"Who? Not queer Billy?"

"Nah."

"Grom?"

"No."

"... Kerry Hart's brother," Jack said. Darren and Thomas choked on their own laughter.

"Fuck off!" Thomas said.

"The filthy bastard!" Darren laughed to himself. He and Thomas walked on, away from the group. "Last chance?" Darren asked Jack, who shook his head.

"Just go canny," he warned him.

"Aye, in a bit mate."

"In a bit."

They walked off into the night; shadows cast from the glow of the estate stretched far ahead of their actual bodies. Jack watched them leaving, disappearing out of the clearing at the top of the road. Eventually they were gone.

Stepping into the house Jack found the warmth shocking. His face prickled like he had fallen onto a million hot needles, and he felt his thoughts become noisy and angered like he was being choked. The light was too intense at first and gradually he allowed his eyes to grow accustomed in the hallway before entering the living room.

Shirley sat on the sofa; her usually creased brow seemed

more relaxed as she stared at the baby – less challenged – or challenging – as though a gentle wave had washed the dirt and debris from a particularly gnarled rock. Her finger swirled around Nicole's cheek in the pram drawing secret messages and shapes that only they would ever know; prayers and hearts etched into her skin, keeping her safe. As the door opened she pulled her hand away as if she had been doing something she shouldn't have, sitting upright and proper the way only the guilty ever do.

"We've got a visitor," she said as Jack entered the living room. He smiled and nodded awkwardly. Suddenly all too aware of his presence in his own home he felt augmented and wrong, as though forced to recite a private whisper to an entire assembly hall; his eyes watered with embarrassment and uncertainty as to how best to act. Jack hated being a latecomer to any scenario; no matter how hard he tried he always felt as though he shouldn't be there, or wasn't being entirely let in on the secret. As she sipped her tea Nathalie placed the hot porcelain cup down onto the table. Being in the same room as him for the first time in months felt oddly powerful, like she'd been tackled. Her eyes filled not gradually but with a large, sudden rush of water that momentarily blinded her.

"Hiya Jack," she said, wavering. "How you keeping?"

"Not so bad. Yourself?"

"Good." She felt her throat beginning to sting. "Missing Ant."

"Me an' all."

She stood up and pushed herself towards Jack, frightened that if she moved too slowly he'd shy away. As she held herself to him she was relieved and happy that he hugged her back, almost as tightly.

"Make sure you stay put from now on, eh?" she whispered damply in his ear. "Please. For us..."

"I'll be here," he said, embarrassed by her emotion but

secretly rather pleased. "Settle down though, eh? You been nicking your Mam's tablets again?"

Nathalie laughed and released Jack, wiping all traces of emotion from her face. Sitting back down she giggled again as Jack joined her, pleased to have said everything she had wanted to instead of bottling it up in favour of safe but unspectacular small talk.

"Do you want some tea?" asked Shirley, herself touched by the pair.

"I'm alright. I had some chips with Darren."

"Good, because we've got nowt in."

Nathalie took the baby from her cot, causing her to wriggle and writhe. It was the first time Jack had seen Nicole with any sort of control over her own body. Before he went away she was just a small, fleshy bean, a fraction of a person, a beautiful tumour that would merge into whichever shape you allowed her to form. Now she was bigger, she was stronger and harder. Hard. You could never be too hard kid, he thought as he looked at her.

She was kicking her legs, showing the dead air who was boss. Her head rolled around too, scanning the room and taking in the sights with those big, empty blue eyes. They were paddling pools waiting to be filled. He felt his heart as he watched her – boompadyboompadyboompadyboom – it skipped like a girl on her way to school. She was the most powerful thing he had ever experienced in his life and all he wanted to do was protect her.

"*Do you want to say a hello to your Uncle Jack?*" Nathalie asked Nicole in the lilting, sing-song voice that he always felt unnecessary for children. "Do you want to hold her Jack?"

"Course." He held his arms out tentatively like he was pressing them closer and closer to an open fire. Nathalie, far more relaxed with the delicacies of her own child, dumped Nicole suddenly into Jack's arms. For a second he didn't know how to act. His initial response was to drop her. Then he imagined that by staying completely still, rigid and straight like stone that she would at least be safe. He caught her eye briefly. Then pulling her towards his body he found that he relaxed with contact; she melted onto his chest, her hand brushing gently against the fabric of his t-shirt, her tired head resting vulnerably on his arm.

"Now then kid, how you been?" he said, stroking her cheek. Jack's affection for Nicole and her comfort at his presence made Shirley want to pull the baby from his arms and take him in hers. He was still a child, in her eyes, albeit a giant one with hardcore attitude and form. But a child nonetheless. His look was untainted: pure and genuine. She thought back to the time he had rescued a bird from the school playground and snuck home at lunchtime to make it better. A cat had broken its wing and Jack stayed at home all day bringing it pieces of bread and cups of water that it was too weak to eat. When he had finally agreed to go to bed under promise that Shirley would look after it she had killed it as humanely as she could. Maggots had already begun to bubble and gnarl through the torn flesh on the broken beast's wing, and a septic liquid oozed from its sores and blended with the crimson of its blood. Jack hadn't noticed this though. The next morning his tears stopped when Shirley informed him that the bird was so well looked after it had flown away during the night.

"She's getting her first tooth," Nathalie told Jack, brushing invisible dust from Nicole's head as she spoke.

"Where?"

"In her mouth, you prat."

"*Where in her mouth*, smart arse?"

"Round the front there."

Nathalie pushed finger into Nicole's mouth, which opened idly, locating the sharp, tender iceberg protruding from her gum. "Go on," she said. "Just have a poke about – if you find anything valuable it's mine though."

Jack pushed his finger into Nicole's mouth. Her gums felt warm and she began sucking his fingers as though it was food or those of her own father. Pushing slightly further along the gum, tracing her mouth gently with the tip, he located the tooth and rubbed the patch of gum from which the angry, jagged spear had erupted.

"Mint." He felt Nicole soothe and relax to the repetition of his motion. "She's got a canny suck on her, this one. That'll come in handy eventually." He said trying to lessen the seriousness of the moment. It was a futile gesture but Nathalie went along with it.

"Fuck off you!" She bumped the whole force of her body gently into his arm. "There'll be none of that or I'll kick her to high heaven." Jack paused for a moment, staring down at Nicole. Her eyes fought against the tiredness but slowly they closed – with each blink they lost the strength to open as wide as before until eventually there were gone. For a moment Jack felt like shaking her awake. To have something so brilliant but keep them hidden was cruel. But her gentle, dreamy breath stopped him from doing it. Nicole slept like she meant it.

"Too right," he eventually said. "And I'll kill whichever filthy bastard ever gets his hands on this one. *Won't I?* There's nowt going to spoil you kid. You're clean page, you are."

"What's the problem with you then?" His mum took the barely eaten tray of food from Peter's lap and carried it into the kitchen. Thick, ugly gravy had congealed over the meal making sure it was blanketed to the spot; safe from germs but unable to move on the plate. He was pleased she had taken it away as the sight was making his stomach churn even though he still felt hungry. He was too tired and preoccupied to do anything about it though: hunger was just a distant voice in a crowd and tonight it was easily ignored. Lights from the TV flickered shadows across his face and body as he rested heavily, his mind full of thoughts that darted and scattered like teenagers in a music shop. Jack was stuck in his mind. Actually he was stuck all over him. He felt like he was under his skin and on his clothes – a sunken grease that wouldn't scrub out. On meeting him he had felt as though he was being compelled to succeed. Jack had already become one of Peter's superstitions – Jack's reformation would ensure Peter's success. There was no logic, just belief. Like the nights in his youth where Peter would wake up frantic that if he didn't listen to a specific song at that very moment then only bad things would happen the following day.

"Cheer up lad." His Dad rested his newspaper on his lap and peered over the top of his glasses. "Whatever it is there's nowt you can do about it at this hour."

Peter smiled hesitantly at his father, the staunch, simple giant of a man who had started looking older recently, somehow smaller. He was the type of man who still wouldn't leave the house without a flat cap on, and whose wardrobe consisted solely of sweaters, shirts and trousers in grey, black, and mushroom. Two ties hung specifically for special occasions: red for meals at restaurants and family gatherings; black for church-based congregations. Sometimes Peter thought he understood him, other times that they were separate species. He had no doubt that his Dad was proud of him – he'd told him once – but they were artist and mathematician; each could see the beauty in one another's craft, yet neither could fully understand their reasoning.

He had hated every moment of his childhood. It was only with time and distance that its appeal became apparent. Primarily, that it was something to fight against, a tide to push potential into results. Nobody who felt comfortable as a child ever went on to become successful, of this he was certain. It was at university he had begun to see its appeal. If you're happy with nothing then anything else is a bonus. 'Expectation is the route of disappointment' was the quote his flatmate had pinned to his bedroom door. Peter had since claimed it as his own mantra. Since leaving the comfy crash pad of higher education life had begun to seem a lot crueller. But Peter would make this work, if only to show his baffled parents that post-sixteen education had its benefits even if he was beginning to have doubts himself.

"It's nothing," he said. "Just this lad I'm working with. He's good, nice enough, but I'm worried about him."

Peter's Dad nodded knowingly. "You don't want to be getting yourself involved in none of that nonsense," he said. Peter's mum sat down on the sofa and nodded in agreement, scanning the TV guide as though it may contain some relevant insight. While his father was pleased Peter was no longer confined to an office his mother fretted constantly – her lad had not been built for day-to-day life. He was born to learn, not to do. A different class of man. She wondered how he would cope when thrown to the lions. Though it was best, she thought, to act as though it wasn't happening. A blind eye can be a blessing as well as a curse. "There's bad things round those ends; different from when you or I was a lad. Things are changing. Nothing good can come from round there any more. Eh Love, down The Ridges?" his dad added.

"Oh aye, gone bad. It's all it takes – a couple of rotten apples and the whole bowl goes to mould." His mum lit a cigarette and let the smoke fall in a tutu around her waist before flapping it away with her hand.

"It could get better," Peter voiced sleepily. "He's a good lad who just lives a bad life. It's easily done. We went to the same school; we could be the same person I suppose."

"Not you my love," his mother said with a laugh. "You were different. You were good."

"No-one's good." Peter sat up and forced himself awake,

plunging his brain into fire and then ice. "Things are blurry, and this lad isn't bad and I'm not good."

His parents laughed at one another conspirationally, a noise that sounded the conversation they'd shared a thousand times over the ten o'clock news in bed.

"Son," his Dad said. "There's nowt you can do about it. You were born good. Some are born bad. That's the way the cookie crumbles. The trick is to learn to make the most of it." Peter exhaled as a means of response and sat back down. Sometimes being asleep is the easiest option. "Now," his Dad went on. "Would a cup of tea make it better?"

Chapter Eight

It was the screwdriver that did it. Thomas's plan of throwing a brick full pelt had backfired in the most literal sense. The red breezeblock had hit the window with a thud and tarnished the glass as though someone had thrown a bag of flour at it, and then bounced back towards them, crashing and crunching across the tarmac of the car park. Its relatively small journey sounded out like a thunderstorm in the night, the noise clicking and echoing off the back wall of the nearby supermarket and causing at least two of the windows from the block of flats behind them to turn on.

"*Fucking twat!*" Darren pushed Thomas forwards as they ran around the corner of the Job Lot, shaken by their own ruckus. "You're a liability you are!" he hissed as he crouched down, eyes scanning the area for security guards or nightshift workers alerted to their attempts.

"Sorry I thought –"

"Didn't think though, did you? Stupid cunt."

"Don't call 'us stupid Darren." Thomas shoved him. Darren's balance was precarious – the tips of his fingers and bent legs supported the entire weight of his body. The single shove from Thomas unsteadied him completely and instead of floundering to regain his poise he simply rolled onto the floor. "I said I was sorry," Thomas continued.

Darren laughed. He allowed himself to stay on the floor for

a moment, eying Thomas from the ground. "Yeah, well, from now on I lead and you follow, right?"

"Right."

After pausing to ensure the silence was not bluffing they snuck back to the chosen vehicle. This time Darren held the plan; Thomas held the rucksack. One jolt – almost soundless, like a gun with the silencer on. Darren had seen his brother do it countless time; it was the expert's method. One sudden point of pressure applied to the most delicate area of any fragile structure and the whole thing fragmented, shattered into a million tiny pieces that could never be placed back together. As the screwdriver pushed into the car Darren felt the same buzz that he used to when casually strolling past guards in shops with borrowed items concealed in his padded coat. The almost sexual thrill pulsed through his body as his masterpiece veined like a dying leaf, the single sheet of glass turning into hundreds of crystal beads that held onto one another for a split second before weeping to the ground in a solidifying waterfall. The pulse hit him again. It was sexual. It was sex. Destruction would be the closest he ever got to creation. "You've got to see the beauty in everything," his mother used to say to him "even if you think it's ugly, some people might find it beautiful." The gaping void in the passenger door looked beautiful to him. He felt like he had achieved something. He felt like God.

"Belter," he whispered. The smoke that trailed in the cool night air was almost louder than the word itself.

"Belter," Thomas parroted.

They threw the bag of tools onto the back seat. Darren allowed Thomas to drive. It was the simpler of the two tasks; all he had to do was put his foot down. Darren was watchman, orienteer and bodyguard all rolled into one. The duty required an alertness and ability to juggle more than one task at any given time. It was a responsibility that out of the two of them he was better equipped to succeed at. He had two GCSEs to Thomas's none. He felt like the bigger man for once, like the boss. Only he suddenly then found himself fumbling and vulnerable, not quite sure how to act around his newfound duty. Darren wished Jack were there.

"Can we have the radio on for a bit?" Thomas asked as Darren stared out of the window. The lights on either side of the street cast giant orange orbs on the pavements like slipped haloes of the lamps themselves. He hated silence, it bored him, and his own thoughts were of little comfort. Thomas was used to large attendances, bustling houses full of extended family and shrieking children – always one feud or funeral to occupy himself with. Because of the sprawling nature of his brood their week was almost always dictated by Monday's *Evening Chronicle*, from which his mother would circle each wake they were to attend. It was a mark of respect, she would tell them, to honour the deceased no matter how infrequently you saw them, or how frequently you wished their demise at the top of your lungs outside of The Comet at one in the morning.

It was also a cheap way of making sure the children had a balanced meal inside of them. Wakes were always good for a decent spread. And there was never a quiet moment – they were the neighbours whose parties you loved to go to but appreciated the ability to leave. As a result, when faced with even the slightest alternative Thomas didn't know how to cope; to him silence was a new word that he could never find an appropriate use for.

"Whatever you like. But quiet. And keep on going steady – I don't want you messing this up tonight, right?"

"Right."

"It's an easy plan. We just need to take it easy, no pissing about."

"I know."

He turned the radio onto the lowest setting. The tinny sound filled the small space and seemed to buffer the silence; it made the journey feel complete by giving everything a soundtrack. Inadvertently both Darren and Thomas found their heads moving roughly in time to the music, craning their necks forward and then retracting them like they were kissing the air – Geordie-style, only in slow motion. As they continued crawling the road slowly they carried on in this way until a chance alteration in both of their routines led them to catch one another's eyes. They shuffled in their seats, pretending to rearrange themselves more comfortably before sitting stone still, their thighs trembling to join in with the beat of the music.

"I love this one." Darren turned the volume dial up a notch as they approached the side street that would lead them to their initial destination. The slight increase in music seemed dramatic.

Slowing down just before the gap between the two rows of houses Thomas allowed only the tip of the car to peek into the wide open stretch of road – the long, winding, sexy black length that went from the darkness of the estates to the lights of the city. It seemed more vibrant at night, Darren thought, almost seductive. Clean snow. All of a sudden he became excited about the thought of tearing the smooth surface up with the tyres of a stolen car.

"Easy does it," he warned Thomas. The car came to a gradual halt allowing them both to take in the view of the road, making sure no police were watching. Shuddering vibrations from the aging engine provided the only movement in the car. They remained stoic and still. Watchmen.

"I can't see nothing," Thomas whispered, suddenly caught up in the thrill of their precision.

"Me neither. Go easy a minute."

Thomas allowed his foot to descend millimetres towards the ground. A gentle purr like a tiger woken from a nap seeped from the engine as they moved forward stealthily.

"We're clear," Darren confirmed. "Just go slow though."

"Plan."

"And none of your fucking stunts either; we're there for the lead, nowt else."

"Right."

He pressed harder onto the pedal, teasing against the resilience until they were travelling at a regular speed. Neither too fast as to raise suspicions from insomniac pedestrians nor too slow as to lengthen the time their admittedly easy plan should take. As they travelled along the road Darren looked up through his window at the sky and realised for the first time that there were no stars – the persistence of the artificial daylight streaming from each lamp created an amber seal through which no natural light could penetrate.

He liked it though, the darkness. Travelling at night felt special to him; it made him feel alone in a good way, like the world was giving him time to think. His favourite journeys as a child had always been those rushed missions to hospital when one of his brothers or sisters had a cold that came with a rash and sent his parents into blind panic, or when his big brother had gotten so drunk that he sporadically stopped breathing as he slept. Everyone piled into his Uncle's van in the dead of night – the victim lain across the knees of those on the back seats – and out they went through the night towards the hospital. Those were the journeys he remembered, the way the noise around him dipped as though the darkness was eating it – stealing the sound so that he could feel peaceful for once as he stared out into the dank midnight air and the familiar streets that became so exotic in the odd sepia of another street-lit night.

He pulled his head away from the window, aware that his

thoughts were already relaxing him. Tonight Darren couldn't afford to be breezy and rested. He needed to be alert; he had to remain focused.

Smoke from Charlie Bowers' cigarette filled the police car but instead of curling around the pair, the waves lay flat and stank. Billie Morgan did everything in his power to stop himself from flapping his arms around, clearing a temporary pathway of fresh oxygen to his lungs – like Moses parting waters, or Tippi Hedren in *The Birds* – the way dedicated anti-smokers like himself always felt the need to do. The tickling inside of his chest was beginning to turn into a burning sensation that made him feel claustrophobic. However, this was nothing compared to the grilling he would get would he dare complain about the situation. "Chill your beans Queer boy," Bowers had warned him the first time he had suggested smoking with a window open. "It'll do your bitch lungs no harm; just relax and have a drag." He couldn't be bothered with another altercation. Their relationship could already be described as stretched as it was.

Desperate for respite he nudged the window handle gently with his elbow, allowing the glass to fall by no more than an inch. The smoke had the right idea and streamed out of the car as quickly and smoothly as it could. Billie envied its escape but wished it well nonetheless. As things stood the momentary grasps of air he was able to steal would suffice.

Charlie noticed the window was open but stopped himself from saying anything. The protest was on the tip of his tongue, eager to jump, but he refrained. Morgan was a foreign species to him. Part man, part *Guardian*. He was new school – more social worker than bobby. His lot were the ones that cared, that felt that every crime had a motive and every criminal a story.

"It's our duty to respond to the individual," Morgan had said on their first patrol together.

"What about upholding the law, maintaining safety and order on the streets?" Bower's had asked him.

"Oh yeah... that as well," he replied.

He was almost alright, as a lad, but failed to notice that the new school of policing was at odds with the new school of criminal. People were different these days. Crime hard; criminals harder. There was a poetic irony, Bowers thought, that as the streets got meaner the cops got greener. Just shoot the fucking lot of them he would suggest – that way everyone's safe.

"Do you know," he said, eying his cigarette. "I think I like smoking more than ale. It just feels... right. Right there, between my fingers. It's as much about the ritual as the actual puffing on the thing. Have you ever, you know, had a tab?"

"No." Billie Morgan's voice forced through the crackle and pop of his throat involuntarily clearing. "Had a drag at school once. Was throwing up so much round the back of the bike sheds I missed metalwork. Got a demerit and everything."

Bowers eyes desperately wanted to roll. Conversation-wise it may have been the first smooth rally the pair had had; he wanted to maintain the momentum if he was to be stuck with Morgan for some time to come.

"What about drink, where do you like to sup?" Bowers asked

"Town mostly."

"Oh aye, don't get down there much myself these days. Better pubs, is it?"

"Better clubs."

They were quiet again. Morgan strained to think of a potential development in their conversation but found himself at a loss. Bowers lit another cigarette with the embers of the last one.

The coarse blast of the radio's message caused them both to

jump. '...*Reports of a stolen vehicle believed to be a blue Ford registration L348 BRG*,' said the black plastic box on the car's dashboard. The voice was almost always female but tonight it was a dull, grey male voice that neither of the men recognised.

"Received, over." Bowers clicked the radio receiver off.

"What do you think then?" Morgan asked with a child's innocence.

"I think," Bowers said, throwing his old end out of the window. "I need some more fags." He sat back in his seat and exhaled the faint dregs from his lungs.

A wheezing noise began to seep like poison through a bandage. Two birds on a telephone wire whispered secrets to one another in the distance. As a car trailed slowly into view and its familiarity caused Billie to sit up excitedly.

"Here we go then," Bowers said, turning the key in its ignition. A rumbling thunder propelled the old police car forwards. It trundled towards the curb and allowed each of its wheels to step daintily onto the main road. They began to gradually move faster towards the joy riders, trailing the stolen vehicle with a gentle pressure as though about to ask whether or not it cared to dance.

Thomas noticed them first. The familiar white and blue car with its confident, steady movement was like an old acquaintance passed in the street. His insides fired like pinballs in different directions: his balls hit the floor, stomach sprung up into his throat, his tongue stuck glued to the top of his mouth.

Then came the lights: neon sparks in the night. The bright blue globes grew bigger and bigger in the darkness before shrivelling back to black; luminous bubblegum blobs inflating and bursting over and over again.

Thomas shifted in his seat and looked over to Darren who was yet to move. "Shit, we've got company." He leaned forward as he drove, willing the car away from the police with his whole body. Darren stirred and sat up. As Thomas spoke he had been disturbed from his daydreams by the lights, or rather the lack of them. The blue flash had not attracted his attention; his suspicions were only raised once they were gone and somehow the whole scenario seemed lacking in their absence.

"Shit," Darren said, staring back at the car. "Shit! Shit! Shit! Shit!" He hammered the dashboard with his hands causing the glove compartment to spring open. Unused tissues tumbled to the floor and were caught like white mice in a trap as Darren slammed it shut again in rage.

"What should we do?" Thomas looked anxiously between Darren and the road. Cat's Eyes flashed warning signs before being crunched beneath tyres. The raised Braille of the road made the car peak and dip as it drove forward as though it were breathing shallow, panicked breaths. For a moment Darren contemplated the likelihood of escape. From the mirror he could see inside of the police car. There were two of them. One he didn't recognise. The other was familiar though – a proper bastard. Fat and resentful, his narrow eyes stared through his balding head like two lost chocolate chips in an undercooked muffin. He knew they were as good as done. They might as well go with a bang.

"Fuck it," he said.

"What?" Thomas glanced at the reflection of the police car that had moved so close it looked like it was about to mount their boot like in a wildlife film.

"In for a penny eh?" said Darren, opening his window just enough to allow an arm out into the night. "We're as good as nicked, might as well make it worth our while." He stuck his arm out of the car window and signalled obscenities at the pigs behind.

"You reckon?"

"A quid says you can't lose them for thirty seconds," Darren challenged him. Thomas felt uneasy. He was frightened by notions of incarceration but bored by the idea of doing the same thing day in day out until the next big plan came along. The more he thought about it the more he realised there was no second option. The immediate thrill of a high speed chase overruled the thought of the repercussions. He dug his nails into the soft leather of the steering wheel.

"You're on."

An irreversible grin spread across Darren's face. "Go!"

The car shot forward as though their freefall had reached stretching point and they were being snapped backwards by bungee elastic. Inches and inches of road churned from their spinning rear-wheels like in a cartoon, increasing the distance between themselves and the police more than even they thought possible. Thomas and Darren both laughed at the exhilaration of untamed speed and the sudden projection that pressed them back into their seats like the best goodnight kiss they'd ever know.

"Looks like we've got a pair of chancers on our hands," Billie said, taking notes as they sped forwards towards the ever shrinking vehicle. Bowers didn't take his eyes off the road; he felt himself burning into the back of the car, his own thoughts tearing it to pieces as he trailed it. He imagined them laughing. Laughing at what they'd done. Laughing at him. He imagined breaking that limp wrist with his bare hands, taking that raised middle finger and stamping on it until it was as flat as the ground it lay on. He knew exactly the sort that would be in a car like that. They were exactly the sort the world would be better off without.

"They haven't got a hope in hell." The quietness of his voice unnerved Billie. Even when completely silent Bower's demeanour was obtrusive; his thoughts were like lighthouses, only they were there to cause, rather than prevent, disaster. Those huge ham-like limbs and square features seemed to be permanently asking for a fight. Everything hung lower than it should. Everything about him seemed to be making a statement, and a loud one at that. He could sit alone without speaking in a room full of people and within the hour it would take both hands to count his enemies.

The siren wailed like a continental widow through the streets, snagging on the concentration of Darren and Thomas. It didn't bother them though – it was there for show. That they could do as they pleased until physically stopped no matter how much noise their predators made in the process. They turned quickly onto a quiet back street and for a moment it was silent. They travelled down it, moving faster and faster until the tall walls either side of the street blurred into one long stretch of shamed, hanging heads.

"Howay the filth!" Darren shouted loudly as they turned the corner sharply and left the trailing blue smudge to carry straight on in a blur. The right side of the car rose slightly from the ground and hovered weightlessly before descending with a thud that caused them to bounce up and down in their seats like nodding dogs. Darren allowed himself to move with the bumps, Thomas remained focused on the road, his eyes narrowing as though directing the wheels over a tightrope.

"Come on you useless twat – quid says you can't do it." Darren ruffled Thomas's hair.

"Fuck off."

"Come on my son!" They sped round the corner. Inside of the car it was as though the world was on fire – it rushed past the windows in a roaring, cackling noise like they were stationary and it was the world itself galloping past like a thousand angry horses. The streetlights stained the darkness like a brilliant crayon; everything else seemed to absorb its colour and the world became ablaze. Darren imagined that they were trapped in the car forever; if the door or window opened so much as an inch then the outside would get inside and burn them alive.

"Howay! Ten seconds...twelve..." He counted to the flicker of his digital watch as Darren fled past the distorted familiarities of the local back streets. Their darkness was interrupted by the glinting blue light approaching from behind.

"Shit." Thomas hammered the steering wheel with his fists as he turned a corner.

"Unlucky mate, back to zero."

"Nah!" Thomas shoved Darren's arm with one hand. "You can add it on; I've got twelve seconds now. I only need another eighteen."

"Not a chance mate. Umpire says... Zero or bust."

"Whatever."

They took a sharp left and entered the shady entrance of a sprawling industrial estate. Prefab warehouses and shabby, low-built factories wove in and out of one another like sticky webs wilting in the heat. Even in the darkness, the rusting facades and slumped roofs – dipped like frowns – made the whole area seem like the sad afterhours of a party that should have ended some time ago. Thomas flicked off the lights of the car and let the darkness engulf them.

"I'll get this bastard if it kills me," murmured Charlie as they watched the car turn into the industrial estate.

"He's handling it alright to be fair," Billie said as he watched the car snap smoothly into the small entrance and then disappear momentarily. "Maybe we should give him a job."

"Mouth shut unless you want feeding through a straw for the next three months," warned Charlie as he reversed tensely. "Hold on." They sped up towards the car, which dotted from one side of the road to the other, turning corners sharply the way avid readers skim textbooks.

They managed to loose the police car again, which wheezed and whined as Charlie Bowers forced it to perform increasingly elaborate manoeuvres at greater and greater speeds.

"Stupid cunt." Thomas laughed as they lost the police. They gained speed as they pulled into a long stream of buildings, at the top of which a beaming security light sprayed sharp rays into the car and cut their journey up into staggered, stretching shadows.

"Come on my son!" Darren screamed as they trailed towards the end. "We might actually make it if you keep this up, you bloody beauty!"

Nearing the end of the stretch they turned a right and were met immediately by the police car, which grew steadily in their wing mirror until it was almost blended with their own vehicle.

"I've got you, you thieving little shit," said Bowers, pressing down onto the accelerator and allowing his bonnet to touch the back of their car like a teasing kiss.

"Shit, they've caught up," said Thomas, pushing frantically for more speed.

"Almost mate. Let's give them one last jump though," said Darren. "Something to remember us by."

"You reckon?"

"I know."

They climbed steadily to highest speed possible. They moved so fast that every so often the tires left the road and they floated weightlessly but poignantly. Approaching a fork in the road Darren allowed the car to slow down and once more it seemed that they were sucked towards their predators.

"Right or left?" Thomas asked anxiously. Each road seemed to lead to the same tangle of buildings and scrap metal littering the pathways, so it made little difference. Yet still he felt compelled to check his own instincts against Darren's better judgements.

"Left."

He turned fast allowing the rubber to tear on the asphalt, leaving dark trails, burnt breadcrumbs, leading towards their destination. The police followed a beat afterwards. They shone through the alleyway, bouncing on kinks in the road and floating, both laughing long, lost laughs at the possibility that their bodies could be travelling so fast, that if only for a split second they were winning. They flew towards the end of the road; each time the police came too close to them Thomas would swerve in and out of the middle of the road, weaving odd black stretches.

He flung the steering wheel left. The vehicle flew to the side of the road and dragged driver and passenger with it; their bodies became limbless and moved like feathers on the wind. A length of scrap metal resting on the pathway clipped the tyre and sent them flying back into the centre of the road with a jolt. They felt the car flip once. It didn't stop. Constable Charlie Bowers allowed himself to slow down as he watched the vehicle dance forwards. It flipped sideways over and over again, dragging sparks from the ground and lighting the alleyway in brilliant flashes that died before they had a chance to catch fire.

The car pounded heavily onwards, inside he could see the boys' bodies moving effortlessly with the movement, bouncing upwards as the roof hit the floor and down again as it returned upright. Their arms tangled around one another's sleeping bodies, both protecting and vulnerable at once. It thundered onwards in an avalanche before stopping abruptly like a broken song when it hit the flat, unmovable side-wall of one of the factories.

The world felt still again. Speechlessly Bowers and Morgan got out of the car and scanned the aftermath. Chewed up and spat out the car had been torn to pieces. It looked like death. Bowers took the lead and moved slowly forward as though the vehicle may use its last ounce of life to pounce and bite. Morgan hovered behind; his hand remained on the safety of the police car as if by staying next to it he could hold reality at bay. There was nothing he needed to be told. There was no chance anybody could have survived what had become the dead black monster that bled clear liquids and broken glass against the hard brick wall.

"Get on the radio. Now," said Charlie as he walked closer to the wreckage. Through the broken window he could make out the faces of two young men. Lads, he thought – barely no longer boys. Their faces were peaceful despite the awkward, angular poses that their bodies had been crushed into. Red streams traced their eyes and mouths and made them look like sleeping stained-glass sculptures. Both were dead. Of that there was no question. However, it was not the facts that bothered Constable Charlie Morgan. More than the loss or the potential repercussions that could ensue, what bothered him was that for the first time in his life he had no idea how he felt.

Chapter Nine

At eleven o'clock on a weekday morning the local Job Centre was as grim as Jack had imagined it would be. The verification of his conjecture was of little comfort to him. Never having been particularly taken by the notion of gainful employment it was a concept he had given little thought to in the past. But as he sat alone with his head down, squirming in the unfamiliar itch of the freshly ironed black shirt that Shirley had left out for him, he couldn't help but wish he could transport himself outside without anyone there noticing.

Already he had sat with three professionals who had required the same information – name, age, date-of-birth, National Insurance Number, employment history. He had recited the short list with ease and nodded politely as he was dismissed once more to a different stretch of thin carpet and thick smoke with plastic chairs designed only, it seemed, to remind their inhabitants that they were no longer in the cushy confides of mid-morning television and lunchtime beers in the ranks of the unemployed. He sat up and tried to discreetly clench the blood flow back into his numb left buttock.

"Would you like to come across now?" A large woman poked her head out from behind two makeshift wooden stands that formed, Jack presumed, an illusion of privacy once inside. He stood up and walked awkwardly towards the empty seat across the desk from her, pulling at the sleeves of his shirt for support. Group scenarios didn't bother him. At best they were a chance to shine; at worst he could always kick off and start some sort of brawl. One-to-one made Jack's blood run cold though. There was no escape, no diverting attention or focusing blame onto a weaker member of the pack. It was just him and his truth, which was something he wasn't all too fond of.

He began to mull over possible answers to hypothetical questions that may impress her as she rearranged leaflets and licked the nib of her pencil. There was no logical reason for his worry. While he had nothing to offer that most would be proud of, he was better than– or at least on par with – her regular rotation of clients. Already as Jack had been there a man had pissed himself while waiting for conformation of his disability allowance, two men were reduced to tears over dole payments and a small woman with red hair had choked the receptionist mildly but effectively with her own telephone wire after a misunderstanding over an appointment card. Comparatively Jack was more than OK.

But still somewhere inside of him he wanted to shine, he wanted people to recognise his determination, or rather his potential. He wanted someone to walk past, raise their eyebrows and say "*Hey, you look like you've got a decent life in you.*" With that in mind Jack began to weigh her up in order to try to find the best way in which to win her support.

She was older than Shirley he had decided and so flirting would be no use. Playful attention is only ever effective if the recipient believes however mildly that it may go somewhere. As she sat there with her badly judged smear of candy-floss pink lipstick surrounding her constipated mouth, not even trying to hold her tummy in or her tits up, Jack got the impression that she was wholly resigned to doing it herself for the rest of her days. His little boy lost routine always went down well with women of a certain age and size, Jack had come to realise, but as he got nearer he recognised a glassiness in her eyes which he knew would be hard to penetrate. She'd seen it all before: a professional lifetime of acts and routines of varying quality and consistency. He sat down and she began.

"What we need to do is to draw up a past history of you as a character – your career being the most important area of concern as well as any necessary information that would be of interest to potential employers," she said mechanically without introducing herself. "*IF –*" she went on, raising her voice for the first and only time during their entire encounter, "– the process is not completed then all requests for income support, jobseekers allowance or disability benefits will be nullified. Is this understood?"

"Yeah," said Jack.

"Good. What was your last job?"

"Never really had one before. Not properly anyway. I was hoping you might be able to help me out there."

"I'm afraid we cannot progress onto the next stage of the form until this stage is complete," she said and looked at Jack coldly.

"I understand. But I've never had a job before. I'm twenty-two. I've been in prison for a few months –"

"We'll get to this section later." She waved her hand as she interrupted him. "No previous employment?"

"No."

"So," she traced the length of the paper with her pencil without allowing the lead to make a mark, "Unemployed."

"Yes," Jack said, relieved after having been made to take the scenic route to a relatively simple answer. The woman pressed her pencil hard into a small square box on the piece of paper and blew away the stray flecks that peppered her page.

"And for how long were you unemployed?" she asked.

"... About twenty-two years, give or take," Jack eventually said. The only thing keeping him from laughing at the ridiculousness of the situation was the idea that this woman was for all intents and purposes his sole link to employment. He shrank flaccidly into his seat.

"I won't lie to you Jack," she said after a brief pause and a shrug of her shoulder. "It doesn't look good. At your age with no formal training *and* form I don't really know what to do with you."

"I thought you might have a better idea than most."

"The prospects just aren't great. You don't exactly offer a handsome package."

"I'm in a Job Centre. I was hardly expecting six figures plus benefits. If you could just find me something I'd do it. Anything – honestly, stick me anywhere and I'll go from there. I'll get my hands dirty. I got good GCSEs."

"There *are* several missing, maths for example..."

"I didn't make it to all of them."

"Why not?"

"Call it a breakdown in communications."

"It's quite an important one to have."

"For working in a factory?"

"For any job. And there aren't as many as there used to be. Why not just leave us with your details, we can keep an eye out here and inform you if any suitable vacancies arise, and until then you'd be entitled to jobseeker's allowance, OK?"

"Whatever you like."

"Now," she turned four pages and checked her watch as lunchtime approached. "What's your address?"

"49 Barron Street."

"Barron?"

"Yeah."

"I don't recognise that one... is that Howden?"

"Meadow Well," Jack said.

"Right." She stretched the word as she filled out the rest of the form hurriedly, her handwriting barely legible towards the postcode. Shortly after that he was dismissed.

Jack decided to walk home instead of getting on the bus. The melodrama of pacing the almost mile in the damp lunchtime breeze suited his own melancholy. Things seemed greyer than they had before. Having never tried to prize open doors of any worth Jack was unaccustomed to the sharp sting of having one slammed in his face.

The streets were almost empty all along the road towards the estate. As he entered the cut leading to the main drag of houses two clouds parted and the dull strain of autumnal light, constant and dead like a migraine, began to drain his energy as though he had been punctured. Across the uneven cracks of the road a small ball rolled towards his feet, bobbing along on the wind and stopping dead at his foot. He picked it up and squeezed it in his hand before clocking its owner from the corner of his eye. A small girl, older than a toddler but no where near school years, stood alone and anxious outside of Ellen's shop, staring at the ball in Jack's hands.

"This yours?" he asked in a whisper.

She nodded vaguely and blushed, taking one step back towards the shop entrance.

Jack walked slowly towards her and crouched down on the floor. "Here you go," he said and handed the ball to the girl. She took it slowly from him and then rushed it behind her back like a secret.

"What's your name?"

"Kayleigh," she said quietly, and allowed Jack one small smile for his troubles.

"Alright Kayleigh, I'm Jack. Where's your Mam?"

On cue the door to the shop swung open and a harassed looking woman with hollow cheeks and enough gold around her neck to make a pirate blush bent down and scooped the child violently from the floor. "Fuck. What have I told you about wandering off?" she said. Kayleigh dropped her ball onto the floor.

"She was alright," Jack said

"Oh *you're* back on the scene, are you? Hoped they'd thrown away the key."

"I was just –" Jack began.

"I still haven't forgot the mess you made of our Keith's face you little thug. And you –" she turned her attentions back to Kayleigh, squeezing her tightly against her body more through anger than love, "Don't want to be walking off on 'us like that again, and you don't want to be talking to shite like *him*." She pointed at Jack and Kayleigh buried her head into her mother's unsympathetic shoulder.

"*Here!*" Jack said "You stupid cunt. I was only giving her the ball back, maybe if you weren't leaving her outside shops I wouldn't have had to."

"It's not even fucking hers." She kicked the ball across to the other side of the road and turned away from Jack. "Do everyone a favour and fuck off back inside," she said as she walked off, muttering about the punishments Kayleigh would receive once she got her home.

He felt flat and angry in equal measures. However this changed the moment he saw her sitting, alone, halfway up the long stretch of road. Nathalie was perched awkwardly like a bird on the hard plastic bench. She hadn't seen Jack and seemed oblivious to the fact that he was observing her. As though caught on a strange gust of wind Jack found himself increasing in speed and steadiness towards where she sat.

"Now then stranger," he said as he approached the bus stop. Glass panes from the side of the shelter had been shattered and their remains blown throughout the street leaving a clean metal structure bearing dirty smudges of flecked green paint. Despite its lack of surrounding walls the bus stop – in its own sensory microcosm – still managed to smell distinctly of human piss. Jack sat down next to Nathalie and allowed his arm to touch hers gently. "What's this? You doing another runner?"

"Oh aye," she rolled her eyes and bumped the weight of her body into his as he sat down. "All the way to the Job Lot."

"Where's the bairn?"

"Tethered her to the outhouse for an hour, thought she could do with a bit of a run around." Nathalie's face burst into a smile as Jack couldn't help but look shocked at her tasteless joke. "*She's with Chrissie.* A lass's got to have a bit of me time you know. Else she ends up going completely off her tits; just look at Margie Patison." Across the street Margie edged cautiously along the pavement carrying a dog leash with no creature attached, whispering instructions to the invisible audience that now constantly surrounded her.

"Bit of pampering down the frozen food aisle and all that?" deadpanned Jack.

"You know how it is." A bus drove into view, which Nathalie looked at before stealing a sly glance at Jack. He glared through the windscreen at the driver and Nathalie thought better of raising her arm and leaving him there alone. The long single-story machine powered slowly forward like a rolling stone away from the pair, the sweet smelling trails of exhaust smoke momentarily dulling the questionable haze of the bus shelter. They both breathed in deeply, enjoying the petrol fumes.

"It was canny seeing you last night. Sorry we didn't get a chance to catch up properly and that..." Jack said, feeling slightly stupid that he had no joke with which to follow this up.

"You too. You were quiet mind."

"It's my Mam isn't it?" Jack shot back "Can't get a fucking word in edgeways."

"Always were pistol-quick with the excuses, our Jack."

"You know how she is."

"I know how you are. Strong and silent, that's what they say about you – the Jimmy Dean of St. Cuthberts... *you bloody love it*." Nathalie grabbed Jack's shy grin between her hands and pinched his cheeks. "*Everyone's favourite rebel without a cause back on the mean streets of the Meadow Well...*" She shook his face in her hands and he pulled away trying not to laugh.

"Get off!" He pressed his finger into her ribs gently and made her jump. "You are off your tits, you know that? No wonder Ant's away – needs the peace and bloody quiet." Jack smiled and lit a cigarette.

"You know they say it's bad for you?" Nathalie took the cigarette from Jack's lips and took two drags of her own before placing it gently back into his mouth. He could feel the dampness of her strawberry lip-gloss on the filter, which made it taste sweet and delicious. Jack enjoyed this more than the cigarette itself.

"They also say it stunts your growth. But six foot four later, what the fuck do they know? Besides, I thought you'd quit."

"I have. Mostly. More of what you'd call an occasional indulgence now."

"'Occasional indulgence' eh? *Check out the GCSEs on Morley*."

"Fuck off," she said, wrapping her arm round Jack's waist. Jack felt his body tighten at first and then relax into her touch. "What you going to do with yourself Jack?" she asked after a long pause. Though not looking at him she could almost feel his facial expression changing at the notion of having to explain himself. She didn't want to upset him; nor did she want to make him think she was like everyone else. She wanted more than anything to let him know that she understood that pulse inside of him, the one that kicked against the currents in search of an exit. "You're too big for this place Jack. I sometimes look at you and wonder how you fit, you know what I mean?" she said hazily as though stoned. "You're just so different. Like Ant. You should do it, just go. Run far and fucking fast and never look back. Well, except to toss me and Shir' a bundle of cash every now and again. *Price of pam - pers these days!*"

Jack shrugged. He wanted to speak but couldn't. Instead he handed the cigarette to Nathalie without looking and listened to the crackle of the burning paper as she took another long, soft pull.

"You're better than this Jack. Better than us," she said through the constricted throat of one no longer accustomed to nicotine exhalations.

"No-one's better than you," he said quietly.

"You know what I mean. You can see it in your eyes. You're not like that lot. You can't just piss about nicking motors for the rest of your days."

"It's a gig."

"Don't do that."

"Do what?"

"Make a joke out of everything you don't like to hear. It's daft; and you know it. Ant'd have a shitter if he knew what you'd been up to."

"You haven't told him have you?" Jack asked nervously, almost angrily.

"Course not. Haven't spoken to him about you. Keep him busy with my own problems when I get round to speaking to him. Sometimes I put it off."

"Why?"

"Don't know really. Suppose I just don't want him worry-ing."

"He would."

"What?"

"Worry," said Jack. "Don't bother him while he's away. He'll be back soon. I'll keep an eye on you, you know that."

"I know." She pushed herself up from where she had been leaning against Jack into a more upright, authoritative pose. "Promise me you're really going to try Jack."

"Jesus," he said into the last inch of his cigarette before flicking it into the road where it bounced and fragmented into a miniature, silent firework of orange and grey. "You're not half off on one today, aren't you?"

"*Jack.*"

"I've been to the Job Centre haven't I?" He brushed his hands down the uncommonly smart attire "... and square root of fuck all that turned out to be."

"There must have been something."

"Not that simple though, is it?"

"It never is."

"Because you can't just go and have a look now –" Jack continued, ignoring Nathalie's interruption. "Got to have an interview and all that. And then when you give them the first syllable of our address you get that look. You know the one, as if they've just found out you've been dumped by your cousin or something."

Nathalie laughed a sad laugh. She knew immediately the look, a combination of pity and disgust. Eyes narrowed, forehead lowered, lips pursed, always joined by a sharp intake of breath "Yeah," she said, "I know. But you've got to get over it. Fuck's sake, people go though worse than being dragged up in a shit postcode. Some people have gotten out. Shirley was telling me about your probation officer, Paul."

"– Peter," Jack corrected her.

"He sounds like he's done alright."

"He's different."

"You're different."

"It's just hard, isn't it?" He lit another cigarette as he spoke in an attempt to make his words seem more casual, less meaningful than they were.

"What is?"

"You know... *trying*, I suppose."

"How do you mean?"

"Like, nicking motors is alright. It's a job. People think you're huge and that. Get in with the hard lads, get to the top, knock some bonny lass up and settle down a few doors up from your mam. Everyone's happy. You get to stay the big man – no risk, no delay, feet first into being someone, even if it is to a bunch of twats and dossers. It's not the right thing but it's easy. But then to try and do something, put your balls on the line. You can do it but..."

Jack paused hoping Natalie might finish his sentence for him. She recognised this and forced herself to stay silent. "It's too much of a risk. I just don't know if I'm brave enough, really. Don't know if I'm strong enough."

"I think you are," she said "I know its scary. But I know you could do it. Or at least try, instead of just smashing things up. We all know why you do it Jack – everyone understands. But it won't get you nowhere."

"Reckon I'm going there fast anyway. This is where it'll all end Nathalie, so why bother kidding yourself? May as well accept it and get on with it. See if we can't polish the turd after all."

"It could be different if you tried."

"I know. It's just frightening, that's all. Big fish in a small pond and all that... sometimes it's just easier. Swimming up stream's no fun anyway."

"Worth it though. And if anyone can –"

Another bus pulled into view and this time Nathalie raised her arm out while still sitting close to Jack. The bus hovered noisily by the curb with a relieved puff of its lungs as it opened its doors to allow a trickle of passengers, each one a different colour, shape, or size, onto the streets like the mis-shape funnel at the chocolate factory.

"Try Jack," Nathalie said, standing up. "For me."

She kissed his cheek before turning and mounting the bus without turning round to wave, knowing that no answer would be forthcoming. He watched the bus blend into the distance until it was a silent spec of dust floating between streaks of light. As it travelled he imagined her silhouette alone, bolt upright, trying to avoid the slurred gaze of another mid-morning drunk. The kiss on his cheek still felt warm and made him happy. But inside Jack felt guilty and halved, as though he had already let her down.

"We need to arrange some sort of structure to your days. Have you been to the Job Centre yet?" Peter asked. It was brighter now though the clouds still hung thick and low in the sky and masked the sunlight into dull shades of constant off-white. Through the net curtains he could see long shadows crawl across the estate in the filthy light, which seemed to be making Jack uneasy. He tried to ignore them.

"Been." said Jack. Peter looked impressed at Jack's efficiency, but Jack shook his head. "Load of shite. But Darren said he was going to have a word with his Uncle Ed though."

"Is Ed back in the picture?" Shirley's voice was punctuated with a plume of smoke that blew across Peter and Jack like drying shirts caught on the breeze.

"Reckons he can get some work for me."

"Brilliant." Peter scribbled in his notes as he spoke. "This is exactly the sort of thing we need to be focusing on. I'm also going to need some sort of proof that this is your full-time residence... utility bills... bank statements... that sort of thing."

"I pay all the bills," Shirley proclaimed proudly.

"Because I don't have a bank account."

"Right. Well, we could sort something out. Shouldn't be a problem. It's all bullshit really." Peter felt himself blush slightly at his first swearword in a professional capacity. He was pleased it was at their house though and not at the office. With Jack and Shirley it felt like an odd initiation. "None of it ever gets looked at properly – so long as you say it's there they'll believe you."

"Here!" Jack raised his voice but playfully rather than angrily. "My rehabilitation should be your main concern, not getting to the pub five minutes early come Friday tea time."

"Your rehabilitation doesn't worry me in the slightest," said Peter. "It's this new case I've got. You'll know them – they went to our school."

"Won't it be breaking every rule in the book by saying who?" Shirley asked

"Technically."

"Well, don't you be getting yourself into bother," she said with concern. "Just nod if it's the right person. Shelly Johnson. Is that her name Jack? She was a right little shocker. No? Dean Collier? Ryan Carr?" Shirley went on.

"Who is it?" Jack asked with a smirk. Peter paused for a moment, pleased to have their attention and their eagerness.

"Gemma Sproat." The boys shared laugh was dirty and sharp like old whiskey.

"Who is she?" Shirley sat forward, feeling left out. "Tell me!"

"Nah Mam, you wouldn't know her; she left when she was thirteen."

"First girl to get pregnant and keep it," Peter added.

"Thirteen!" Shirley widened her eyes "Not in this whole fucking creation!"

"What's she been in for?"

"Guess."

"On the game?"

"Got it in one."

"That'll be a piece of piss compared to some of the nonces and nut jobs they'll send you round to," Jack said staring back out of the window. Dark figures with heads hung low like death row ramblers floated past the front garden and disappeared into the day.

"You're kidding! Have you seen the fucking state of me? There's no way they'd send me round to any of the high risk cases." Peter blushed at his own self-deprecation. However Jack's small brute laugh – one syllable and unnoticeable to the untrained ear – cushioned his sudden embarrassment. Shirley placed her hand understandingly on Peter's knee. "I didn't want to say anything hinny, but I was thinking about that the other night – what with you being all skin and bone. Some bruiser could break you in half if he didn't like the colour of his mood board."

Peter and Jack both muted their laughter. "I mean it!" she went on. "Maybe you want some sort of extra protection, take a breadknife in your little suitcase or something. Just in case."

"I'm sure I'll be fine, but cheers anyway."

Jack's eye was caught once more by shadows floating towards the other side of the street. Craning his neck to try and steal a better look he found himself unable to gain any further information as his newfound social awareness had him glued to the seat, physically engaged in what Peter had to say. Shirley noticed Jack's interest in the bustling outside but found herself pleased and in some small way proud when he sat back down the way a proper host should do when guests are present.

"Why's Gemma such a pain in the arse then?" he asked, the corner of his eyes still edging towards the window.

"Because most of her work she gets through her boyfriend, who's also her pimp," Peter said, preoccupied with the filing system he had created himself one bored day and now couldn't seem to remember the logistics of. As a child he would spend so long creating colour coded, geometrically perfect time sheets for revision that four hours later he would be too exhausted to even contemplate home-work; he was the boy who spent so long applying sunscreen that he missed the rays completely.

"And?"

"And he likes to sit in on our meetings. You'll remember him too."

"Who?"

"Scott Seamark."

Jack's attention was immediately diverted to the centre of the room as if it was water and Peter had pulled a plug.

"Fuck me!" he said. "She might be right you know, better take a breadknife with you just in case." They laughed once more, though Peter emitted a noticeably more anxious sound: his laughs tapered and flicked at the end with a nervous into-nation that made him gently writhe in his seat.

More and more action bustled outside and with each minute it became harder to ignore. Raised voices and misfired obscenities gently strummed through the quiet pauses and Jack found himself unable to resist the lure of his own curiosity.

Shirley could tell; she too knew that something was hap-pening. Even from the calm of her own living room she could feel the estate pulsating like a spot desperate to be popped. More than anything though she wanted to keep Jack away from it – whatever was going on – partly to ensure the straight and narrow but also to show Peter that Jack was a changed man. As far as she was concerned Peter's seal of approval was the first step in getting Jack up and over the fence he had been stumbling at since he went from being one of the lads to being one of the angry young men that tore through the estate like warning sirens.

"Nah, something's going on out there," Jack said as he stood up.

Shirley, panicking, responded louder than she had intended.

"Sit down you!" she yelled. "You're going nowhere even if I have to hold you down myself."

Grudgingly, Jack did as he was told. Shirley, desperate to dull Jack's craving for involvement, turned on the television to its lowest setting; too quiet to be able to distinguish individual words but a loud enough whisper to mask the increasing noise from outside. On the screen a dour-looking newsreader looked to a video of coolly distressed students in torn denim and matted hair clutching banners and yelling politely through loudspeakers. Their cause was undetermined and their placards so elaborately designed that the text had become an undistinguishable jumble of bubble lettering and abstract smears of red and black.

"Ban..." Jack could make out on one placard. "No more..." Peter saw on another. Jack's mood altered back to the person that Peter had been faced with on his initial visit. Those prolier than thou eyebrows rose disdainfully towards a higher being, angered at what he saw. "Fucking typical that, isn't it?" he said.

"What?" Peter asked despite knowing all too well the tracks on which that particular conversation was travelling.

"That lot get together and kick off about something and it's a protest, but when we do it's a riot."

Peter struggled for a moment as he tried to best formulate a response which was articulate yet provided Jack no further fuel to go back to loathing him. Unable to express any insightful comeback he found himself relieved when Shirley snapped back. "Oh you're a one man martyr you are Jack! *Bloody hell.*"

Jack opened his mouth to respond but wasn't given a chance, "Yeah," said Shirley, nodding towards the television, "maybe so, but I'm sure that their *protests* don't end up with the offie being burgled, a motor being burnt in the middle of the playground and Kenny Adams losing his middle finger to a petrol bomb." She stopped herself to take breath and then politely leant in towards Peter, "he forgot to hoy the bloody thing after lighting it. The daft bastard."

Peter nodded.

"Oh and that's another thing you missed when you were away. Tourettes, the doctors reckon it is now. I blame the parents myself. Your Nana had a funny turn the time he had one of his little flits in the Post Office queue." She shook her head in disbelief "Oh by the way I didn't tell you love – she's been barred from the corner shop again so we're having to get her bits in for her until after Christmas."

"What for?" Jack asked, still annoyed from his argument having been quashed but eager not to seem like a sore loser.

"Shoplifting"

"What did she get?"

"Two bars of soap and a roll on deodorant. I wouldn't have minded only she still stinks of piss."

"What were the riots for?" Peter asked.

"Protests," Jack corrected him; Shirley shook her head before finishing her tea in one gulp.

"Sorry, yeah, protests."

"Can't remember."

Shaking hands with Peter as he left Jack noticed the anxious, small crowd building up outside the Pearson house. Peter noticed too but was preoccupied with his own thoughts as he left the estate – pleased with the progress Jack seemed to be making. Progress that he felt was partly his doing. It made him feel for the first time that what he did mattered, or rather that he was good at what he did. Perhaps they were one and the same. He felt taller as he got into his car. He no longer wanted to make himself so small that he blended in or disappeared completely. Waving clumsily at the car as it pulled away Jack noticed Darren's father, Chris – a transient fixture in their household but a caring man nonetheless – as he chatted uneasily with extended family members and neighbours that congregated in the overgrown garden. His eyes met with Jack's and they seemed to ask a million and one questions, none of which Jack was able to answer.

Slowly and hesitantly a police car drove onto the Meadow Well. Unusually it was met with the silent, respectful anticipation that the estate now only reserved for hearses. It slowed down towards the Pearson's house and Jack felt something inside of his body change; it felt like a piece of wood splintering and twisting inside of his stomach, winding his organs around until he almost couldn't breathe.

"I just need to –" he yelled into the house but was interrupted by Shirley.

"Get yourself back in here, now!" she barked. Jack did as instructed and sat with her on the settee. They were quiet for a moment. Jack's mind sloshed around, thoughts wrapped around other thoughts and tangled on his increasing sense of dread. He found himself unable to form one sensible or coherent idea about what may be going on outside.

Shirley didn't care. It was outside: it didn't count. Her bid to distract her son was the first time she had, in her memory, turned on the news while at home. "Once I'm inside," she had once told Jack, "the world can go to shit for all I care so long as we're sorted." She meant it too and now she had her son back he was all she cared about.

"It will be alright," she said eventually, taking his hand in hers and hoping that he would not overreact to compensate for his uneasiness. Thankfully he didn't and for a moment they sat silently, neither one feeling the need to say another word.

Then the noise came. A woman's voice. Long and sharp it harpooned their moment so brutally that neither could ignore it. The worst sound in the world is a scream when it's meant and at once both Jack and Shirley knew that whatever the worst was it had just been confirmed. Shirley stood up, pressing her hand onto Jack's knee, silently signalling for him to remain seated.

Out of the window Shirley saw two policemen staring red-faced at a small, ghostly audience outside of Debbie and Chris Pearson's house. All of her children were there apart from Darren. Chris wept silently into the shoulder of his eldest daughter who in the space of seconds seemed to have taken on the deep, bottomless, tired look of someone who has known great sadness, the sort of look that can fade but never truly leave a person. The noise had come from Debbie, who was still screaming in the direction of the policemen from the floor. Her middle son, Alex, tried to help her up but she looked pathetic and frail, like a puppet whose strings had been cut.

"You might want to look at this," she said, verging on tears.

The front door swung open and flapped like an almost severed limb as Jack flew from the house. He walked as fast as he could as he steamed forward towards the house where the police still stood and Debbie still wept. It seemed to take him just one giant stride to make the relatively short journey across the road and it was only once he found himself standing there outside of the battered gate and crumbling wall he realised that for at least a minute he hadn't breathed. He looked around frightened to speak. If he spoke it became real.

Debbie was sitting on the floor weeping, mumbling prayers and wishes about her baby boy. Alex looked up from where he cradled his mother in his arms; he stared at Jack and shook his head.

"They fucking killed him," was the only sentence Jack could make out through the smudged ink of Debbie's monologue as the police nodded professionally before retreating to their car and exiting the estate. A speck of rain dropped from the sky and landed sharply on Jack's forehead as he stood silently on the outskirts of the crowd.

He sat rigidly. That was all Shirley could think of, the way he felt hard and brittle. Not quite living. She knew it was his way, but she also knew that it was hard and brittle that snapped the easiest. Her eyes stung from crying secretly in the toilet with the taps running full power so that Jack couldn't hear her. With him behaving so properly she felt like her instinctive hysterics would have been unsuitable. Sitting close enough to feel his breath she was frightened to touch him in case he shattered. In her hand she held the photograph. By looking at Darren as a young boy she could at least pretend that he was an adult when he had died.

"Speak to me," she said in hushed, pastel tones; gentle toast on a sensitive stomach. She knew Jack and she knew his moods. "Just tell me how you're feeling, please... it's always better out than in no matter how hard it seems at first."

"You're not a social worker," he said drily, turning his head away from her.

"I know."

"So stop fucking talking like one then."

"There's nothing could have been done. Sometimes things just happen; it doesn't make it right but it doesn't help to think any other way."

"I should have been there."

Shirley felt herself grip the photograph so tight that the edges began to dig into the palm of her hand.

"Oh aye, and then it could have been me out there on the street with Debbie Pearson and Gayle Eastlake. That'd have been a massive bloody help, wouldn't it?" She noticed the sound of her voice rising as though she was separated from her own functions, staring down at the scene like a CCTV camera on which she was both robber and security guard.

"Look love," she said, placing the photograph onto the edge of the table, carefully ensuring she kept her voice to its lowest, most soothing level at all times. "I know how much you cared for Darren. For both of them truth be told. We all did. But nowt could have been done. They made their decision. Life's not always fair and it's seldom nice; neither's easy to get your head around but once you do it makes everything a fuck of a lot easier. Things happen –"

"And most of them happen to our lot –" he stopped his sentence abruptly. Both he and Shirley knew that there was more he wanted to say but halfway through his words Jack felt his insides quiver and tighten. His throat was a tightrope on which each noise balanced precariously before stumbling from his mouth. He swallowed hard and stayed silent, forcing himself into propriety. His breath gave it away though. Like cracked paving it was staggered, jaunty and uncontrollable. Shirley went to place her hand on his, but he straightened up once more. He knew that one gentle touch – even the slightest act of kindness – could break him at any point.

"We've all got our crosses to bear sweetheart, just some of them are heavier than others. Life's not easy."

"They'll have killed him." He spoke like a sawn off shotgun, his sentences finished with a succinct, glinting polish that shattered on impact.

"Who sweetheart?"

"You know who."

Shirley breathed out deeply through her nose and felt her body deflate and lessen until she was too weak to react with the force that she wanted to.

"They were doing their jobs. You know that." His mourning was something Shirley was more than happy to accommodate for as long as it took Jack to recover, but she knew that before long it would turn into something uglier than sadness. A series of sickly thoughts trickled through her head and down towards her stomach, irking her with all the what-ifs that she had hoped would disappear once Jack had been frightened by the reality of prison.

"Well they weren't doing their jobs the night Kenny's ear was still missing," Jack said matter-of-factly "Or when Mark was bleeding his heart out, getting forty winks on a glass mattress." Once more he stopped himself short. He felt a wave travelling through his body once he stopped speaking, an energy that he neither wanted nor knew how best to utilise.

Without thinking he kicked his foot out sharply towards the coffee table where Shirley had placed the photograph. It edged forward with a phony looking jerk of its chipped mahogany legs and reminded him of the shoddy footage of poltergeist activity on the late night documentaries he sometimes scanned on one of the many nights where sleep forgot him. It was only as he saw Shirley move the table casually back to the dented carpet marks on which it belonged that Jack realised it was he who had caused its movement.

Shirley was eager to provide an answer that was of some comfort if not some use, but she couldn't. Jack's opinions were warped but his logic was infallible. Instead she just sat, stroking her hands against the soft edges of the sofa.

"I do remember that day though," Jack said, nodding towards the photograph. His smile was the shimmering throw that masks a filthy armchair. "Do you?"

"Bits and pieces," Shirley said cautiously. "I remember getting the bus there with yous and you saying I couldn't stop. I only said yes because Sharon was there. It was the first time I'd left you; I knew she'd keep an eye on you."

"We did drink cider."

"I'm sure that's not all you did." She moved her hand again towards his, but he pulled back, slowly enough as to be polite, but sternly enough to imply that such contact was not welcome.

"We waited outside the shop behind the chippy, got this old feller to get three bottles of White Lightning. Drank them in one go. When we had our first tabs that day too, tasted like shit. Darren reckoned he had to keep at it though because his dad and his brothers did it; reckoned you couldn't be a grown up if you didn't smoke. He made his Sharon promise she wouldn't say nowt to his Mam."

He moved the photograph with his hand. But instead of pulling it nearer he pushed it towards the furthest edge of the table until light from the window bounced off it, making the image painful to look at in the afternoon's sharp glow. "Driving and smoking he told us – the only two things he ever wanted to do with his life. Do you think that's what they would call irony?" Shirley smiled but didn't let herself laugh. "He spent the whole day picking butts off the floor and lighting again, all day until he said they were starting to taste nice."

"Daft sod," she said quickly.

"Then these lads started having a go outside the amusements. I'd picked up this stubbed out half for him and they reckoned we were scroungers. Gyppos. One of them started on 'us and do you know what Darren did? He ran round the fucking corner."

"You never got done in that day, did you?"

"He wasn't gone long." Jack ignored her and carried on. "I thought 'little twat.' Sharon was kicking off but this lad didn't take no notice, just carried on shoving 'us against the wall. Then he came back smiling. Darren comes up with his cider bottle and empties it onto this lad... Empties a bottle of warm piss all over his head and shirt. The lad's mates were even laughing by this point like; he was fucking fuming... Suppose you would be. We just legged it; hid down by the promenade. It was the funniest thing I'd ever seen, probably the funniest thing I ever will see. Ended up spending my bus fare on bags of chips for us all, that's why we walked home."

Shirley noticed his breathing change again. Fast and sharp he stole breaths that he held tight in his lungs and then released bitterly. He felt the pulse again – a tingling in his bones that rippled through his body and out of his skin. Memories snapped and stung like static and the world felt like it was changing colour. With the full weight of his leg he struck the coffee table upwards and forwards. It tumbled once and hit the fireplace with a sour smashing sound as it stopped dead – legs bent awkwardly, contents scattered across the floor; a slight trickling from Shirley's almost empty coffee cup made the patterned carpet cloud and storm. It looked like a GBH victim found days after their attack. Hairs on the back of Shirley's neck rose. From the base of her spine to the top of her head prickled and she found herself unable to stop herself shuddering. It had happened: Jack had taken two steps backwards, slid down the snake. She looked away from the table and her son as he stood up – his footsteps grew fainter as he mounted the stairs but then became louder again and more erratic as he slammed the bedroom door above Shirley's head.

It made her imagine him dancing on her grave. Her tears fell like cherry blossom in summer but Shirley didn't allow herself to cry properly; instead she just sat alone, breathing hollow breaths and looking down at the white backing of the photograph that lay face down on the floor.

Chapter Ten

There was a lull in The Comet to mark the passing of the boys. Baritone whispers filtered throughout the foggy room. They spoke of wasted youth, lovely boys – couldn't hurt a fly between them – and the bastard coppers always bothering their lot.

Bill sat alone at the bar chatting with Janet solemnly as she poured pints and blinked back tears.

"I haven't paid my respects yet," Bill said. "I'll pop round tomorrow once I've given my shirt an iron."

"Me an' all," Janet said. "I might take them a bit of food too. You can never be doing with cooking when something like this happens."

"Got to eat though," Bill said. "Just kids, eh?"

"Don't Bill, I'll start again," she said croakily with just the faintest trail of crocodile tears. "Wonder how Jack's taking it. Have you spoken to Shir' yet?" she said as she poured a pint for Simon, a classmate of Thomas and Darren's who seldom frequented the pub.

"Nah." Bill looked into his half empty glass for an answer. "Best give her a bit of space now that her Jack's back."

"He walks a fine line at the best of times that one. Best let him settle down before causing too much bother." She went quiet and pursed her lips as she tilted the base of the glass, allowing a thick head to form on the beer. "Did you hear about the crash though," she said to Bob. "Fucking shocking. Ellen reckons the police were going almost a hundred, no lights on or nowt. Practically ran them off the road." She passed the pint to Simon who handed her the exact change before returning to his table.

"Just rumours Janet," Bob said. "Wouldn't surprise 'us, but they'll never get no answers on that one. Our lot's not worth the ink and paper."

"Have you heard about the crash?" Simon asked as he sat down. Michelle poured some of his beer into her lemonade to make a weak shandy and took a sip.

"What?" asked Rob as he stubbed out his cigarette out.

"Reckon they did them in proper. Going over a hundred and all that – smashed them off the road, just left them for dead or something."

"Wouldn't put it past them," said Michelle "That time they nicked our Keith they knew it wasn't him. Record for life now because of them."

"Yeah," said Rob. "That's one thing, but to kill them... where the fuck do they go from there."

"Bomb the Meadow Well. They reckon it'll solve everything."

"They'd be lucky," said Michelle. "We're like pubes we are – you take one out and six grow in our place!" Simon and Rob laughed guiltily in such solemn circumstances.

From the table next to theirs Alex stood up and knocked his chair over in the process. He had been sitting silently, invisibly, cradling just the one drink and leaning against the warmth of the fruit machine for support and protection from the chattering masses – who were desperate to probe him for insider information. From the bar Janet nodded to where he stood and Bob turned to look at the ghostly figure staring at Simon's table with a murderous glint in his eyes. The entire attention of their table turned towards him, shocked at his presence.

Michelle smiled sympathetically but Alex ignored her.

"Is that true?" Alex asked.

"I don't know Alex. Just what I heard," Simon stuttered.

Alex finished the final dregs of his whiskey before pushing through the crowds towards the pub's exit, slamming the wooden frame sharply against the wall as he left.

"Shit," said Simon. "Why didn't you tell me he was there?"

"We didn't fucking know," Michelle said, taking another sip of her drink. "He probably knew anyway."

Their deaths were sad, she knew, but Nathalie found herself unable to muster up the emotions of the others on the estate who had taken so badly the passing of Darren and Thomas. She remembered them from school mostly unfavourably and every now and again bumped into one or the other in the street when she hadn't been able to cross the road quickly or subtly enough. She knew it was a tragedy and would never have wished their demise, but felt neither a void nor a regret that they would no longer be a day-to-day fixture in their life; as though someone had told her that a perfume she stopped wearing years ago had been discontinued. Death had been good to Thomas and Darren though. In just over twenty-four hours they had gone from barely worth mentioning to all that was good about the estate. The young thugs that had once tormented Nathalie had joined with other gangs and were rampaging through the streets, all in the name of their dead brothers.

From her window she watched, frightened, as the groups grew bigger and bigger. Stones arched through the air and poked splintered peepholes in the glass fronts of shops and houses. Some of the lads and their older brothers – even one or two fathers she recognised – carried bats and were swinging casually at gates as they walked past, chanting out of tune about pigs and filth, murderers and children. A gang had grown outside of the chip shop and were spraying the word 'KILLERS' in high, bright letters against the side of the wall beneath which they managed a smaller tag of 'DARREN AND THOMAS RIP'.

Nathalie watched them and their destruction, moving from one side of the street to the other like dogs without leashes. There was no order or control to the damage that they caused, no plan or purpose. There was barely even a point. The names were painted on the wall but already Nathalie felt as though it had stopped being about Darren and Thomas and rather about those that were left behind, one more excuse to vent some of the venom that had been growing and seeping through the sutures of the estate for some time. She always thought that funerals were about the living, not the dead, anyway. She knew too that it was going to get worse before it would get better.

A vacant woop-woop began to sound from one of the shop alarms as she placed the fire-guard in front of the window, locking it in place with thick electrical tape that croaked as she pulled long ribbons. In the distance she heard a sharp smashing sound that made her jump. Nathalie tried to ignore it and carried on taping the cage to the window. The baby was sleeping peacefully in the middle of the room, blissfully unconcerned and breathing a gentle, careless breath as she sighed her way through sweet dreams.

The back door had been secured with the living room table but it was the faulty front door that was her main concern. She checked her improvised locking system once more. Two kitchen chairs sat in front of the door, their high backs perfectly positioned to made the handle impossible to turn from the outside. She had also managed to tightly press two brooms between the lip of the bottom stair and the door frame, which made her feel safer despite looking far more secure than they actually were.

She turned off the main light and switched on the television for company. The quiet voices swallowed some of the noise of breaking and shouting from the streets outside and if she concentrated hard she found herself able to dull out the sound completely. Nathalie sat on the floor beside the baby's cot with her hand touching the skin of her child's forehead ever so slightly, the warmth of her skin and steadiness of her breathing soothing her mother. Eventually she too found herself falling into a deep sleep on the floor of the living room, hoping hard that her husband would come home soon, that as if by sheer force of will she could convince him to take impromptu leave the way she used to stare at stranger's backs to see whether the intensity of her will could make them turn around.

Were she to telephone him then he would come home immediately, but something inside of her couldn't do it – if only to spare him the unbearable anguish he would feel on the long journey back to their house. She dreamed of fires and blood. Dark red images filled her head until eventually they forced her back awake, shivering in the darkness. The television had gone silent and the only picture was that of the unnerving small girl grinning smugly at Nathalie as she clutched her toy clown. Outside the noise hadn't stopped, but it had moved further away, which was better than nothing Nathalie managed to note through the unshakeable haze of interrupted sleep.

The swearing tipped her over the edge. She could abide most things in life – petty theft, vandalism, drunken misbehaviour. But excessive and unnecessary foul language irked her more than anything. She knew that they were spraying their walls. It happened all the time. Were there a competition for graffiti removal then she would unquestionably claim gold. But the words that were coming out of the boys' mouths made her feel physically sick.

"I'm going out there," she said, dropping the spatula onto the metal bench, leaving her husband to finish cleaning the fryers.

"Don't love," Eric said, placing his own spatula down before going over to his wife, gently stroking her arm. "It'll pass, it always does, just let them get on with it and they'll be gone before you know."

Before he had a chance to reiterate his point she was at the front door, chest puffed like a proud hen. "I want you lot away from our wall, away from our shop, and off this street *now!*"

May was a hard woman with a soft heart and vowels that purred like a sleeping cat. With her head held high she would walk straight through gangs at night time as she strolled through the streets allowing her trembling dog to empty its bowels, greeting them with a "hello" before carrying on where others would have taken detours. Because of this she was mostly left alone.

The one attempted robbery since their purchase had lead to a hooded youth's ear being seared with a plastic fork melted in hot oil and another knocked unconscious with a jar of pickled eggs. Perhaps more impressive was May achieving full reimbursement for said eggs from the boy's mother as well as a grovelling apology. Apologies were few and far between throughout the estate and this saddened her. Poverty she could handle – a lack of money seldom destroyed a community. Lack of manners, the death of courtesy, was to her unforgiveable. As far as May was concerned this was the reason that the Meadow Well was as good as fucked.

"It's for Darren and Thomas," said one child as way of explanation

"For their memories and all that – they've killed him" said another, taller boy.

"You lot will be nowt but memories if you don't scarper. You've got five seconds starting from now," she said, placing one hand on the doorframe and eying her watch with an animated exaggeration.

"Fuck off man May –"

"And watch your language else there'll be war on!" she yelled. "Go on... *Now!*" They shared a glance before trundling onwards. As they faded into the unlit backstreets May shook her head. "This is the biggest we've had in a while," she shouted back into the chip shop as she eyed the graffiti. "At least they spelled it right this time."

Turning back inside she noticed for the first time that day the intensity of the stench of grease and fish. The smell was one she had become accustomed to after spending more years than she would care to see in print frying for a living. And it was only when she sampled the alternative – a visit to a friend's house for a coffee and a chat, or a stolen moment at the front door with undiluted air filling her lungs – that she realised just how intense and oppressive the odour was. It was ingrained now: in her hair, her skin, her pores. Even when others reassured her that she had no such taint she could feel it on herself. Such stenches were for life.

Alex walked briskly through the streets. Or rather his speed was brisk, his manner was heavy – a bucking horse trying to thrash from its headgear – and he knew that the first thing with which he collided would spark an explosion. The long knife he carried in his hand like a bat; it had been the first thing he'd thought to take with him. Somewhere inside of him he wanted to destroy; break things like a petulant child the way Darren did when he was younger.

They'd been tethered to two awkward ages that never quite fitted until they hit common ground. Alex was four when Darren was born. Bang! *Jealousy: An Introduction*. The floppy pink mouse-like creature had been pushed from his buggy and dragged from the back door by Alex on an almost daily basis after his requests that he be returned from where he came went ignored. It was a trend that had continued late into their teens when their lifestyles began to blur and merge with one another's and, eventually, Alex began to feel more like a big brother than a reluctant opening act. He had become his protector. And an hour and a half ago he had been his identifier. The skin of his face was still tepid but to touch he could tell that it was just an illusion; beneath he was turning cold.

The light outside was the same. Harsh rays that you had to squint to look at made everything look warm and satisfied, like a post-coital doze. But the estate was cold with a crisp chill that hurt if you breathed in too quickly. Inside he felt frantic and desperate, a thin film whose too heavy contents were bulging and boiling, urgent for release.

"I wish I knew more words..." he'd said to his mother in arch tones in the escort car back from the hospital. With her hand wrapping tighter around his he was unable to speak after that, frightened that he might explode if he did.

People and groups dotted about the street making pithy statements on brick walls as though they had even the faintest idea how it felt. How it felt to lose a part of you that never really was, or how it felt to wake up as one thing yet go to bed that night knowing you no longer were, and never would be again. Behind him he heard a group gathering. A flutter of whispers tumbled after him. In one crumbling garden a new tree grew resiliently, its branches fighting the chill of autumn with green patches grabbing the dusty brown like sailors going down with the vessel. With one sharp swing of his blade branches snapped painfully, crushed with grief. The crowd behind him gasped. One more blow and the tree fell completely. It made him feel better momentarily, but it was a shortlived respite.

As he stormed off, severing every protruding object he could reach, the crowd watched him go.

"Poor lad," said Jane, dropping her alcopop bottle onto the floor. "My Mam said they'd done such a number on their Darren and Thomas that his Mam fainted when she saw his body."

"'Fuck would your Mam know?" Michael asked incredulously.

"Used to work at the hospital – she's got contacts she said,"

"As a cleaner!" he shot back, "And she was fired so shut the fuck up."

"Chill out I was only trying to help."

"Well you're not."

"And what are you doing that's so helpful."

He looked at her smugly, calling her bluff and buying himself a moment's thinking time before his response became obvious to him. Michael picked up the glass bottle she had dropped and without a moment's hesitation threw it with all of his might. It twisted in the air, flipping up and down like a party trick, before smashing through the upstairs window of the house. He looked at her and shrugged as though having provided a perfect and concise answer. A dark smile surfaced slowly on Jane's face like a body floating to shore. She pushed Michael playfully before picking a stone from the floor. Throwing it hard it hit the door with a clunk, chipping the red paint so that a fragment of white etched into the middle of the rectangle.

They all followed, mimicking their actions, hurling stones and bottles at the house. Taking anything they could find – a snapped wing mirror; a half empty can; any stone however small; the child's toys that had been left behind in hurry – and with a growing zealousness showered them towards the house until it was completely without glass. Staring at the aftermath of their attack, the silence seemed wrong, as though the decrepit two-up-two-down should be impertinent at its unjust abuse, not speechless and stunned like a real victim. Some of the girls looked between one another, flashing remorse in their wide, almost clear eyes. The boys looked too, only with a different sort of remorse. They wanted it to be bigger, more explosive, climactic. As the tattered door snuck open with a creak they turned in unison and ran.

Chapter Eleven

Through the afternoon light Jack could see the crowds getting bigger, bulging uncontrollably without structure or control like barely set jelly. He'd heard his mother stirring through the night; her tiptoed footsteps to the window to investigate the bigger noises that tore the night and punctuated her already fitful sleep. He'd heard her crying too. This he resented, especially as he'd had the common courtesy to smother his own sadness – face pressed tightly into the pillow, blanket over his head surfacing only occasionally for breath when the smothering cotton and the restrictions of his own tightening throat and teary, dribbling insides made his face pound and redden through lack of oxygen. He'd allow himself one deep, rewarding grasp of air before cocooning himself again, moaning and weeping into his pillow like he used to when relieving a different sort of pressure. The act of not being heard became a game to him. The guerrilla tears he allowed himself were a mission in themselves, and the stealth that the operation required provided him with a temporary distraction from the hurt.

It was looking shabbier than it had before. Not entirely broken, but neglected; beaten and bruised though not quite dead. There must have been more than fifty people already stomping through the estate clustering and disbanding like fireworks. Each object they passed seemed to wither and wilt, starve to half its original size. They were the biblical locusts Jack had been taught about. A plague.

From the noise he could tell that there were less than there had been last night. Riots were better at night anyway; he knew this from experience. The day was too open, night time provided more cover – a communal mask – and then the revealing buzz of the harsh light of day pulled back like red cloth from an open wound, allowing the entire legacy of your anger to be observed backlit and framed like the transformed living room on Christmas morning. He felt a brief but painful stab of sorrow like a single pluck of a violin's bow.

Everything inside of him wanted to be there. For Darren and Thomas, mostly. But partly for himself. His knee jerked uncontrollably as though he was listening to a fast tune and he began to feel itchy and unsatisfied, like he wanted to eat even though he wasn't hungry. In his hand he held the photograph tightly, folded into a sharp square and pressed deep into the palm so that only he would know it was there. With his hand dampening around the tightly bound wrap of paper he watched them running, groups zigzagging in and out of one another like cars racing on a circuit; no-one yet realising that there was really no end, nothing to travel towards and certainly no conclusion – just the beginning decorated in different coloured ribbon.

Shirley could hear the noises too but chose not to look. The sleeves of her drab dressing gown frayed between her fingers as she pulled strand after strand of thread from the already bare cloth. It was an activity that she had begun simply to preoccupy herself with but before long she found herself doing it instinctively, almost hypnotised by the repetition of the action, teasing threads and watching the fabric ruffle and tighten before the string snapped back and the creases resumed; back to normal but one thread thinner.

The cigarette next to her had burnt itself out. She knew how it felt. Fucking waste nonetheless. The smell of dead ash made her empty stomach turn once and squeeze into a tight fist. She felt her throat constrict and moved the ashtray away from the arm of her chair to stop herself from vomiting. It would usually have rested on the table but that remained sprawled and damaged on the floor as neither she nor Jack had bothered to return it to its upright pose. She had felt volatile for the past day: a combination of anxiety, depression and the hollow, dreamy nausea of pure exhaustion had turned her body to stone. Each movement dragged through a sea of treacle. She was neither erratic nor maudlin, which at the back of her mind worried her. She was flat – low and flat. Resigned to the facts and the likelihood of where they would lead. Nothing about the situation was right. But still she couldn't quite bring herself to scream, to shout and kick like she normally would have. She felt as though she had leaked overnight. All the good that she had planned had disappeared. She heard him come downstairs and she forced herself from her daydream. She knew he was going; she just didn't know how long it would take.

He strolled through the living room casually gripping a long red baseball bat. Shirley didn't move; she barely breathed. In the kitchen she heard the hiss of a pop bottle open. After forcing down three glugs of the generic sweetness – more fizz than liquid – Jack screwed the lid back on and placed it as quietly as he could on the counter. He stayed stone still, frightened and anxious as though he was about to dive from the highest board. Why did she have to be there? He wished she had gone out. It made everything seem so much worse. He felt bad enough that he was going; it made him feel distant and resolute, like pressing extra hard onto the full stop of his own suicide note. But with her there it was tenfold. It was the difference between the time he had been mugged one night after five-a-side and the time Bobby and Paul had kicked the shit out of him in a packed dinner queue. The wounds were similar but the disapproving crowd – the shirking looks of pity and regret – had left a bruise that had lasted longer than those to his eye and abdomen.

Perhaps he wouldn't join in? It was an option he had considered. Maybe he could go out, just to see, and try to bring an end to it all. That way everyone was happy.

Somewhere outside he heard a smash and a yell followed by the flurried patter of running feet like summer rain bursting onto the pavement. The neighbour's dog barked three times at no-one and nothing in particular, just a loud, angered yelp that nobody would tend to. Maybe it was hungry or cold. More than likely just livid. It was a black beast of a canine with thin, hard fur like the carpets of an old people's home and the eyes of the devil himself. Jack used to imagine it was a monster and it would catch him in his dreams. Sometime's they'd be friends, walking through streets together, but then it would turn and bite him, shaking its head as he bled on the ground, glinting teeth chewing through his flesh; he would wake up just as he felt the smooth ivory spikes crunch through his bone and cause him to fade in and out of consciousness in whichever scenario his mind had created.

He'd once heard that if you died in your dream then you don't ever wake up. It was a stupid theory but one that had yet to be disproved and so he grudgingly respected its likelihood. As he lay panting into his duvet, the vivid memory of the imagined attack still rang in his leg or throat the way amputees felt pain in their severed limbs. He shuddered at the thought. It should have been put down years ago after having got hold of Chrissie's young niece one Christmas time. Afterwards her arm looked like it had been badly sewn together from scraps of dead bodies, but the dog was part of the family so it stayed. He never saw the niece again. He ignored it and swallowed the metallic taste that had been building up in his mouth for hours.

He walked straight past Shirley in the living room who was yet to make a sound. With his hand on the hallway door he turned briefly to check that she was still alive. The moment he turned he knew that he had made the wrong move.

Shirley didn't move and spoke in dead notes like the lower end of an organ. "Please don't go out there," she said. She immediately wished that she hadn't. If she hadn't said it then he couldn't go against her. Perhaps he would have gone out there thinking she didn't mind, like a mistake. Crossed wires.

"I have to," he said to the floor, staring intently at the swirls and scuffs of the carpet like a new girl in a familiar pub. "I'm going to try and stop them."

"You can't pet, just let them be. They'll burn out fast."

"For Darren and Thomas. I could stop it for them. They'd have not wanted this," he said innocently – pure and honest as though it were a foregone conclusion. The way a child reasons that the sole purpose for keeping a stray cat is simply because they love it.

"For you, you selfish bastard," she choked on her own words. She hadn't meant to cry, nor had she meant to get angry. As things stood she was sure that Jack's intentions were innocent – or at least good – but she knew that his destruction always began with baby steps. In a way it was a relief, cutting herself to remind her that she still felt. Sitting alone since the small hours Shirley had given passing thought to the idea that her insides had in fact died, that she was just an empty, leaden shell left behind to go through the motions without any of the reward. She'd felt something similar in the months following Jack's birth. It always passed though. As painful as they were the tears comforted her. She could still care even if it did ache this much.

"What about me?" It was out in the open now though. She may as well follow through. If Jack wasn't going to stay for himself then perhaps he would for her. It was her last card and one she seldom liked to resort to. But desperate times, she thought. Desperate times. "What am I going to do – sit here alone and hope a bloody petrol bomb doesn't go off?"

"You know they'll not bother you; I'm going to stop them. Honestly. I'll not get involved. It'll be alright. They'll listen to 'us. You know they will if I talk to them. The police'll not do owt and someone's got to."

It was a pathetic and Jack knew it. He felt himself writhe the way Peter often did when he said something simply to fill in the void where an answer were needed. He knew as well as Shirley that his curiosity was taking him outside. He would try, he thought, to stop them. It seemed only right – for him as much as the estate lest it jeopardise his shiny new life. But Jack had a growing itch that he knew could only be cured by stepping out into the mess and at least observing it first hand.

"They're not thinking straight Jack, no-one is."

"I'll be alright, I won't be long," he said as though popping out for a last minute loaf of bread. He'd said exactly the same thing when he had been sent down. Shirley remembered this; Jack didn't. She stood up and walked towards him unsteadily like she had just come round from a general anaesthetic. She placed her hand on his solid, tense arm and grabbed the bat with her other hand lightly. The wood was warm from where he had been gripping it upstairs, passing it between his hands without realising it as he sat thinking, looking out of his window onto the streets below.

"What's this going to prove?"

"If I go out there I might be able to stop it; it'll be over then we can all get on. You want it to stop; don't you?"

"I want you to be safe. I can handle a bit of bother Jack. I can't handle losing you again. What good'll it be if you get caught up once you're out there? You could you know. I know what you're like"

He looked at her and wished he had a proper answer. "I'm

going out," he said quietly.

"Please Jack, please don't go." She became more frantic and her voice rose in pitch and tone like background music. "Please don't leave 'us again. I can't do it. You're all I've got. I've got nothing else. I've got nothing else to fight for."

"We've got plenty to fight for."

"Jack, Jack please."

"I have to. I'll be alright. I'll come back. Just give 'us one hour and then I'll be back here." He shrugged her hand from his arm but she gripped the bat tighter and tighter.

"One hour," she said with tears in her eyes, gently releasing the bat.

"That's all."

"Alright." She sat back down and lit another cigarette. "But please, for me, don't do anything stupid."

He nodded vaguely and left.

There was an eerie sound. Silence. It was the quietest he had ever heard the estate. No noise, hardly any traffic, none of the across-the-road banter that would seep into your conscience like cooking smells in the corridors of a tower block each time you left the house. It was the quietest it had ever been save for the sound of smashing and breaking – wood from the gates of houses being broken, glass shattering, bricks on concrete. A distant hissing noise slithered in the background from spray cans putting words to the emotions running through the veins of the carnage like lead through blood. The only sounds were those of destruction, of decay. A corpse cremating rather than being left to rot. It reminded Jack of the gentle rustling noises he used to pick out as he laid his head on the grass in summer. A group of six, maybe seven, of the younger children walked steadily past his gate carrying a lamppost in their wake like exhausted pallbearers. It scratched and squealed on its journey and left a faint white smoke trail of flint etched into the path.

At the entrance to the estate stood a group of acquaintances and old friends who Jack recognised from back in the day. Dean and Simon had been with Jack the first time he had been suspended. They'd all set the fire, but Jack took the brunt of the consequences as it had been his lighter and according to the others his idea entirely. The rest he knew though not by name. The nucleus of the group – pulsing and fervent with an implacable rage – was Alex.

In his hands he cradled an axe the way most would hold a newborn baby: head supported delicately in one hand, the long stretch of the body gripped tightly for security. Jack walked over to the group and was greeted with a single nod from each member. He and Alex shared a secret glance; a nod of pity for one another, unspoken condolences, a silent determination for different sides.

"What should we do?" asked Alex, immediately marking Jack out as a superior figure, the foreman to their factory hands. The tacit responsibility felt like an achievement to Jack and he couldn't help but smile slightly, a facial twitch that he was careful to manipulate into a malicious sneer as to avoid any suspicions.

"I think yous should stop," Jack said. The improbability of his response caused Alex and Simon to gather round him as though he was leading up to a great plan. The rest of the group were oblivious to his speech.

"Are you pissed?" Alex asked angrily.

"What are you really hoping to achieve?"

"Show them not to mess with us."

"Fuck's sake Alex, they know that. But where are they now, eh? No-one's here to see this – there's nowt being done, no-one's being shown anything except making this shithole just that little bit worse for them who've still got to live here."

"They need to know that they can't –" Alex began.

" – *They know*," said Jack. "This is mad though – tearing

the whole place down. There's no-one to watch. Look –" he opened his arms to the streets, empty save for the rioters themselves. "Do you think anyone gives a fuck?" Jack heard himself speaking but somehow it didn't ring true even to him.

Alex thrust the axe into Jack's hands "Show us how it's done then."

The uncontrollable weight of the axe's head felt wrong in Jack's hands. But within moments it felt right; a pair of shoes that he had broken in swiftly. However, against all of his instincts he handed it back to Alex.

"Just think about it, eh?" Jack said. "This is helping no-one."

Alex glared at Jack and walked towards the patch of trees at the entrance to the estate.

"What you doing now Alex?" Jack asked.

"Marking our territory." He said eventually

The crowd cheered as Alex swung the axe over his head and brought it down brutally in a diagonal arch that bit into the shins of the tree causing a v-shaped splinter of wood to disappear beneath the pressure. He swung the axe again and this time the tree snapped cleanly at the base like a magician's finale. At the other side of the road he did the same. The second tree fell the same way and created a barrier across the entrance to the estate, slender but definite. Jack observed the poignancy of the makeshift barricade in a moment's silence.

"What now then Jack?" Alex asked. Having riled himself up like an athlete he looked ready to charge or pounce. "Are you in, or are you out."

Jack didn't respond.

"So you're one of them then?" Alex yelled.

"Fuck's sake!" Jack said "There is no us and them."

"You *know* that's not true." Alex stopped for a moment and looked around at the infant riots. "So if what we're doing's so useless then what would you suggest?"

"Well," Jack said, unable to help himself from showing them that he could, if he so chose, commandeer the entire proceedings. "If you want to make them see, then you're not going to do it by smashing in a couple of shop fronts, are yous? You need to make them look. Fuck holding their heads to the window; you need to push them through."

Alex smiled and Jack shrugged. "Don't say I didn't warn yous though. It'll not end the way yous want it to." added Jack before forcing himself to turn to leave.

"If you change your mind mate, you'll know where we'll be," Alex said.

As he walked back home the conglomerate of minions swathed the smaller trees either side of the road like flies to shit, shaking and kicking them until they too fell to the floor in tangled layers.

They waited for quiet. Other gangs skulked through the streets but they wanted to claim this one as their own, to take things to the next level. Alex had separated himself temporarily from the larger group and had initiated himself as leader of another, smaller pack.. Ed, Thomas and Ashley looked obediently to him, awaiting their commands.

"Get in and pour it about. Be quick though, then get the fuck out. *I'm* lighting it," he said quietly. For the children hearing him speak was odd; the past two days he had seemed almost like a ghost – visible but silent – patrolling the streets with his long, rusted knife. Listlessly tearing gashes out of any surface that he though he could beat.

They did as they were told. In unison they threw bricks through the window of the shop. Hitting the window roughly at the same time the glass tumbled to the ground and carpeted their entry. As they walked over the damage their steps crunched and cracked like a gentle autumn stroll. Ed entered first. He felt a buzz being the only one there at night. He skipped through the aisles of sweet packets and tinned goods, kicking over the small rack of spices that Bangladeshi Mary stocked for her friends and relatives. It hit the floor and bounced; the cheap metal structure fell onto its face and packets of red and gold scattered the floor like treasures. Ed picked one up and opened it, spilling the contents onto the floor. Holding the pack to his nose he coughed as he inhaled some of the heady mixture.

"Fucking rank!" he shouted "Get a whiff of that." He thrust the packet at Ashley, who slapped his hand away and pushed him jokingly onto the chest freezer.

"Stop messing about," she said. "Someone'll hear us."

"Chill out," said Ed, pocketing two packets of the spices. "No point in it all going to waste." The three disbanded throughout the small shop, filling their pockets with bags of sweets and packets of cigarettes. Thomas crammed as many bottles of vodka as he could beneath his skinny arms. Ashley lugged the red drum to the till and began pouring its contents onto the counter.

"Wait!" Ed yelled, running beneath the barrier to the cigarette counter. He took three more boxes of cigarettes and handed them to Ashley. "Can I do some?" he asked, stuffing the last few lighters into his back pocket. She shrugged and stepped back. Ed took the can and began hurling it around his head in mad, frenzied swings of his arms. Petrol spilled onto the walls and the floor, and rained droplets onto his forehead that tingled and smelt sweet.

"*You stupid bastard!*" Ashley scuttled to the broken entrance of the shop, away from Ed's makeshift downpour and began wiping her hands across the front of her sweater.

He continued to pour, gradually weaving in and out of each aisle, dribbling up the counters and onto the food and tins. By the time the can was almost empty he was confident that no surface was untouched by the fuel. He walked backwards towards the window and poured the remaining pool over the small fridge at the front of the store, paying particular attention to the plug beneath the broken window frame.

Crawling out of the shop one by one they stepped backwards cautiously as Alex observed the damp, potent unit. He walked back to where they stood and poured the final drops of liquid onto a scrap of cloth which he wrapped around a brick. Lighting it in his hands the flames crawled slowly towards his fingers. He held it for a moment, daring it to burn him. As his small hairs began to painlessly singe he tossed it like a bomb into the shop.

The fire appeared quietly at first, an intense flash like the television screen turning on with the sound down. As it ate its way hungrily throughout the shop the flames began to roar and grumble; the aching architecture of the shop hissed and spat as it diminished in the heat. Crowds fled to where they stood, watching their masterpiece fall in on itself. The roof opened up to allow the flames room to crawl up towards the night sky. Then it began to frown and wilt. It tumbled into the main body of the shop and with it took a large portion of the two main walls until all that was left was an unrecognisable mass of heat and noise as hundreds gathered to watch.

Chapter Twelve

Lying in bed was somewhat of a fallacy. She'd simply ascended the stairs clumsily on instinct after sitting in the thickening dark for a few hours. Hadn't turned on the lights. Why bother? She knew she wouldn't sleep but still she felt it necessary to at least maintain the basic boundaries of normality while her tiny world tore itself to pieces around her. She'd had only one visitor that day. A man from the electric board. He had a foreign sort of look; foreign sort of walk too. Polite enough lad but not the type that comes from a quickie with Him Next Door.

Shirley had invited him in and allowed him to give his prepared speech. She had managed to place the table back where it belonged and so the house was, she felt, as suitable for visitors as it would ever be. Even his pauses were scheduled. She didn't really hear him. The only detour he took from his script was for minor jumps at the sudden thumps and thuds from outside. As his words blurred past, Shirley found herself dipping in and out of her own daydream.

Jack had been alone in his room since he had returned the evening before, staring out of the window at the destruction he had been unable to stop, although Shirley still felt a toxic snag of doubt that it was really his lack of involvement that was causing him the most unease. She only noticed that her visitor had stopped speaking as he held out an array of supporting materials – pamphlets on upgrading her residential electric system.

"You new on the job sweetheart?" she asked, finally forcing herself to focus on her guest.

"Yes Madam," he said. The way he said 'Madam' sounded odd, as though someone had been forced to pop a twenty pence piece in him to get the last half. He sounded exotic and sexy but this only served to make her gruff, hearty accent feel more gauche than usual. Brushing her hair back behind her ears she shook her head sympathetically and rolled her knowing eyes. Another one she had to keep right.

"Look, I don't want to put you off, but take a look around –" she nodded outside and he glanced briefly at the picture-postcard destruction, "– the only thing keeping this place alive is the fact that none of that lot can afford guns." As though on cue the sound of a smashing glass bottle ruptured through the living room.

The electric man nodded as understandingly as he could without appearing patronising. Sensing that his newest potential customer was on the verge of tears he scanned his clipboard for an 'In Case Of Emergency' list of answers but found no such information. "Someone's obviously having a laugh sending you round here. General rule of thumb is that we're a no-go – not for police, not for non-residents and certainly not for salesman. You're a brave one, I'll give you that. And obviously keen. But take my advice hinny – turn around and run as fast as you can. There's nowt good that can come out of this. And most of them've got the meters so well fiddled they'll never need an upgrade in their lives."

"Thank you Madam," he said. Shirley nodded and stood up.

"Watch how you go flower," she said as she showed him out of the door. She watched him to the bottom of the gate. Hovering for a moment he turned right instead of left, venturing further into the estate rather than towards the exit as she had warned him. She considered shouting after him – instinctively she filled her lungs with the force of a yell, to warn him to take her advice and run. But she found herself unable to. If he was too thick or ignorant to take her advice in the first place then he'd have to learn the hard way. It was only a matter of seconds before she heard a wail. Lighting her cigarette at the window she saw him running the opposite way down her street, papers from his briefcase scattered in the air and spun to the ground like sycamore seeds. He had been given a kind head start, but the Mackenzie brothers were trailing him as fast as their legs would let them. Their twin Dobermans were pulling tightly at their leashes, keen for a bit of that foreign-looking flesh.

"Howay our lad," shouted one of the brothers. "He only wants to play." She pulled back the net curtain and followed their progress. Luckily the salesman managed to jump the felled trees at the front of the estate, which even the dogs recognised as poignant. They drew to a grinding halt behind the spindly, dead branches and watched menacingly as the quivering speck on the horizon threw his briefcase into the back of his car and drove fast and far.

It had been a relatively quiet day. Hungover, a Sunday-ish sort of day. Though as dark began to spread so had the noise. It crawled like fog. She had tried not to listen but she couldn't. Not looking was hard enough. It felt like the time she had been forced to stand behind closed doors when Jack had his stomach pumped; she felt impotent and helpless. Smoke from her cigarette had already made the clicky fabric of her bedclothes stink. She knew that the second she left and re-entered the room the scent would be too much to bear. Perhaps not leaving was best for a while. Realistically, she wasn't too bothered about the stench of her soft furnishings even though no smoking upstairs was one of her main house rules, laid down the day she found Jack's first pack of Lambert's in his backpack.

Anything, Shirley thought, to soften the sharp tug she felt. She'd been trying all day: stroking her hand across the brushed fabric of her armchair; wrapping the cloth of her dressing gown around herself although she was fully clothed; sweet, gentle foods like jam on toast and tinned custard. If only Jack would talk to her then her mind would be partly at ease. Selfish, she knew, considering the damage that was going on outside; but she couldn't help herself.

She concentrated hard on each moment, feeling the smooth sting of the tobacco entering her lungs as she breathed as deeply as possible and waited for the momentary wave of tranquillity that usually came with a deep drag. No such luck. She was stuck, alone, listening to the sound of the outside. Tear marks stung in two long, thin icicles either side of her face but she was too tired to wipe them away. In the orange glow of the streetlights she began to feel her eyes grow heavier though not sleepy. She closed them, too exhausted to sleep, and sat in the darkness as her cigarette cackled and burnt to a halt between her fingers.

A long, white car with brown panels and scabs of rust drove towards the entrance of the estate and stopped dead at the tree barriers. From inside the car Tommy turned on the lights that he had dimmed for security purposes and glanced as far as his eyes would let him. A cool breeze drifted across his face from the broken passenger window. In the distance he saw a group gathered on the grass verge. A few shadows floated around the entrance, patrolling the barriers like prison wardens. He thought about driving dramatically across the threshold, sending the branches scattering to the sides as he sped to the crowd with his borrowed goods like an action star. Instead he reversed sheepishly and turned left towards the estate's back entrance.

People hammered bats and sticks into the damp grass in the

centre of the estate; brown patches that had once been green spread until eventually the surface was a slick, sticky layer that stuck and stained anything it touched. From his bedroom window Jack spotted the clapped out old car cruising towards the entrance before retreating back into the night.

Across the estate over a hundred people had gathered. It made him feel proud in a small way, as though they were there in place of him, a thousand words to his one picture. Everyone looked searing with mad, dead eyes that just wanted to break and ruin, tear everything down like flimsy pantomime scenery. For the first time it was as though everyone on the estate felt the way he always had, felt the simmering fist deep in his belly that he spent most of his life trying to extinguish. Maybe they'd always felt the same way and it had just taken something like this for them to show it. Whatever the case it felt comforting to him. Only he wasn't there; he was stuck in the observation booth with both hands pressed against the pane.

Behind the mound on which they all stood Jack saw the same shitty white car coughing and grinding towards the assembly. Alex noticed it too. It moved fast, though the noise it made suggested far more complex stunts. It drove straight through the crowds that parted and looked sceptically at the rusted beast parked at the exact centre of the heap like a sacrificial altar. Alex walked to the car like a soldier. The crowd made way for him faster than they had for the vehicle itself. He glared into the filthy windshield as he tried to work out who was driving. He didn't recognise the car – it was grubby and tired and he wouldn't have taken it for free. But he relaxed when he saw the smashed rear window.

The driver's door opened and the crowd took a communal step backwards. Tommy got out of the car and stood proudly with his foot on the driver's seat, spreading his hands across the dirty metal of the car's roof.

"Evening lads and lasses," he said in his showman tone. "Guess who's been shopping?" he yelled and then jumped towards the crowd. They cheered as Tommy went over to Alex who playfully punched him before drawing him in close to his chest and ruffling his hair. Tommy pushed him off and pretended to be embarrassed. Watching the scene from afar Jack felt like he was observing a family party to which he hadn't been invited.

"Where did you get that bastard from then?" Alex asked, walking over to the car.

"Never you mind, Alex my son. Just enjoy the moment." Tommy kicked the foot of Alex's axe. With a smirk Alex raised his weapon across the bonnet, high above his head until his shoulders felt as though they were being stretched on a rack. He heaved it downwards as fast as he could, slicing through the air and pounding into the long sheet of metal with a thud. The bonnet dented in the middle; the sound was short and sudden and not nearly as dramatic as Alex had wanted. He hit it again – he wanted an echo, a long, piercing ring of metal on metal. He hit it again and again but still the sound he had hoped for didn't happen.

A few members of the crowd gathered around with their various weapons as the others assembled to watch. A circle of more than a hundred people surrounded the car as the small team ripped it apart like a carcass. Two boys pushed bricks through the windows and the old glass of the discontinued model snapped back into the car in long shards like a drunkard's teeth. One of the boys cut his hand on the glass and in a fit of rage opened the door and peeled it back like a bird's wing. Teasing and pulling with all his strength he was joined by two of his friends who together managed to pull so hard that they fell back, taking the passenger door with them.

Alex put the handle of the axe through the windshield and the loud, empty noise caused a cheer from the crowd. He felt more encouraged and continued to hammer the bonnet with the blunt head of the axe until the dents began to take on shapes like a bedroom wall in the dark; strange faces and ghostly blurs stared back at him as he pounded. In front of him a gang of three young girls gripping bricks and sticks filled in each of the remaining windows. The crowd around them cheered and chanted. One girl swung her brick high above her head and brought it down hard onto the wing mirror with an erotic groan of relief. The mirror tore off, an ear in a fist-fight, and in its place three thin, frail wires hung like blood.

With bats they caved in the skull of the car until the roof was level with the headrests of the seat. The remaining three doors were peeled off in grim, sadistic crunching noises. As they continued to kick and beat the car Alex bent to his knees and pressed the blade of a Stanley knife into its underbelly and allowed a few cool, clear droplets to seep onto his hand before standing back up.

Within seconds the smell hit them and the assembly of destroyers found themselves stopping dead in their strides as though only just awoken to the reality of their own violence. In unison they walked away from the car with their heads drooping – silently aware of the procedure – their arms hanging low from the sudden and feverish workout. They blended in seamlessly with the larger circle as a narrow trail of petrol wept away from the vehicle and towards the furthest edge of the crowd.

The circle grew bigger – wider and more dispersed like an atomic bomb. Alex joined them. Out of nowhere someone handed him a bottle from which a piece of filthy cloth poked out of the top. He lit the rag with three clicks of his cheap lighter and crouching down he threw it smoothly beneath the car. There was a moment's hesitation. Baited breath. And then the blast hit them. Warm ripples stung their eyebrows and noses as they gasped and wooped in excitement. White flames burst from underneath the vehicle and engulfed the battered victim as though it were being murdered by its own arms and legs.

Worst-case scenario. Ridges. Three complaints that a car was burning had been phoned in and they'd been sent. It wasn't usually their patch. They patrolled the more genteel environs – North Shields, Howden, Wallsend. It was a fucking nightmare – without speaking they knew that they were in for trouble. They never quite saw eye to eye. One or two of the bent coppers would pop in and out to shift some confiscated gear every so often but in a professional circumstance it was generally understood that so long as the estate kept it within the boundaries then they'd be left to their own devices. Usually their calls weren't answered. Not the same day, at least. Give them a chance to cool off and it'd be alright.

This time though it hadn't just been them that had called in about the fire. Neighbouring streets that had smelt the smoke and heard the shouting rang to complain. The fire engine had been alerted but by the third call the fire had practically burnt itself out so they'd marked it as a follow up case.

With those two lads having been killed on a chase (there'd already been some little shit caught spraying the station wall) they were never going to win. But even they were shocked. It always had been a shithole, though this was different. It looked like a ghost town. They had entered via the back entrance to create as little fuss as possible. The long stretch that lead from the main road usually alerted someone's attention, who alerted someone else, and by the time they arrived at their destination there'd be a large, defensive mob awaiting their arrival. This, they thought, was their safest option.

From inside the police car they saw gates hanging from their hinges, their wooden slats splintered and smashed. Brick walls crumbled and doused in graffiti of varying quality. The themes were all the same though: condolences for the two dead boys; curses for the police. Glass and debris littered the floor and a thick, choking smoke danced through the streets like a warning signal. Constable Stevenson felt herself blush as they drove through the decaying rot of the main thorough-fare. The police car that usually made her feel proud and tall suddenly felt like something to be ashamed of, as though she was the only person to have turned up in fancy dress. She started to feel guilty, too.

As they continued further and further into the estate figures and shadows began to emerge in the darkness. Some looked on with hate, anger and resentment. Others, behind the bravado, looked longingly, almost hopeful. She suddenly felt that part of this was her fault. Constable Tait didn't give quite so much thought to the matter. He just wanted out. Pulling up to the verge the crowd turned their heads in unison towards the police car. On top of the dank grass the blackened car sat, still smoking in the chilly night air.

"Fucking hell," Jane Stevenson said as quietly as she could and without moving her lips, as though faced with a pack of wild animals.

"They've finally done it," Mickey Tait said, "They're burn-ing the Meadow Well to the fucking ground."

It was only when they allowed themselves to turn their attention away from the broken streets and the burnt out car that they realised the scale of the gang they were facing. As an estimate Constable Stevenson would have said one hundred residents were gathered on or around the grass verge, staring wicked, angry eyes at them. Constable Tait would have guessed nearer to two hundred.

A burning bottle curved through the night sky and narrowly missed their passenger door. It hit the ground next to them and an almost perfect circle of flames burst on the road. From the top of the hill Tommy yelled something that neither Stevenson nor Tait could make out as the crowd began to chant..

'*Filth... Filth... Filth... Filth*'

With each syllable they seemed to become angrier, like each word was pumping another blast of air into an already full tyre. From the front of the group they began to run towards the car. Like hour-glass sands the entire mob followed smoothly until the entire wave of bodies were pouring down the hill towards them.

"Shit! Shit! Shit! Shit!" Tait struggled with the car keys. In his panic he honked the horn twice and accidentally knocked the switch that caused a spray of blue lights and pithy sirens that battled against the din of the crowd. Constable Stevenson couldn't speak. She dug her hands into the sides of her seat and closed her eyes. Just as the first members reached the car the rumble of the exhaust kicked in and Tait managed to manoeuvre quickly and smoothly around the crowd. Inside it sounded like a heavy rain as legs and stones pelted the doors and roof.

They sped down the main street towards the entrance. The crowd followed them tribally, tossing broken bricks and stones. Occasionally petrol bombs showered onto the ground beside them. A few of the faster members of the pack caught up with the car as they reached the entrance, crunching and bobbing over a pile of crushed trees as they sped away into the distance. Alex walked to the furthest point of the estate yet still wouldn't let himself cross the now tattered pile of trees that marked the start line. Trailing the police car with the length of his axe he tucked it beneath his arm and closed one eye.

'Boom,' he mouthed.

Chapter Thirteen

Bob was there when he came downstairs. This didn't bother him in itself but as it stood he resented even Shirley's company and the extra presence only added to his unease. As he entered the living room their voices dipped and faded, suggesting to Jack that he had been the topic of conversation. On the sofa where they sat Bob moved an inch or so from Shirley as discreetly as he could. Her eyes were red and bulbous, which Jack had come to realise meant either alcohol or sorrow. Noticing the half empty cups of tea in front of them Jack concluded that it must have been the latter.

"Alright Jack, how you keeping?" asked Bob.

"Been better," he said as he sat down in the single chair that Shirley usually occupied. The curtains were still closed and the television had been turned to its lowest setting. The only signifier of morning was the glossily preened presenters mumbling their way through makeover segments and true life love stories. A pastel weather girl stroked a green map of England, tracing formidable grey storm clouds to the top right-hand side of the country. If only they knew, Jack thought to himself.

It hadn't rained yet. Shirley wished that it would; that way it may clear the air. The whole world felt like a pressure cooker slowly sweating a tough joint. Too cold for summer and too tepid for winter there was an aching dampness to the air that made her whole body prickle.

"What are the curtains closed for?" Jack asked Shirley.

"Because if they stay closed then I can't see," she said in a voice as cracked as the old photograph that Jack had pinned above his bed.

"Don't be like that," he said, unable to restrain himself from at least partially defending the riots.

"Your Mam's just a bit upset," Bob said, taking hold of Shirley's hand.

"Fuck makes you think you know more than I do?" Jack said angrily. Shirley pierced two silencing eyes in his direction and Jack knew that it was a good time to stop while he could. He already felt uncomfortable and agitated in his own living room, as though he were a passing guest and an unwelcome one at that.

Bob didn't respond. Shirley stood up and cleared the mess around them. "I'll make you a cup of tea," she said to Jack. "Do you want owt to eat?"

"I'm alright. I think I might go back out. See if I can help again," he said without looking at her. Shirley visably deflated. "God's sake Jack!" she said as she fussed and flapped around the cups and plates on the small table. "What makes you think you can help?" She had become more cutting than he had heard her since his return, angry rather than concerned. "Huge load of good it did last time you went out, eh? Things have gone from shit to shitter. There are some things bigger than you, you know? It's gone too far – there's nothing anyone can do except keep your head down and try and stay safe."

"But if I don't try –" he began.

"There's no good that can come out of going back out there. At best you'll get your head kicked in. At worst you'll get... you'll get sucked in flower."

"Nah," objected Jack. "I'm not going back inside. Not for no-one."

Shirley shook her head and took the cups into the kitchen without looking at him.

"Just do what your Mam says, eh?" Bob tried eventually as the sound of the kettle's steam rose in the kitchen. "She's upset about the whole thing. It's a right mess out there Jack. And she's worried about you, worried that you might end up back inside. I just reckon –"

"Would you like that Bob?" asked Jack.

"What?"

"If I went back inside?"

"Nah son, no-one would."

Jack smiled wickedly at Bob. "Only I'm not your son, am I? And Mam's not your wife. Must make it easier to pretend though, if I'm out of the way."

"Jack lad..." he tried "...we're all tired and worried, but there's no need to be talking like that. There's no-one wants you back in that place. Least of all me and your Mam."

"'Fuck are you on about – *me and your Mam?* When I'm around it's *me* and *my Mam*. You're an afterthought, *mate*. And don't be getting above your station. I know what you've been up to. And I know how much better it was when I was away."

"Your Mam, me, everyone Jack – we're only trying to help the best we can. Why are you being like this kid?"

"Maybe I am like this. Maybe this is how I'll always be."

"There's nowt you can do out there lad, just stay inside. I know you're trying to help. You're a good lad –"

"Maybe I don't want to do good no more," Jack interrupted him. "Been trying it for a couple of days now and I'm not sure it's all it's cracked up to be."

Bob shook his head and as the kettle reached its peak in the background Jack went on talking quieter than before. "If I want to go out there now and torch the whole fucking world I will. And there's nowt you or her could do about it. I could, too."

"What?"

"Bring the whole place to the ground. Do you think that lot know what the fuck they're doing?" Jack nodded to the closed curtains; Bob looked but didn't say a word. "Give us an hour and I'd make them something to really remember."

Jack smiled. He was goading Bob though he didn't really know why. He wanted to break him somehow, or at least destroy any trust or support he may have for Jack. Perhaps, he thought, it was simply because the sly bastard had had the audacity to believe he could grope Shirley in secret and assume Jack wouldn't know exactly what they were up to. But maybe he was doing it for Bob's own good – if Jack cut him off now then it would hurt less when he really did fuck up. Just as he was about to continue Shirley entered with a cup of tea for Jack and a freshly lit cigarette for herself clenched tightly between her teeth.

"Here you are." She placed the cup on the table in front of him and sat back down next to Bob.

"Don't worry about it. I'm going back out for a bit, see if I can do owt. I'll be home in an hour or so."

"Jack –" Shirley went to stand up but Bob held her hand. She looked at him sceptically but he shook his head. "Please son, just stop here."

Jack looked at them but making eye contact only with Bob. "I'll be fine. You just stop here with Bob. I'll not be long."

"*Fuck's sake*," she whispered as she heard the front door click and lock. She gripped Bob's hand tighter. "It's happening again, isn't it?"

Nathalie's house had become a prison to which she held the key though chose not to leave. Like the tramps and beggars that would break shop windows so they could spend an evening in the comfort of a cell: fed, watered, and protected. The only problem was that increasingly Nathalie was achieving neither food nor protection. Another car had been burnt the night before outside of her house. It was smaller than the one on the mound and paled into insignificance compared to the blazing cornershop that had lit up the streets in a pulsing glow, but it had been so close that the glass of her bedroom window was warm to the touch. Frightened she had watched the car burn, transfixed by the flames that danced like the damned until she smashed through her own dreamy mood and realised the seriousness of the situation like a date rape victim combating the haze of their chemicals.

As the fire of the car grew bigger and angrier – spreading onto the path outside of her gate – she had taken the baby and hidden in the bathroom, every so often leaving Nicole asleep in the dry bath so she could check on the progress of the flames. In the early hours it had died down and the young boys keeping warm by the glow moved on. Unnerved she found sleep more difficult and feeling safer behind a lockable door she had set up a mattress and small travel cot in the cramped bathroom.

Back in the living room, Nicole cried and popped her hungry jaw from the settee where she lay. The tub of milk was entirely empty and Nathalie had become too scared to carry on using diluted milk. Through the small holes in the fire gate she watched more men patrolling the streets. It looked like hell, she thought, and reminded her of those films where the last human being wakes up to find that his homeland has been destroyed and evil forces lurk in the shadows. One man looked into her window accusingly. Shocked, Nathalie jumped back from the window and sat down in her armchair facing the opposite direction. She then slumped onto the floor and crawled over to where the baby lay.

Tiny, famished noises spat from Nicole's mouth and

Nathalie felt something inside of her break. She no longer felt frightened; she felt angry. Like the boys out there but worse. Angry at them, not the world. She wanted to get a bat, to find the hard girl that she had buried inside of herself years ago, and to smash the faces of each and every one of them – to tell them that they were the reason they lived like this. She wanted to stop it all on her own and momentarily the thought passed her that she might actually be able to. But she was kidding no-one. Instead she just stroked her baby's head and picked up the phone from the floor, untangling the curled wire that Nicole had taken to chewing to soften her teething pains when unattended.

Holding the receiver she pressed the first three buttons of Anthony's work line. The 'family emergency hotline' he used to call it. He had told her to use it whenever she felt the need. Before finishing the number she found herself going over in her head what she was going to tell him, how best to let him know he had to come home immediately without worrying him. Suddenly she was fourteen again and trying to vocalise to her parents why she had been suspended for whacking a teacher. She couldn't tell them that he'd tried it on with her. Girls like her fared poorly in sexual assault cases. Their chapters were over before they had begun.

Flustered and upset she slammed the phone down and without warning burst into tears. Like the best kind of friend – distraught at their loved ones upset and eager not to let them blub alone – Nicole did the same and began to weep quietly. This made Nathalie cry even harder. She gripped the settee to try to settle herself but found it difficult; tears flowed softly but there was nothing eloquent about her wails. She picked up the phone and quickly punched in the number.

"Hello?" Shirley's voice was thinner than usual like too-diluted juice. But it was a comfort nonetheless and Nathalie began wishing that she had phoned sooner.

"Shirley..." Tears pushed their way rudely past words in Nathalie's throat.

"Hiya pet."

"Shirley I'm frightened."

"I know you are. We all are."

"Shir' I need some help. I've got no milk. I need to get my tokens to the shop – there's nowt for Nicole. I've stretched it as far as I can go but –"

"Calm down sweetheart; you'll be alright. We'll sort it out eh? Just you settle down. You stay where you are. I'll give Ellen a ring and I'll come and fetch you."

Shirley hung up after being thanked a million times. She was a good girl, but sometimes Shirley missed the little lass that used to spit blue Panda Pops at boys from her front gate. She felt bad for her, though still she shivered at the idea of leaving the house. This way she had to face it. She dialled another number and after three rings heard the click of a receiver being lifted.

"Ellen, its Shirley. I need a favour."

Being outside felt wrong and instinctively she found herself wanting to run back in, slamming the door behind her. Instead she locked both locks and turned to the estate with a stony, funeral face. She felt winded when she saw the moribund streets fallen and tattered. Six youths walked past her gate with their baseball bats, one holding a machete. They hovered for a moment in contemplation of her front gate, which unlike the rest still stood upright. Shirley maintained eye contact and took one step towards them, sneering. The largest of the group jostled what looked like his second in command and muttered something before they walked off in unison.

"Pathetic little shits," she muttered before walking out of her garden and taking a proper look around. To the left the trees had been cut down and lay scattered across the threshold. Glass made the paths look like they were paved with diamonds; the concrete shimmered like an expensive dress in the sun's light. Walking towards Nathalie's house blackened skeletons of cars looked sad and dejected. Dotted sporadically – some on their sides, some upside down completely – they looked as though they had fallen burnt and crushed from the skies like a horrible curse. Through the gaps in the houses she could see the gaping facade of the burnt shop – its insides black and wretched like a dissected smoker. Its burnt innards spewed onto the street from where the gas canister had erupted. The lightest black scraps occasionally caught on the breeze and danced upwards in a sweet cyclone before disbanding and falling back to the floor. School children led by those that should know better were sitting on the wall and small grass hill opposite Nathalie's house, graffitiing more letters onto the concrete.

Each surface held so many sprayed messages that they had tangled and mulched into a thorny, unreadable jumble of colours and shapes. None of the words were decipherable, like a million prayers all screamed at once. Waving into the front window she only had to wait a moment before Nathalie timidly dragged the pushchair from the house, shutting the door carefully as she did.

They walked briskly but steadily through the streets, the hard wheels of the pram rat-a-tat-tatting across the broken glass and chipped pavements. In the pram Nicole stirred but remained relatively peaceful, closing her eyes from the hard grey sky and sleeping weakly through her hunger pains. They were silent as they crossed the road to the shops. To the left a gang caught their eye sitting in the caved in front of a shop that had been abandoned for some time. The insides, Nathalie could see, had been desiccated – every item broken and upturned. The few remaining fittings and fixtures were crushed and the space had been used as a makeshift office from which the main players of the riots sat smoking – drawing up plans for their next mission.

Amid the group Shirley saw him but she couldn't bring herself to turn her head. Even though he stood taller than most Jack seemed lost within the group; the leader that didn't know quite how he had arrived there. His mother didn't look up and even with the distance between them he could tell that it was taking every ounce of her strength not to. All he could stare at was the pram. He wanted to be with the baby, to have something that simple and untainted to hold. He thought that would make everything better, clear his head like a scalding bath after a long day's work.

Nathalie felt an ache as she saw Jack standing there; she imagined him orchestrating the violence that frightened her as if a familiar dog had bitten her savagely. Parting slightly and silently her lips were a broken heart through which Shirley managed to hear the word "Jack". "It's alright flower," she said sternly, holding herself together and linking Nathalie's arm as she guided them across the street to the shop. "He's only out there trying to stop them all from doing something really stupid." Shirley spoke hurriedly but bluntly, trying to convince both Nathalie and herself of her words "He's trying his best, one of the good ones, eh? Now let's get this over with then you can get that one back inside where it's safe."

Nathalie allowed herself to be dragged onwards by Shirley but felt her body turn cold as she spoke. Unable to dull her own morbid curiosity her eyes trailed behind as she craned to neck to catch one final glimpse of Jack in the hope that she could see for herself that he was actively trying to stop them. Then they turned a corner and he was gone.

Perhaps out of respect for the long-serving member of the community, or perhaps simply because it was located as near to the rest of the world as to almost not be classified as a Ridges dwelling, Ellen's cornershop had been relatively untouched by the riots save for a small patch of graffiti marking the side wall. 'In memory' it said. Still, Ellen had decided not to open up the shop. A closed sign hung permanently in the window and iron boards had been placed behind the windows in an attempt to discourage the arson attacks that were becoming more and more frequent in the estate. She'd been fire damaged once before it had almost finished her. As well as the business theirs was a single storey structure with the shop at the front of the building and five small rooms to the rear in which she lived with her husband and her son – a lumbering baobab of a man-child who had the beady, glazed stare of someone lacking in all the necessary components.

"Ellen! Howay Ellen it's us, open up." Shirley hammered on the kitchen window at the back of the building. The curtains were closed but she knew it was where Ellen sat perched during the shop's less eventful moments. The off-white fabric trembled with the pressure of an unsteady hand before peeling back nervously. Ellen poked her greying hair around the gap she had created to check that the face matched the voice before drawing the curtains back fully, nodding understandingly at the pair. Opening the small gap at the top of the window she passed two boxes of baby milk to Nathalie in return for the small tokens that had faded and smudged in Nathalie's nervous grasp.

"There you are sweetheart," she said as she checked the tokens instinctively.

"Thanks Ellen, you're a lifesaver."

"I don't know what's happening," Ellen said, shaking her head as she lit another cigarette – chewing the filter between her thinning red lips that reminded Nathalie of dying roses.

"No-one does hinny. You've got the right idea with your boards though. What's a bit of missed business for peace of mind eh?" Shirley said.

"It's like the end of the world, isn't it?" she said through the glass, waving her cigarette towards the tip of the estate.

"You're right there. And you want to count yourself lucky

you can't see the worst of it."

"Hey, you must be worried, what with that little one to keep safe."

"I am," Nathalie said, placing the milk bottles beneath the pram's small holder. "It'll be over soon sweetheart – they'll wear themselves out. They always do. Mind, this is the worst it's ever been." She paused for a moment, contemplating her own words. It hadn't always been like this, she thought. Ellen, along with Shirley, was one of the few people who could remember when there was little but good on their streets.

"Mind," Shirley said. "Them useless sacks of shite could have done more to stop it."

"Aye," Ellen agreed. "Not like the old days when you got proper coppers – not scared of owt that lot."

"They'd have sorted them out in seconds. None of this'd have happened if we'd still had the Kinners and their lads in force."

"Oh no." Ellen laughed at the memory of the hulking policemen who once patrolled the streets – all built like brick shit-houses and proudly decked out in her Majesty's finery. "Tough love they'd have called it."

"Tough alright. But they got the job done. Cheers Ellen," Shirley said, linking Nathalie's arm once more. Ellen nodded and waved at the baby as she closed the window and pulled the curtains tightly shut once more.

"Are you sure you don't want to come and stay round ours?" Shirley asked. Standing outside of Nathalie's house a light breeze picked up and dragged her hairs uncomfortably across her face.

"I do Shir', I really do, but I have to be in 'case our Ant rings. Maybe he could at least get Jack to..." Nathalie went quiet as she saw Shirley's eyes begin to fill. She knew that Shirley said he wasn't involved; not properly, not the way the rest were. But she had seen the way Shirley had looked when

Jack came into view across the street. Her face was old and deep with lines now permanently ingrained like carvings on a tree. She was a weeping statue, the tears protruding awkwardly through her thick skin, and nothing Nathalie could say would make any difference.

"Are you going to be alright on your own?" she asked, gripping Shirley's hand hard.

"For now." Shirley rolled her eyes to try and absorb the tears. "Jack'll come back soon enough. Once he's had a chance to sort them out a bit. You know what he's like."

Nathalie took her in her arms tightly and although she resisted the embrace at first Shirley found herself sink into her grip. As they let go Shirley kissed her own finger and traced it onto the baby's head before waving Nathalie silently back indoors, waiting to hear the click of the door before making the short walk back home in the growing breeze.

Chapter Fourteen

Local news had been running bits on it for a day or so. Even the nationals showed a few pictures. Not as much though. It wasn't that uncommon Peter knew. And they seldom bothered with anything up North when a similar event could be reported nearer to the Thames. Two helicopters had flown over. One was the police and the other one was for television. They'd shown the estate at night. Gangs had been streaming through the streets – bent over and travelling fast like wolves. Houses and shops blazed an odd orangey glow and cars dotted the streets like dead beetles on a windowsill. His mum had counted four as they watched as though it were the end of a quiz show.

"That's what you get for trying to help that lot," she'd said over a garibaldi the night before. Peter had sat silently. It felt like he was there, like it was his world falling in. He didn't care about the cars or the shops that were being lost. He didn't even care about people's houses being destroyed. The whole time he scanned the screen with a surgeon's precision, absorbing each particle of detail in search of only one thing. He didn't see him, but inside he knew that somewhere, somehow, Jack was there.

No-one else on the estate could have orchestrated such intense chaos so quickly or expertly in such a small amount of time. Were it left to the masses then there'd have been some superficial damage. Maybe the odd car burnout and a fight that got out of hand. But they'd have grown bored and stopped by now. He had a feeling only Jack could have achieved this.

"You're not going out, are you?" his dad had asked him that morning as Peter tied his laces nervously.

"Yeah, just popping out for a bit."

"Lad," he looked up from his newspaper, "Tell me you're not serious."

"I'll be alright."

"Don't go. Please." He looked more concerned than Peter had ever seen him. A grey cloud of terror stormed his face like those of the parents he saw on television whose children really were lost forever.

"It's just a visit."

"You're not at work." He put down his newspaper and turned to his son. "Please son, for us, don't play the hero. You're not cut out for that sort of thing. You'll be helping no-one."

"I have to. I won't be long."

"Peter, please." He stood up. Peter made his way to the door, pleased in some small way that his Dad cared this much. Though he wasn't affected enough as to do as he said.

"I'll be back soon. I promise. In and out, honestly."

"They'll eat you alive – look at the bloody state of them at the moment." He pointed to the lunchtime local news headlines showing snapshots of the riots.

"I'll be back really soon. Don't say anything to Mam."

He left the house and got straight into his car. Primarily to ensure the safety of Shirley and Jack his visit was also, secretly, his own way of verifying his concerns that Jack had become involved. And though still confident in his decision to enter the riots he felt it best all-round if he reverted back to parking outside of the estate. Just in case.

A slight figure began to take shape in the distance, long and lean without any definite shape like someone was squinting at a star. It walked around the trees at the entrance and continued further and further onto the estate, its blurred edges hardening into a more human shape as it did so. There was a rustling among the group as it grew closer. People picked up their bats and stood up, calculating the force required to take down the intruder.

"Who's that?" one boy asked loudly at no-one in particular, taking the cigarette from his mouth. Jack, with his back against the entrance, turned around and was shocked to see Peter approaching. Jack had moved further into the estate from where Nathalie had seen him, into the heart of the riot.

"He's alright," he said, slightly flustered. "He's one of us." He felt like he had been caught on a date by his wife: his two lives coming face to face for the first time. However Jack felt as though they were crashing headlong into one another, each one destroyed somehow in the process. Part of him was pleased: Peter would only have entered the estate for him. But part of him felt broken. Peter, he thought, was clever, sensible, Peter should have been able to curb his own curiosity the way Jack knew he never could. He felt disappointed and vulnerable like he had seen a parent trip over for the first time. He blushed and turned from the figure approaching, pretending that he hadn't seen him. Peter carried on walking with his head down.

Inside the house was strangely quiet considering the mess outside. With the windows shut and the curtains half drawn he could have been anywhere.

Shirley sat down uncomfortably. "You're braver than I thought," she said.

"It's my job." They both knew that wasn't true. Peter had none of his usual paraphernalia and was dressed in his civilian clothes – a tracksuit top and jeans with old trainers that he'd had since school as they still fit him.

"You knew he wouldn't be here."

"I honestly thought he might be."

"You're a good lad," Shirley said. She felt bad that for a moment she had wished that Peter was her son, or even that her own son would act a little bit more like him.

"I didn't think Jack would –"

"He didn't," she interrupted him before he had a chance to say anything more, "at first. Went upstairs. Said he wasn't getting involved. But he did. Reckons he's trying to stop them all, says he might be able to make a difference. I know it's only a matter of time before..."

"He's only doing what he thinks is right. And maybe he is," Peter said as believably as he could manage. "I saw him, when I walked in. Perhaps he is trying to stop them all from getting worse. Perhaps people just need to have a bit more faith in him."

"No." She shook her head. "Faith's one thing I've got coming out of my ears flower. But I know Jack. And I know what happens when he gets like this. He's not trying to do good anymore."

"He might be."

"Four days ago he was doing what he thought was the right thing. They all did. They've not got words or people to talk to. Not like, well, not like you. It's how they say things. How they pay their respects is to smash something up so we'll all know how they feel. Happens all the time. Not like this though. Not for this long. And now... God knows. Is there something inside of people that I'm missing?" She felt her insides cloud with tears again but managed to push them down and seal them tight shut like a full suitcase. "You know? Something that likes it, that likes to break things that needn't be broken; to take your whole life and turn it to shit just for a few minutes of fun?"

"Sometimes..." Peter tried, though was unsure of where his own response was leading. He attempted to find the right words to say to Shirley as though she were his friend but he found it too difficult. Instead he found himself sounding like a bullet-pointed handout from one of his Sociology modules. "Sometimes circumstance can...What I mean is, if you're born into a world that seems to be one big obstacle then destruction can seem like the easiest option. Maybe Jack's scared – maybe they all are. Maybe he's feeling vulnerable."

"Maybe they're stupid; stupid and thoughtless. And angry," Shirley added resolutely, though weak with attempts to justify their actions in her own mind.

"They don't seem to be angry out there though. If they were angry they'd have made mistakes. Someone would have got hurt. I think they want to be stopped."

It was a thought that hadn't crossed her mind, although as much as she wanted to believe him something about it just didn't quite stick. "How do you do it?" she asked.

"What, stop it?"

"How do you get out? Get somewhere, be someone, more than where you were born, more than where you went to school?"

"It wasn't easy."

"You managed, though."

"Jack's a fighter." Peter said and meant it. "He'll sort himself out."

"Jack fights. He's no fighter though. It's people like you that really fight."

"I don't think I do."

"I do. We're all fighting in this shitty world. It's the best ones that pick their battles wisely – the ones that take on the world and win, or at least strike even. You won. What's that lot taking on? A few nicked motors and the back wall?"

They laughed futilely. For Shirley it was either laugh or cry and she'd done enough of the latter over the past few days.

"It will be alright you know," Peter said.

"Sweetheart," she said, still smiling like she'd been given gas and air, "I invented that one. You and I know it's the biggest lie in the book."

She hugged him at the door as he left. Turning to walk away from the estate he noticed the gang had moved across from the park area where the burnt car sat like a throne and had regrouped outside of a chip shop. They were smashing the windows with shiny nylon tracksuit tops wrapped around their hands. The gang wasn't that big, much smaller than the ones he'd seen running around at night on the news. He knew he shouldn't but he found himself drawn. His legs carried him across the road, past the burnt patches and detritus and towards where they stood. A few looked over unsurely at the stranger approaching but most were so occupied with the task at hand that his presence went almost entirely unnoticed. As he joined the group a small girl – thirteen, Peter thought, and that was being kind – offered him a cigarette.

"Thanks anyway." He shook his head and pushed through the spectators towards the front of the group.

"You'll need plenty of petrol if you want it to be the big one tonight. And get a car if you can," Jack said to his apostles who ran off loyally without pause or question. He glanced at Peter approaching and shiftily separated himself from the main body of the gang, resting against the rusted, glassless shell of a phonebox as he lit a cigarette. Peter joined him and took the creased roll-up that Jack handed him.

"Peter."

"Alright Jack... What are you doing?" Peter asked sceptically.

"Here, *I tried*." Jack opened his hands widely in his defence. "Tried to stop them. They didn't listen."

"You're not trying to help now though. You're making them

worse, working them all up into something they probably don't want to be. You know –" Peter dipped his voice so he couldn't be overheard "– that lot'll do whatever the fuck you say. They've not got a proper idea between them. Why are you doing this?"

Jack paused for thought but didn't answer Peter's question. "What do you think?" He nudged his head towards the estate. It seemed that not one building had been left untouched, each surface marked or demolished somehow.

Peter was unsure how to react. "I think you're not thinking," he said it quickly, pulling off a bandage swiftly to minimise the sting. It was the first direct criticism he had ever given Jack and even as the words came out he was certain it was a bad move.

"What?" Jack looked baffled though slightly amused.

"You need to stop this Jack," Peter said desperately. "I know they want someone to stop them but they won't, not anymore. It's gone too far. You could have helped by now if you'd really wanted to but it's not too late. You have to stop it all now. You could if you wanted to."

"You don't know what the fuck you're on about. I tried."

"Hard?" Peter asked. Jack shrugged and Peter continued. "Just think about it. You've made a point; no-one's going to forget it, *ever*. Just leave it Jack – there's still a chance you won't have to go back inside."

He ignored him. Clasping his cigarette tightly between his teeth Jack picked up a broken brick from the ground and handed it to Peter with the pride of a child giving his first gift.

"Go on," he said, pressing the jagged square towards him. "Have a go."

Peter took the brick from Jack and looked around. There was a window upstairs in the bookies that remained untouched. It was small but shiny and seemed out of place in the now ruined exterior of the ugly red brick structure. The brick was heavy and clumsy to hold and throwing it would have been a relief as his hand started to sweat. Dropping it would have been just as easy. But then he thought about how much breaking something might please Jack. Canonise him, even, so that Peter could finally become one of them.

He eyed the window and measured it against his own admittedly meagre upper body strength. He had been dismissed from PE as he had found that the javelin proved too tricky, the shotput too heavy and the discus too awkward. He could never see the point in just throwing an object when all that resulted was the need to walk and pick it up again. Same with running – why bother unless you're being chased? He narrowed his eyes and found his shoulders moving backwards in preparation for the shot.

It was only when he caught Jack's face – eyes wide and excited, like he'd found another convert – that he managed to stop himself. He dropped the brick, which splintered dust onto the pavement and tumbled off the curb.

"I'll see you Jack."

"Whatever you like." He seemed disheartened, almost let down that Peter wouldn't join him, and watched him intensely all the way to the exit of the estate until he blurred into the distance.

The sound dipped in the evening light. Jack walked home through the back passages of his street, dawdling under the brick archways of the tattered semis. White chalkmarks from hopscotch pyramids faded beneath the damp September air and weeds grew defiantly where grass had given up long ago. He dragged his hands across the outhouses in which he used to hide as a child. He would wait for his mother's voice to grow to its most frantic crescendo as she called his name for tea before stepping out casually, acting as though nothing had happened.

The back windows to most of the houses were still boarded up but they'd been like that for years – protected in case of emergency. They were the old ladies who carried umbrellas even in summer '*just in case*'. From this angle there was little damage and it was almost quiet. For the first time in days it was like he had rewound, gone back to before his friends had died, to the fleeting moment where he had, for the first time in his life, felt as though he had a chance to move forward instead of circling in the same pack, around the same spots, going nowhere. It was a happy thought but a passing one and it only reminded him that while he may once have been going nowhere, he was now travelling there fast – too fast to do anything about it. He knew he couldn't stop, not on his own, and not now.

He flicked his lighter and took three short drags of a roll up that he exhaled in almost perfect smoke rings. They stayed in shape for a moment before disintegrating and disappearing into the air. He made a fourth ring and poked it with his finger fast and hard before it had a chance to melt. He thought back to jokes Darren and Thomas used to make about fingering smoke rings and laughed. At that moment all he wanted was to go inside and act as though nothing had happened, to be met with a sharp comment and a soft smile from Shirley who'd have made something a little bit too cold on the inside and a little bit too black on the outside for dinner. He stubbed out his cigarette and brushed himself down, ready to face the music.

Then it barked. Just once at first. But then another and another. He jumped. Through the gates the black dog howled angrily at Jack, pushing its head towards the slats, trying to break through the barriers and tear into him, eat him alive and spit out his bones. His instinct told him to run, to get inside the safety of his home, and for a moment he considered it. Then he felt the hairs on the back of his neck stand on end and his insides turned to glass; one wrong move and he felt like he would shatter.

The dog carried on barking, bearing its lupine teeth and rolling its head from side to side. Jack felt a fear he hadn't known in a long time. For some reason he thought of Nicole, asleep in the pram. He imagined she was there with him and he had to protect her. Inside he managed to change his fear, grab it like clay and squeeze it hard until somewhere in his stomach it turned into anger. He no longer feared the dog; he hated it. He hated the sort of world in which such a creature might exist.

It continued to bark and thrust its head against the side of the fence, its clawed feet pounding into the soil and leaving imprints ingrained like fossils.

Jack bent down to its level; his heart jumped up and tried to crawl out of his mouth. Slowly edging towards the fence he took out a small pocketknife and flicked the blade into battle mode, pointing the business end at the dog. He edged forward with his knees bent. Balancing on the fingers of his left hand he began to tremble and resented himself for it. Curious at its newfound company the dog stopped barking and cocked its head with a look of intrigue in its black eyes that made Jack briefly imagine it as human, as though it knew all along how it was behaving and did so only to frighten him. As he edged closer, the dog appeared to relax.

"Here boy," he said quietly. "Come on..."

The dog looked at him again and as Jack's face was practically touching the fence it flew suddenly forwards, barking a long, loud howl as it chewed at the crumbling slats of its makeshift prison. He sprung back, pressing his hands into the pavement and pushing himself as far away from the dog as possible. He watched it for a moment from its own level – biting and screaming at dead air. The thin metal leash that kept it in place had snuck beneath the fence in its frenzied attempt to escape. Jack edged forward again, staring into its black eyes as it chewed at the wood. He grabbed the chain in his left hand

and gripped it hard. Standing up he glared at the dog and stood still. It continued to bark and bray, oblivious to Jack's new-found pole position.

Yanking the chain with all his might the dog's head flew forwards and pressed against the other side of the fence. It writhed gently in its concussed state as he pulled tighter on the rope. He crouched down again, retaining the pressure on the leash to make sure that its head stayed in place, before sliding the knife quickly into the centre of its throat through the largest gap in the fence.

Retrieving his arm rapidly he stood up and released the chain. Without sound it sat on the floor. It hadn't fell, which surprised him, rather it bent its legs and lay down like a civilised creature, placing its head delicately on the ground. Blood oozed from beneath its heavy head quickly at first and then slowly, gushing in spurts before becoming a steadier, constant stream that pooled around its dark fur.

Despite the wicked crimson in which it lay the animal looked peaceful for the first time since Jack had known it – as if it was sleeping, not really dead. He wiped the knife on his tracksuit bottoms though the stain didn't show. Black can't get blacker, Shirley used to say. For once he was glad to concede that she had been right.

Chapter Fifteen

He had washed and shaved. Changed his clothes, too, the way he used to quickly before zipping out to The Comet for a couple of pints and half an e. Every so often he heard his name being shouted from beyond the front garden – voices he didn't even recognise screaming for him by name as though only he could conduct the evening's events.

Shirley had been dropping in and out of sleep all evening on the sofa. The walk to bed seemed like a wasted journey and so she sat heavily, merged with the fabric of the couch like a whale whose tide had gone out. Physically she could have gotten up, but somewhere along the line she'd convinced herself she had forgotten how. Movement was a distant memory. Her mother had called, concerned for her wellbeing, but she had played it down for both of their sakes.

After voicing her disbelief over and over again, "but I seen 'em on the news!" she kept protesting, "like animals they were! Fucking monstrous round your end these days our Shir', You want to get yourself a nice little flat like what we got ourselves – and you want to get in quick, too, because these young lassies with the bairns are snapping them all up." However, she had eventually accepted Shirley's PG version of the X-rated events. "Well," she had surmised, "if it's not that bad could you get us a few bits in and drop them round ours tomorrow? I'm busting for a bit of Madeira cake and that coffee you picked up last time's no use to man nor beast. Like dust it is" before hanging up hurriedly to catch the beginning of her programmes.

Walking quickly past Shirley to avoid eye contact Jack closed the kitchen door as he raided the fridge. Clunks and clanks of glass jars toppling over sounded through the narrow walls. *Growing lad*, she'd found herself thinking before remembering that she was as vexed with him as she had ever been before.

"This has to stop," she said as firmly as she could as she felt his bulking figure pass her on the couch in a waft of warm air; it felt powerful and determined – unstoppable – and all the other words they used on the sunny aftershave adverts. He didn't respond at first. Her eyes were red and veined like undercooked meat from where she had been crying. He knew that she was upset. Frightened, maybe, certainly disappointed. But he had gone past the point where he could change that.

Basic business sense, he thought – to upset one person is surely better than upsetting a hundred, which was what it had become. Damage limitation, that was his philosophy. They were outside now. He'd seen them from his bathroom window. Split up into small groups and patrolling the streets like the opposite of riot patrolmen. Perhaps had the actual riot police made an appearance, they'd have stopped already. Though probably not.

"It's been days now Jack," Shirley went on sleepily. "What's going to have to happen for this to stop? What's it going to take?" She stopped feebly like a hospital patient too weak to continue talking.

"Don't you want to pay your respects to Darren, and to Thomas?"

"Yeah," she said and smiled. It was the first time in days she had heard their names mentioned. Their deaths felt like a distant memory. "Yeah son I want to pay my respects. I want to pray for them, to keep them safe wherever they are. I want to get the readies together for a nice bunch of flowers for their grave." Jack felt his insides tremble as she spoke. It was the first time he had considered the reality of where his friends were, and where they were going. He imagined them in the earth, disappearing. He had to stop himself from crying. "Not pulling down the place they called home all their lives though," Shirley went on. "That's not respect flower; it's stupidity at best."

"They..." Jack corrected himself "*We're* proving a point," he said as calmly as he could, suddenly angry that his mother refused to accept his intentions.

"Yeah yous are, you all are. Proving a good point too. What point is it again pet? That we all deserve to live in some shithole." She sucked the last moments from her cigarette and pressed the filter into her ashtray. "It's true what they say about us lot. And I never thought I'd live to see the day I said that."

"Fuck off! They killed him!" He stood up and walked to the door.

"Jack –"

"And they make this place the way it is. You know they do. Once you're here you're stuck for life. You know that. You're living proof."

"Right sweetheart. Alright, so it's the police that burn the cars in the middle of the green is it? And it's the counsellors who piss in the bus stops, and it's them from Cullercoats and Tynemouth who come down here of a night time and brick all our windows?"

"You know what I mean."

"I know what you used to mean. I don't anymore though Jack. Debbie and Gayle had their sons taken from them and God only knows how they're coping. But at least theirs were taken from them – they didn't run and jump with both feet like what you're doing. Do you know how it makes me feel? I've just got you back Jack, and God I was so happy, and now you go out there – risking it all to prove some stupid point. What kind of life is that eh? I have to go through what they went through time and time again, and each time I get you back for a day here, a fortnight there, and then you decide that you've had enough, that going inside's worth it for some stupid fucking mission to prove a point that's never going to get proven –"

"It's not –" he interrupted her but she waved her hand disparagingly.

"You say this was all happening for them, out there. They're dead, Jack. I'm here. What does that say about you and me? You'd sooner go out there while this is going on for the memory of two lads that'll never be brought back, and leave me here alone – scared to shit and not even my own son for a bit of comfort, a bit of protection." Jack blushed and went to speak but wasn't given the chance. "Every day this goes on you're becoming lost to me. And the worst part is that if it goes on for much longer you won't be lost at all, you'll be taken. And I don't know how many more times I can go through that sweetheart."

"They need to pay for what they did."

"That's what the courts are for Jack. You know that."

"And when've the courts ever done their bit for us, eh?" Despite remaining fervent in her objection Shirley didn't know how to combat his warped logic. Eventually he continued. "What was it you used to tell 'us when I was a bairn? If you want something to stop just go faster. Well, it'll stop tonight."

To Shirley the words felt like she was having the most beautiful dream and the most horrible nightmare all at once. They were the words she had wanted to hear for days but now they frightened her. Before she had a chance to say anything Jack opened the door and left.

It never got dark on the estate anymore. Not properly. With all the fires and the fuss it was like the whole world was gently cooking – baking in a non-stop, amber haze. The Meadow Well was on fire, burning to the ground, coming down to dust and ash. As he looked around he felt proud, like he had created something, rather than destroyed it. Poetic, he thought, that when it rots it will look just like any other torn down street. Stagnant whispers of smoke floated through the air, polluting his breaths and marking his clothes. Two more shops had gone up, or at least that had been the plan and by the looks of the flames and the crowds they'd managed without him.

More people were out than ever before. It felt like a minute to twelve on New Year's Eve and he wanted to kiss each and every person there. Tearing forwards with its whirring engine – the most anal and pithy of all the emergency service hollers, Jack had always thought, like a siren on the rag – a fire engine ripped onto the estate. Proud and red it crushed over the trees at the entrance like a smug social worker dusting the settee before they sit down. Another followed shortly afterwards, heading over to the main drag of the shops where the fires still soared high above the houses. Obviously aware of the situation a police car followed the pair pathetically and limply; quarter of the size of the fire trucks it was the sinewy child that hunches next to the school bully and snitches on gossip. 'Just the one lads?' Jack thought to himself, but was interrupted by the chopping air above him – the sky staggered and stuttered like the bad foreign cartoons they sometimes showed after the lunchtime news.

Helicopters – two – danced in and out of one another above him like dragonflies mating. They weaved in zigzag patterns across the estate. Bright lights that shone straight through you like a parent's stare sliced the streets up in strips. He laughed at the sight of them, useless in the air. There was nothing they could do. They knew it, he knew it. Why bother? Too little too late boys! He stuck his middle finger up as the beam approached him, insulting the bulbous, black belly of the machine as they passed him without pausing.

Running to join the crowd he picked up two bricks from the ground. The fire engines curled like a seductive lip at the commercial stretch. Fires marked the opposite ends of the shops like jumpers for goalposts; both eating dangerously into the adjoining buildings. A collection of salvaged goods lay on a pile on the central grass verge. Some of the younger kids had forgone the riots temporarily and were tucking into melting chocolate bars and sly cigarettes, taking their first bittersweet tastes of alcohol and grimacing as subtly as they could. One young girl was throwing up as her friends cheered – flicking their cigarettes at her as she tried to stand up on her puppet's legs like a newborn horse.

Fire fighters emerged from the trucks but sharply retreated back inside as a hail of stones and bottles cascaded towards them; a impenetrable wall that became more frantic and violent as they tried to edge further towards the flames. They got back inside of their truck and sat momentarily as the crowd moved towards them.

A large group surrounded the police car and began pushing and swaying the car until the wheels levitated from the road; raising one at a time before stomping back down like an old man trying to don new trousers. Slowly it moved forward, defeated. The people in front moved grudgingly from its pathways but managed to smash the windscreen with their heavy fists before it drove off in a shower of more stones and glass, popping like angry confetti on the roof and road around it. Fearing the same fate the fire engines chugged into gear and slowly drove forwards. Initially attempting to turn to the rear of the buildings, gangs followed them round and eventually they harrumphed off into the night.

A girl Jack used to know put a fag in his mouth and lit it for him as he observed what felt like his own masterpiece. The police car and fire engines faded from the streets as the helicopters continued to scuttle aimlessly overhead. Running through the streets, regimented like soldiers, they tore down everything they hadn't already. It felt like he was watching his thoughts played out on a cinema screen. It was apocalyptic. His whole world was crumbling to the ground once and for all. It was the happiest he could ever remember being.

Upstairs in bed they heard the sirens but ignored them at first. It was background noise in The Ridges; it was the hissing of summer lawns, or Sunday jet streams blasting dirt from the four-wheel drives on the nicer streets. The other sounds frightened her though. May listened to the crowds outside and wondered how things could have been allowed to get that bad, how no-one had helped. For every terror there were a dozen good people living on those streets – but even she could see why they got swept under the rug. And the police took their lives in their hands, she knew, so stayed at arms length wherever possible. Still, she prayed quietly that it would be over.

There was a cracking sound – sharp and succinct – like the ice beneath them was beginning to give.

"What was that?" she asked.

Her husband stirred and turned over. "Go back to sleep," he said only half-awake. "It'll just be the pipes."

Footsteps. Sudden and light. The patter of a million mice – vermin – scurrying about downstairs.

"*They're in*," she whispered so loudly that the act of whispering became somewhat redundant. "Get up, now!" Shoving him in his arm he groaned again and turned over. Her heart became a caged beast inside of her chest, bashing itself hard against her ribs in frenzied hurls that she couldn't control. Each breath was staggered and sudden as though capped with their own full-stops. Fear wasn't quite what she felt.

Reluctantly she stood up in her nightgown and felt the warmth of the bedroom floor on her bare feet. Pulling on her slippers out of routine she felt her back creak slightly with the pale white signs that middle age was becoming an increasingly stretched term. Walking towards the bedroom door her house felt different. Angry and poetic it was speaking to her with a hushed rumble – like a roar moving further and further away.

The handle was hot. Well, tepid, but for want of drama she would later talk of a blistering sensation as she opened it with trepidation. Whoever let truth get in the way of a good story? Her lungs were pushing breaths from her throat like she had been held underwater and could no longer control her body's need for fresh air. In the hallway smoke lay quietly like a cat burglar. On opening the door it turned in one dark mass of soot. Blinking twice to verify its reality she eventually concluded she was not mad; it was there. Brushing forwards like a slovenly creepy crawly its stench snuck into her nostrils and mouth, choking her like a lover's hands inside of her throat. Retching she slammed the door shut and turned on the lights.

"Get up!" she shouted as she pulled the bedclothes off to wake him up and mask the gap at the base of the door frame like they did on TV. She slapped his bare thighs with a sharp snap of her wedding-ring hand. "They'd done it; there's a bloody fire!"

He sprung up and looked around the room, dazed. "Eh?"

"The shop. It's up in flames. We've got to get out. Now," May said.

Pausing for reflection a small tear bulbed and sprouted in his right eye, which he wiped away with dignity. It had been his idea to come in the first place. "*Everyone needs chips*," he'd told her as they pulled up outside of their new home and business, her face as drab and unflinching as the January morning. "*Even this lot*."

It wasn't just about business prospects though. Somewhere

inside of him – perhaps next to the part that still longed to succeed as a local politician, or the memory of the time he'd taken an entire day's stock to the hungry strikers slouching staunchly by the pits – he'd thought that together they might be able to make the slightest bit of difference to the area. Streets that reminded him of his own childhood: the grey, real estates of Glasgow with the harder accents and harder attitudes. Perhaps, he had thought, what they need is a good example; role models, manners. Apparently not. The truth was gently simmering beneath his feet. A woody, sticky smell began to creep through the peppered hairs of his nostrils.

"Come on!" May looked between the window and the door frantically, estimating the most likely chance of escape. "We've got to go. Now."

"Alright sweetheart," he said quietly. "Let me just get my coat and cap and we'll be off."

"How?"

"We'll use the back-stairs. We'll be fine. Don't you worry my flower."

They stood and watched it burn with a delicious relish: villagers destroying a witch. The most impressive yet, even Jack had to concur. The chip fat had exploded gloriously in the fryers and the fire was at its angriest. Red and orange swirled around the open shop, occasionally poking its head outside to lick the night before finding itself sucked back inside to cackle and groan. Dark mist swirled through the crowd that had gathered outside. The distant whirr of helicopters still sounded in his ears.

"Fucking epic," Jack said to a group he had become integrated with. Fire hypnotised him like magic. There was still plenty to do. What exactly he didn't know but he knew it was to be done. Yet still his eyes were glued to the flailing building as though he was watching a loved one die gracefully;

relived of their pain as they slipped away – happy and sad both curdled in his stomach.

"What we doing next then?" asked Dean.

"Something big. Bigger than this."

"Oh aye, Jack's the man with the plan, eh?" Jack ignored him. Something inside the shop exploded with a bang and as silent and huge as a rocket an orb of flames shot from the building and twisted uncomfortably in the night time. The estate blasted into a moment of brightness as the crowd stepped back from the heat like a soundwave, moving smoothly and together.

"Ah, my fucking eyes man!" Dean tripped as he stepped back. With his trance broken Jack dragged him to his feet using only one arm.

"Cheers Jack."

"Just shut the fuck up and go and find some fuel," he said. "We'll need plenty."

"In a minute, yeah?" Dean said, blinking the sting from his eyes.

"Yeah," Jack said vacantly.

"We're going to walk forward, straight, towards the back door..." he spoke slowly and calmly, holding her hand in his as she grew increasingly hysterical.

"No it's too hot," she interrupted him, unable to conceal her own fear. "We'll get burnt. What if we can't do it? What if one of us falls?"

"Sweetheart," he took her face in his hands and stared sternly into her eyes, "There's nowt going to happen to us, eh? Tough as old boots we are. It'll take more than a bit of warmth to finish us off."

He became convinced by his own encouragement and held her hand tightly. The door handle stung as he turned it and a dry, cutting heat blasted them both. Accustomed to the change in atmosphere they walked together to the other end of the hallway. At the base of the stairwell they could see orange flames hanging smoothly over the back of the door leading to the stairwell.

May's ankles stung on the short walk from bedroom to the emergency exit at the back of the house. Thank God, she thought, for his neuroses. Health and Safety fascism was not something she herself was led by – if it's going to happen then it's going to happen was her attitude. But he was insistent that they should be covered in case of such emergencies. Still, at the back of her mind she was furious. Even allowing them- selves to be smoked out was like a miniature defeat.

Pushing the green safety door open firmly, a blast of cool air soothed her skin and lungs. They stepped onto the cold metal of the stairs and drew breath. The door slammed behind him with a terminal thump as they paused for a moment.

"See flower," he said, "I told you it'd be OK." He kissed the top of her head. Already she had begun to smell like sweet, thick smoke as if she'd spent the evening at a barbeque.

"But the shop. We're not OK. What are we going to do?"

"We'll be fine," he said softly. "We've got each other. We'll move on, we always do."

Jim and Chris sat at the foot of the stairwell but hadn't heard the noise above them. The warmth, they thought, was simply a by-product of the mellow high from the resin they were passing between one another; sucking at the tip with pursed lips, holding it inside of their lungs for as long as possible, then exhaling gently, eager not to tarnish the buzz with an intense coughing fit.

"That's the thing about tac…" Chris said philosophically. Jim leant his head back and allowed his thoughts to sink to the bottom of his brain where they no longer mattered. Smoke tickled his insides and he felt like laughing but couldn't be bothered. "... it's much more effort, but worth every second in the end. Like trying to get your missus to take it up the wrong 'un."

He choked on his last word and began a fit of giggles. His eyes narrowed and like a yawn Chris followed, laughing so hard his sides hurt. A sharp foot in the base of the spine interrupted his good mood. Looking up he saw the old bird from the chippy and her husband, who was looking ever more like a Labrador. They'd seen better days. She stared at him sternly; black smudges marked her face, the most prominent of which was a thin, dark line above her top lip.

"Hold on," Chris said between giggles, "it's Hitler!" They fell into one another in bursts of laughter.

"Move, now," May said in a voice that invited no compromise. The boys stood up and collected their beer bottles and stubbed out joints to satisfy the inevitable early morning cravings. "*Filthy junkies.*"

Turning the corner she joined the mob and was faced for the first time with the reddish glow that was once their pride and joy. "*Oh our shop!*" she moaned into her husband's arms.

"That'll teach them to mess with us!" Dean shouted, dancing around May with flailing arms like a chimp trying to woo a mate. Without warning her fist jutted out sharply and met with his lip, which burst red like a blooming flower. He hit the ground immediately, clutching his mouth, whimpering as he writhed in his own shock and agony.

"Stupid little fuck!" May shouted at the top of her voice before curling back into the arms of her husband, keeping warm by the light of her home as she wept.

The night became more alive as he descended further and further into its heart. It also felt septic and volatile, like he had waded too far from shore and found himself treading water amid an oil spillage. There was a pull though. A current.

Despite having left the house with no such intentions, Peter found himself being drawn closer to the Meadow Well even though for the first time in a long time his heart and head seemed to be in unison, holding painted banners, yelling at him not to go.

It was almost a mile from his house – a distance that seemed so much further at night. Perhaps it was because 'back there' disappears faster minus the benefit of daylight. More than likely it was because, though reluctant at first, he had become both desperate and terrified of what he might find there. And in a strange way anxious to see how far he would allow himself to go, whether or not he would have the courage or the nerve to hover for more than a moment – staring into the belly of the beast, watching as it tore itself to the ground.

There was no danger of him entering the estate again though, he thought. He'd never had the bollocks or the inclination even when it wasn't burning alive. The majority of his pre-pubescent tormentors resided there. Or if they didn't they usually pretended to as a means of boosting their credibility; rubbing shoulders with the hard kids on their home turf. The most gossip-worthy school bus had been the one that terminated at the Meadow Well. He knew he wouldn't go in. He only wanted to. Just a bit. Just to see what it was like to feel part of something that strong.

He drifted downhill. Maybe it wasn't as bad as people had said? Maybe they were just messing about. What's a minor fire here and there? Most of the shops there needed tearing down in the first place. Perhaps they were doing the council a favour. They say getting started is the hardest step. It had been at university – the first sentence is the trickiest; the first inch the worst (this always made him blush.) After that you can only go upwards; onwards and upwards. Maybe from here they could rebuild and start afresh. Probably not though. Jack seemed driven to ensure there were no foundations left on which to build, for them to disappear forever.

"Here, mate," he heard a voice from behind the corner that he was approaching. A child's, almost, but with the grainy staccato swoops, like a bare torso scraping down a coral reef, of someone still teetering anxiously on the edge of puberty.

"Here, mister," he said again. Turning the corner two youths were hiding in the shady entrance of a long alleyway – known locally as Crimestopper's Cut – with pockets bulging full of small plastic bags.

"Alright lads," he said nervously in his deepest, most intimidating voice. Taller than both of them and with at least a decade's advantage he still felt underwhelming and vulnerable in their presence.

"You want any gear?" he asked. "We've got the lot. Proper good green – straight from town. Es, whatever you like.

"No thanks."

"It's good man," the boy protested, his friend nodding in agreement. "I'll give you a good price an' all. Whatever you like, try before you buy and all that."

"No I'm alright."

"Just buy something."

"Fuck off home."

"You're a twat you are mate," his friend piped up from behind the muffler of his black scarf – shrouding his face like an assassin's mask. It made his voice sound old and serious beyond his years. Peter carried on walking.

"Here, Mr... Where you off to anyway?" The question stopped him dead in his tracks. He didn't know. Or rather he knew where he just didn't know why, and certainly didn't feel like attempting to vocalise his decision to two amateur drug pushers.

"I'm off home," he said. The boys looked at one another.

"You live up there?" One of them pointed down the street towards the Meadow Well.

"...Yeah." no-one likes a tourist, he found himself thinking. He blushed, embarrassed at his own lie, secretly hoping that they would mistake it for discomfiture at what may politely be described as his humble background.

"Fucking hell," the deeper voiced boy said.

"Well you'll not be living there for long," said the friend with the gear. "My dad said the whole shithole's going up in smoke."

"Yeah well your Dad probably couldn't last five minutes round our end." Peter said, suddenly enraged as though he were in fact a lifelong resident. It was only a moment after saying it that he prayed the boy's father wasn't in earshot.

The main drag leading to the estate had been lined with police cars. A gesture of sorts. Inside they sat and smoked. One policewoman had fallen asleep, her blond hair flattened unattractively against the window. Helicopters made the whole area seem electric; a copied video on which the drone of the recording could be heard high above the dialogue.

The stench of smoke overpowered almost every one of his senses in the same way fire makes everything look the same. He felt only one thing – something that he couldn't quite place, something that he had never felt before and as such had no specific name with which to label it. Gentle white flecks cascaded from the sky and swirled in glinting sheets through the air. It looked beautiful, like snow, and patterned his dark clothes with a million speckles that when touched smudged into ugly stains.

Staying close to the low-rise walls of the neighbouring streets, Peter approached the entrance pensively. Each police car he passed with a sense of relief, only to be met with the mounting anxiety of another and another. Top to tail they queued patiently and two riot vans were parked idly opposite the entrance. Little movement seemed to be occurring inside.

A single watchman stood at the entrance in his blue uniform. Chewing a cigarette he was fatter than a policeman ought to be. Fatter than most men should be. There were no ripples on his body. The fabric of his doleful uniform clung tight to his perfectly bulbous frame, fat like a card-shop toy cat; the sort of man that seems to be filled with nothing but too much air. One subtle pin-prick would be enough to send him spluttering and flapping through the night like an untied balloon. Facing the dark curvature of his back Peter walked quietly towards the entrance and contorted his slight frame into the space between the thick stump of a lamppost and the wall of the estate's first house.

Holding his breath he felt protected by the darkness and somehow warm. It was only when he turned his head that he realised why. Orange and bulging the streets were on fire. Burnt cars littered the roads like empty cans. Groups were running deeper in the estate. He could hear shouting and footsteps on cracked pavements – untold decades of bad luck, his Dad would have said. Another loud 'boom' sounded somewhere in the distance and reverberated through his body in a deep, healthy pulse that made his blood warm. It felt like a shock; the first heartbeat of a silently born baby. Something clicked with the unseen crash of another building that made Peter feel suddenly alive.

Three sharp clicks of a car's window stunned him into a moment of temporary paralysis. He heard the window roll down in a gentle whoosh and the fat copper turned his head.

"Chief..." the woman from inside the police car said. The fat man turned around and met her eyes. She signalled to Peter who remained frozen to the spot.

"What's this then?" The fat man walked towards Peter. He thought about running – he could surely outrun him. But perhaps not the infinite line of waiting police that he'd have to clear before home turf.

"You up to something son?"

"No... I'm... no... I work..."

"You work!" A wicked laugh belched from lips flecked with hungry white spittle. "Here, Clare – get this, one of this lot *works!*" He laughed again and the young policewoman shook her head, whispering something to her colleague who sat behind the steering wheel playing with a Rubik's cube.

"And you think," the fat man continued, "that makes it better?"

"Look," Peter stepped out from the shadows, "I was just..."

"Think this is a laugh, do you?" The policeman waved his arm to the estate. "Think you're all proving something?"

"I don't even –"

"Do you know there's a reason why you lot live like this," he said as he walked slowly closer to Peter.

"*What?* I was just –"

"And what were you doing creeping around back there? Thinking of cashing in and robbing one of your own? Thought that was a major no-no among your lot. Thick as thieves and twice as poor, that's how the saying goes isn't it?"

"Please, my name is Peter and I was –"

"Or were you going to play a little trick on me?" He carried on towards him. As big as a coffin and twice as deathly he looked like a child's drawing come to life: flimsy limbs with small, awkward hands and feet jutted from his frame. His roly-poly smile was a sinister tear in a muddy dress. "Going to sneak up behind me and have a bit of fun – do in the rozzer because they did in your lot?"

"This is ridiculous I was only –" Peter tried. The policeman stepped further towards him and Peter edged back cautiously.

"That's what it's about, isn't it? You lot think we killed them – the two little joy riders."

"This is bullshit. I wasn't doing anything wrong I was only here because I know –"

"Fucking filth. That's what they were. They weren't killed though."

"Well actually there's been no development in the inquest –" Peter became possessed by his professional self; a cloud of coloured sheets and bold-type lists rushed to his tongue.

"If you don't keep your mouth shut I'm going to rip your jaw off its hinges. Do you understand, big man?"

"Come on, I just want to..." He couldn't continue because he didn't know the answer. He didn't know why he was there or what he was hoping to achieve; what could be gained. He knew very well what could be lost. But that wasn't why he was there. He just wanted to see it; just wanted to feel what it was like. Maybe then he could understand why they did it. What it was that made it worth it. "I was just going; I'll go now."

"Because you lot think you've clever, don't you?" the policeman went on, edging towards Peter who took two steps back for each step the policeman took forward. "Think you're all so fucking worthy – salt of the earth. United we fall. And that's all it ever will be – falling. You don't want to go up; you want to take everyone down to your level. Drag them to the gutter and lower because you can't be arsed with the alternative. Do you think this is the way? That someone's going to stop you?"

"It's not like you haven't got the resources, is it?" Peter's face suddenly burned with humiliation and anger in almost equal measures. He nodded back to the police cars "What's the point in this lot? Cheaper than the pictures is it? Because you're certainly not making any attempt to help –"

"We help people you little shit. Not vermin –"

It came from nowhere. Words were lost in his brain and blocked in his throat like a six lane pile up. He spat, hard. It landed square in the policeman's face and dragged down his nose like a drunken sentence. Peter widened his eyes as he shot towards him. This is it, he thought. This is how I'm going to die. But then the policeman stopped. His head turned like a wounded animal as a pebble hit the floor with the click-clack of a sharp heel. A small trickle of blood curved down his face as he turned his head to the attackers.

"That got you moving didn't it? You fat cunt!" A gang of ten maybe twenty people Peter's age stood beside the car-shell nearest to the entrance. Two boys bared their backsides at the policeman who reddened and steamed in front of Peter's eyes. Girls held baseball bats and bit cigarettes tightly between their teeth as they made wicked eyes at the policeman; part come hither and part fuck off and die.

"Oi, mate," one lad shouted at Peter. "What you doing down that far – you coming or what?" The policeman swung back round to Peter. This hadn't been the plan but suddenly the alternative seemed unthinkable. With a sly shrug Peter ran into the estate as the policeman took a desperate swipe at him. The car door opened behind him though instead of pursuing him the policewoman tended to the injured party, dabbing his graze with a dampened handkerchief.

"We're going up the top now," said one of the boys.

"Right." Peter followed them as they trudged further into the heat. There were no more words. No confusion or verification. No We-Accept-You-As-One-Of-Us as he had always imagined the case may be. He just blended in quietly, subtly, like the ascetic final moment of a jigsaw puzzle; Peter just fit.

Chapter Sixteen

More fire engines pulled onto the estate. Splitting into separate strands like a peeling banana they pushed through the crowds towards the fires. At one end the chip shop stood tall and bright with thick, proud flames the colours of autumn, while the betting shop had fallen inwards and was sinking to the ground in shimmering embers that looked menacing and hungry. Hundreds of people had gathered around the warmth – shouting and chanting. Around them smaller, younger groups still ran without rhyme or reason. With little left to destroy they hurled bricks and bottles of fuel into the burning building – feeding the monsters despite the fact that by morning they'd be gone; disappeared to nothing.

Peter watched from the outskirts of the largest group. Carefully positioned he wanted to seem neither like an outsider nor be caught up in the thick of the action. Were things to reach their climax tonight he wanted to be able to make a clean getaway – stepping over anyone in order to do so. Already he had scanned the estate carefully like the laminated safety procedures on an aeroplane. To his front and rear were the main exits though these were the most likely to be cordoned off by the authorities if things got even worse. His ideal means of scarpering were at the sides of the estate – in the branching arms and legs of the area that lead to the walls and barbed fences. He could clear one of the walls. Only he'd have to select wisely – were he to hop into the long cut to the side of the estate then he could easily find himself trapped from either end. He knew though that while logistically plausible his plans were practically futile. He had become involved – reluctantly, maybe, but purposely nonetheless. He was on the vessel, swirling nose first towards the ground in flames and broken metal. How useful, he thought, would an inflatable vest and flashlight really be were you crashing from the skies?

The crowd turned as one away from the fire. Attentions became fixed on the fire engines. The first stone was cast and bounced from the side of one of the engines. Then another. And another. Bottles shattered on the loud red of the machine's bodies as they tried to force their way through. Rushing over they started to push and shove the machines meaning that once more they were forced to retreat.

He slowly moved himself around the group like at an art gallery in the vain hope that perhaps a variety of vantage points would all of a sudden spell out the meaning. Like the head-tilters outside of Athena who after hours of being rooted to the one spot with their chins touching their shoulders and their eyes facing opposite directions would suddenly declare '*A DOLPHIN!*' Peter's main problem was that in such situations he had always been inclined to nod "...*Oh yeah*." He had passed two decades without seeing that elusive water-based mammal emerge from the Technicolor fuzz. And now, standing amid the braying mob, he was sure that once more he would not get it. The anger he could feel like sound from giant speakers; it tingled in the air and made his skin feel edgy and chilled even next to the warmth of the fire. But it came from them, not from him. It just wasn't inside of him.

It was only as he shifted from place to place within the group, shimmying through the rows and clusters of revellers, that he saw Jack. He stood on top of the hillside looking down on the crowd stoning the tail end of the fire engines' departure.

Watching with flaring eyes it looked as though he was controlling it all through sheer force of will. Peter began to move back through the masses – pushing his way through small gaps between bodies, pressing himself away from the possibility of Jack altering his stance, seeing Peter. He didn't know why he was scared, but he was. Not frightened of whether the police may show up – well, maybe a bit – but more than anything scared that Jack might see him, as though he had to make him proud or at least not disappoint him. Peter didn't know whether he felt like Jack's responsibility now or whether Jack felt like his, but either way he knew that he could not be seen.

Jack hadn't noticed. He was too enthralled with the feral masses. As he watched them he imagined them on all fours, the sophistication of fully-formed words having left long ago; instead shrieking and grunting as they clambered over the remaining burnt cars, pulling at attachments and bashing them against the ground like prehistoric beasts trying to cause another spark.

His daydream was stirred by Tommy's hand on his shoulder. Tommy's miniature minions – none of whom were older than fifteen – surrounded them like the apostles.

"What's it to be then Jack?"

"We need more petrol," Jack said matter-of-factly. "And can you get a car too? Quick."

"You'll not even notice I'm gone," Tommy said as he ran off.

"What do we need the petrol for?" said one of the younger boys, cradling his dad's baseball bat in his arms.

"Last touch," Jack said. "We'll do the community centre in."

"And the health centre?" the boy asked enthusiastically. "No," Jack said resolutely. "We need that to stay standing. The community centre's going though – been closed for the past month anyway so they can't fucking complain. And make sure that lot know that this car's not for wrecking. We might need that too."

"Aye, right," said the boy. They scattered in different directions, frenetically sniffing the night for resources and tools. Tommy had already exited the estate through the back entrance. Others darted between the streets.

The camera van drove along the street cautiously towards the glow. Navigating his sandwich as carefully as the roads Carl tried desperately to compromise his falling saveloy dip with the jut of the regimented police cars.

"Ten points for a wing mirror!" Dan shouted from the back. Phillip guffawed but Melanie sat quietly, her mind having momentarily relocated to somewhere inside of the estate. She was pretty in a local TV sort of way – all traces of natural beauty had been buried by the android battle mask of industrial foundation and drawn on eyes and lips. It was a wiser investment in the long run. Get them used to the mask early on and then no-one will notice a decade down the line when it becomes a necessity rather than an optional insurance. *Drawn on eyes and lips never care*, her first editor had told her after she'd been ribbed by some of the old time boys on her first day in front of the camera.

"You two can fuck off as well," Carl shouted from the driving seat as he pulled in beside two police cars at the estate's entrance. "Here, you talk to them. I get fuck all sense out of this lot."

Opening the small window Dan stuck his head out and nodded at one of the seated policemen closest to the Meadow Well. "Evening officer," Dan said in his most professional voice, hoping that the authorities would see him as director, rather than runner.

"Sergeant."

"Sergeant. My apologies. We're from the BBC –"

"Kept that one quiet." The policeman nodded to the white block capitals on the side of the van.

"*Yeah*." Dan laughed a short *what-are-we-like?* laugh. "We were wondering whether or not we could do a brief spot on the developments of the riots, just there." He pointed to the scattered pile of trees. "It'll only take a minute – we won't get in the way."

"Son, you're already in my way"

"But sir, it'd be of public benefit to highlight the issue... we're with you on this one. We want to raise awareness, to –"

"Look." The policeman marched to the van and stood beneath the window like executioner beneath a guillotine, staring disdainfully at the Dan's lolling head. "Just do one. There's no filming here tonight. Or any other night. This isn't some old slag off telly bathing in baked beans outside the new Kwik-Save; these are people's lives we're talking about. And the longer you carry on pulling my dick and getting in the way the longer it's going to go on getting worse."

"Well," Dan said, reddening. Acknowledging his loss of the battle but eager to make a bid for the final word, he added, "In all fairness we wouldn't be interrupting that much now would we, *Sarge?*"

"You pompous little shit." The sergeant moved towards him with definite intent. Dan pulled his neck back through the porthole and slammed the window shut. Outside he heard the dead thumping of the policeman's hands against the side of the van.

"Nicely handled," Melanie said in her soft voice.

"Looks like it's a no," Dan said drily.

"You don't say," added Phillip.

"There's a back entrance," Melanie said. "Just round that corner."

"She's right – just up the road there," Carl spat through the munched dregs of his sandwich. "Want me to try it?"

"Anything," Dan sat back exhausted in his seat. "Let's just get this over with."

Driving around the corner Dan stuck his head against the darkened window of the vehicle. Shadows of fire and discarded shrieks filtered over the battered roofs of the houses and filled the van like an old smell.

"They're tearing this place to the ground you know?" he said. "Reckon the damage is well into the millions."

Melanie shifted uncomfortably in her seat, gripping her nervous hands beneath the weight of her body as she tried to shift the sticky, nauseous feeling that she had been unable to discard all day.

"Nah," Phillip said, kicking a stray wire beneath the seat. "There's not a million's worth in The Ridges. Built that shit-hole on a tenner and still had change for a pint."

"I grew up here," Melanie said quietly, staring into space. Dan and Phillip shared a surprised glance like schoolboys who've just found out a secret about their friend's sister. "So then Mel," Dan said as he scanned the van for his audience of one, "Is it true what they say about Meadow Well girls then?" Phillip let slip a small laugh.

Melanie smiled innocently and turned her head with dignity, staring out of the window. "I don't know Dan –" She shot forward and gripped his balls in her fist, squeezing tight so he doubled over sharply into her grasp. Screaming in agony she gripped tighter. "*You tell me!*" As he yelled for release she eventually let go. Dan returned to his upright pose as much as possible, but still cradled over his aching organs like a mother protecting her child. They made the rest of the small journey in silence. Melanie stared out of the window; Dan and Phillip looked solemnly at the floor.

"Here we are then," said Carl as they pulled to a slow stop. No-one moved.

"Come on," said Phillip. They marched out of the van in unison.

She'd seen it on television. Pictures in the grainy local rags had showed a fraction of the destruction but black and white makes everything look gentler she had found. It's why it was so much easier to fall asleep in front of old comedies than modern blockbusters. In colour the estate was hellish. Hot and burning the streets were drawn like mourners – sad in a way they had never been when she had pounded through them as a child. Fire and crowds now tore through streets; dented houses looked frightened and spoilt. The sound of the helicopters dulled the swarms of rioters but not enough.

"Do you think we'll be able to do it with the noise?" Dan asked, pulling wires from the van and plugging them into the standalone camera that he aimed at the bull's-eye of the estate.

"Shouldn't be a problem," Phillip murmured, fiddling with the lens of the camera. "You alright Mel?"

She walked unsteadily to the side of the van, transfixed with the burning estate. In the background their voices blurred and mellowed. Children stared at her in the distance, enthralled by the van but anxious about approaching until given the go ahead from a higher authority. She felt her body fill up – tears formed in the corner of her eyes but she blinked them away. Her throat stung and her legs felt weak and unreliable. She felt it coming and couldn't control it. Heaving once she threw up beside the van. It hurt but made her feel lighter and more relaxed. Wiping the acidic trail from the corner of her face she stood back up and rubbed the redness from her eyes.

"Mel...?" Phillip said, still fiddling with the camera.

"I'm fine," she snapped, grabbing the microphone from his hand and taking her place four steps back from the lens. "Let's just do this and get out."

Dan and Phil retreated to the back of the camera. Bumbling

through his mandatory shot numbers and time codes she heard Dan mutter "Action" harshly. Inside she felt the switch flick and professionalism steered her through the motions like a guide dog.

"You join us outside of the Meadow Well estate in North Shields where for days now a series of violent protests have taken place following the death of two young joy riders – Darren Pearson and Thomas Eastlake. The area – formerly known as The Ridges..." Dan stared between her and his watch and nodded in agreement at the valuable footage. From behind a rusted red car with broken windows sped onto the road beside them and ground to a halt inches from their legs.

"Hold on!" Dan yelled. "We've got company."

Phillip clicked the power button of the camera to red and Melanie relaxed – her shoulders dropped and her stomach pouted an inch as she returned to her civilian stance. The car door flew open so hard that it locked immediately at an awkward angle and Tommy stepped out violently.

"You!" he shouted, pointing towards the camera.

"Excuse me, sir," Melanie tried, "We're from BBC Newcastle and we're reporting on the riots. I grew up in the area and we were wondering whether or not you would like to comment on –"

Jumping from the car Tommy stormed towards them. He thrust Melanie to the floor and grabbed the camera in one hand. Hurling it to the ground the glass of the lens smashed and scattered onto the gravel.

"Oi!" Phillip walked towards him furiously before realising the physical difference between the pair.

"You want some do you mate?" Tommy screamed, marching towards Phillip, who shirked backwards towards the stability of the van. "Because we've got plenty of supplies in there – could have ourselves a little Guy for the fire if you like?"

"Look mate –" Dan said

"*I'm not your fucking mate!*" Tommy yelled. The veins in his neck bulged and writhed like snakes trying to consume his head. "You lot want to watch what you're saying. And *you*," he turned to Melanie, "should know better!" He picked up the broken camera and threw it angrily at the side of the van. It dented the metal, narrowly missing Dan's head.

Tommy got back into the car and sped past them, missing Melanie by inches and disappearing around a corner.

Dan and Phil moved towards Melanie who remained on the floor. "Come on love let's get you up" said Dan, placing his hands beneath her arm.

"Get off me!" she said, pushing him away. He did as instructed and took two steps back. "Phil get the other camera quick and let's get this over with."

Pulling the secondary camera from the van – a larger, more archaic beast than the premier one – he set it up in the exact same spot. Melanie looked behind her into the estate once more as she brushed herself off. Mostly she still felt pity, but she also felt bitter from the altercation. She was still bereft for the mess in which the estate was rotting and burning its way to the ground. But a tiny part of her had become angry. Tommy's actions had reminded her of just what it was she had pulled herself up by the bra straps to avoid; the sort of people that had turned her home into the reality of the rumours she had heard all the years she had grown up in it, defending its honour even after she had stopped believing her own praise for the mean streets. With the camera rolling she took her place once more and pulled her hair back to its unnatural resting place.

"Action!"

She breathed in deeply and began.

Chapter Seventeen

She kept the volume low. The blue TV screen light masked the red pulsing that shone even through the closed curtains. The gentle, inaudible hum of the tinny voices combined with her bopping knee had managed to lull Nicole into a state not too far from sleep. Her eyes fought off the tiredness that crept over her body, but she remained resilient in her effort: too tired to fight completely but too anxious to give in to rest. Murmuring, Nicole took another sip of warm milk from her bottle and moaned just once.

"Enough is it sweetheart?" Nathalie asked, knowing that no answer would come. "I know that feeling babe." She placed the milk on the bed and stared intensely at the television, lip-reading to occupy herself while she swayed the baby back and forth like a gentle tide.

The TV showed clips of London – glittering and golden. It was the furthest she had ever been and the sight of it made her nostalgic. London had been the only time she'd actively tried to escape it all. To sever the umbilical chord with her bare teeth and flee to pastures new.

She'd gone just after her first pregnancy. The one that got away. The one that she hadn't known about until the pain came on the dance floor at Jumping Jacks disco. Halfway through the closing song the feeling had arrived with three brittle thumps before settling into a more established stream

219

that crushed her bones beneath the ache. And then the blood. A tiny trickle like the opening bars of the rag. Then it had gotten unbearable. Three paramedics had to carry her out though she quickly checked herself out of hospital, eager to keep her dignity having just lost her baby. She walked home feeling halved.

Of course she had never known it was there. Why should she? Her tits had ached for a few weeks but she wasn't done with growing by that point. And the curve of her hips was surely because of her sudden fondness for pints and shorts. Afterwards no-one knew save for the friends that she'd been with that night. And they were so full of their own secrets that blowing hers would have been a bad move. But she missed him. It had been a Him, she'd decided. Strange how you could mourn something you never really had.

She left the school three days after that. Her GCSEs had been acceptable but none of her friends were at sixth form so there was little reason to stay. Sweet sixteen and empty as a yawn. She had nothing to lose. She wanted to go where the streets glittered with diamonds not blood and glass, and the air felt fresh and prosperous without the lingering scent of smoke. She'd imagined it was going to be one big chance, like a city-wide careers convention with dancing and drinks, sophisticated conversation with fast, beautiful friends. A city that felt like a shimmering glamour model not a traumatised rape victim. Only she hadn't accounted for the fact that on her budget no where's different. Same bastards, different accents.

She'd returned a week later with her tail between her legs and her lovebites masked in stolen foundation. Soon after that she met Anthony and things began to seem a little bit more bearable. That urge had never left though. Once you've even tasted the possibility of escape it consumes you completely, hiding in your thoughts and dropping at inconvenient moments like a leaky tap. Sometimes she would be feeding

Nicole, or washing the dishes, or putting on lipstick for no reason in particular, and she'd get the thump. An urge or a craving that she could only describe as lying somewhere between panic and ecstasy. How easy it would be to leave. She'd done it once before. It wouldn't take any forethought. She could pack up a spare set of underwear, grasp the few remaining pounds that littered the house and fade away. Jump on a bus with no number and arrive at a new life somewhere else. Maybe with a new name. She could change her hair, dull her accent and teach herself about history, art or politics. She could become anyone or anything.

Nicole whined again. "Come on sweetheart," she said, placing the baby in the cot that she had rested on the bed. "Let's try and sleep properly." She turned off the television and sank London in the gradual blackness of the static, which cackled and fell silent. "Let's rest and see if tomorrow's not better." She moved her photo album onto the floor and checked the security of the ironing board that held the bedroom door in place. "Safe as houses, eh babe?"

As she turned to get into bed she felt a brief chill. A draft snuck under the door and whispered up her spine and across her neck. Pin-pricks tickled her back and her stomach turned to lead. Slowly she removed the ironing board from the door and, checking that Nicole lay safely, she walked into the landing of the hallway.

"Hello?" The creak of the floorboard was louder than her voice. "Is someone there?" No answer. The draft in the hallways was intense. The whole room felt chilled, like outside had gotten inside. She walked slowly to the landing.

"Come on," said Johnny, dragging Paul through the streets by the loose fabric of his sleeve. "We need fuel."

"Let us finish this first." Paul sucked the tail end of his cigarette before throwing it into the window of a burnt car.

"Priceless that one was." He chuckled to himself. "I helped set that one alight," he said proudly to Johnny.

"So fuck. This is going to be bigger than that. Where should we go? Is the shop still standing?" Paul asked as he scanned the streets for potential resources.

"Ellen's is. The bottom shop's been torched. So is the offie. Reckon Ellen might have some left though – she's got tons of shit there all the time. And everyone knows she keeps a week's worth of stock out the back."

"Try there then."

"No." Paul stopped dead in his tracks and pointed. "There."

The house was dark but the windows still intact, which to Paul implied occupancy, ergo supplies. And the door was open wide. Practically an invitation. "*If they're daft enough...*" He ran towards the house and Johnny followed him.

"Belter." Johnny said as he ran. "Who's is it?"

"Ant's, I think."

"Fuck that." Johnny took two steps back towards the curb. "He'll do us in."

"He's away. Rigs."

"He'll find out."

"Will he shite. They'll never know it was us."

"He'll find out."

"And we'll say Jack told us to."

Johnny paused and thought for a second, still unsure. "Alright then."

"Hello?" Nathalie walked to the top of the staircase and saw the door, which had edged itself open. She took one step down, relieved that it was nothing more sinister. She took a further step before she heard the footsteps.

"Come on," the child's voice said in the background. She froze. The footsteps grew nearer, practically at the door. Terrified she managed to order her thoughts momentarily and pulled herself back up the stairs, hiding behind the banister as the footsteps entered the house. With her hand over her mouth she listened. It sounded like an animal moving – four feet, light and lilting like a flippant typist just before home time. The scuttled through into the living room. She began to feel wrong – like it was her that shouldn't be in the house, making their intrusion so much more complicated than need be.

"Hello!" Johnny shouted from downstairs. He picked up the baby's blanket and threw it at Paul.

"Fuck off man." Paul bundled the blanket and threw it at the television. Two family photographs and a small clock – an engagement present from Shirley – fell behind the television and banged loudly against the uncarpeted floor where the wires lay. Nathalie jumped at the sound. Without standing she turned and edged forwards on her hands and knees, slowly avoiding the floorboards which she knew to be weak. Just before getting into the bedroom her hand slipped and she pounded onto the floor.

"*Shit*," she whispered. Aware that she'd failed in her stealth mission she gave in to temptation and scurried clumsily into the bedroom and slammed the door behind her, barring it with the ironing board.

Nicole stirred with the noise and began to writhe in her cot. "Shhh baby, it's OK. We're fine. Nothing's going to hurt us." She said, pulling another chair in front of the door. "Come on now, don't be silly," she said as Nicole's sobs increased to a gentle wail.

"Hear that?" Johnny said to the thumping ceiling above them. He smiled and picked a half empty cup of water and smashed it off the floor.

"Here! Missus!" Paul shouted. "Missus, we need some fuel, you got any?" No-one answered.

"Stupid bint," said Johnny. "Let's check the kitchen."

They pulled drawers onto the floor. Upstairs Nathalie heard cutlery smashing against the lino and closed her eyes, desperate to block everything out. If escape wasn't an option then complete denial was often second best she had found. It was no use though. She tried to concentrate on the ringing in her ears or the soft feel of the baby – wriggling and breathing beneath her trembling hands – but she could hear them. Footsteps pounding on her floor, the slamming of her cupboard doors and laughter as they touched and joked with her things.

"Here." Johnny passed Paul a kitchen knife.

"What for?"

"Just in case. May as well. I'm taking one." He tucked the knife into his trouser belt and Johnny did the same. Finally when each of the drawers lay discarded and emptied on the floor they walked back into the living room.

"Fucking useless this." Paul kicked a baby's highchair over in a rage. "Going to have to try the bedrooms."

They moved quickly. Upstairs Nathalie panicked. "Come on," she said in a whisper. "Come on; we're alright." With Nicole held tightly to her chest she crawled into the small walk-in cupboard that Anthony used as storage. The wardrobes were full of her clothes – old pieces of brightly coloured material that she could never bring herself to throw away. She'd never have fit inside. But the cupboard was practically empty and in her stuttered thoughts it was the only safe place she could think of. With her feet pushed against the door and the baby at her chest she pressed herself tight against the back wall of the tiny square box – pitch black like a coffin – and held her breath.

There was a thud. The floor trembled and then it was still. Voices whispered outside. The second thud was bigger. It shocked the baby who raised her hand to her mother's mouth as though trying to silence her.

The ironing board and chair flew across the bedroom and smashed into the dressing table where Nathalie kept her sparse makeup selection.

"Here, missus," Paul said as he entered the bedroom and walked straight to the door of the cupboard. "We need some fuel. We'll not hurt you."

Nathalie didn't move.

"I'm not fucking kidding!" He pressed his head against the door.

Nathalie jumped at his raised volume but stayed silent.

"We'll get you if we have to," Johnny said, shoving Paul out of the way and pushing at the handle of the cupboard. It opened by a fraction and Nathalie heard a small whimper that could only have come from her. A stream of light pushed through a gap by the door as Johnny slid his hand inside. "Just say and we'll leave you alone." She released her feet fractionally from the door, allowing him to sneak his hand in a little further, before slamming them back. His fingers splayed in agony and she heard him scream. He pulled his hand away and fell onto the bed.

"Fuck off!" Nathalie screamed in the darkness, pressing her feet tighter and tighter against the door.

"*Fuck are you playing at?*" hissed Paul, pushing Johnny back onto the bed as he tried to get up, nursing his throbbing paw.

"Look, Mrs," said Paul gently, pressing his forehead against the cupboard door. "We only want some fuel. We'll leave you alone if you just say. Have you got owt or not?"

"Please go away," she said wearily.

"Just tell us where it is and we'll be gone," Paul tried again.

"Fuck's sake!" she screamed at the door as Nicole began to cry. "Just try the cupboard under the sink and please... please go away."

"Right." He moved away from the door and dragged Johnny with him. Passing the cupboard he kicked it hard as he walked past, still tenderly probing his wounded hand.

"*Bitch!*" he shouted as he left the bedroom.

Nathalie heard them move beneath her once more. Down the stairs and into the kitchen they crunched on the broken plates, kicking knives and forks that scattered the floor. She heard them move back through the living room. Another crashing sound. Something breaking on the coffee table, maybe the coffee table itself. And then with the crack of the front door slamming but not shutting they were gone, and it was quiet once more.

Jack saw the front door hanging open as he skulked on the pavement, waiting for Tommy and supplies. He ran forward to shut it and make sure she Nathalie and the baby were OK. He felt a passing nausea once more but swallowed it awkwardly like a bad taste. He was in too far; there was no going back now, not for anyone. Then a noise. He saw their shadows move through the living room and then the boys came out of the front door, looking satisfied and proud. Laughing, one of them held a can of lighter fluid in his hands as they skipped from the garden and through the front gate.

"Here," Paul shouted to Jack who stormed towards the house murderously. "We got some lighter fuel. Had to tear the house apart a bit to get it like but it was no bother, just one lass and her bairn hiding –"

Before he had a chance to finish his sentence Jack swung his fist as though Paul's face were a car window that had to be broken. His words stopped and so did he. His small body flew backwards silently, blood checking the surface like grubs after the rain. He groaned and rolled over too dazed to retaliate. Not that it was an option. When Jack acted he did so for a reason.

"Think you're clever bothering lasses with bairns?" Jack swung his foot into the centre of Paul's stomach and watched as he snapped in two, hunched around his injury.

"Nah," Johnny stuttered, frozen to the spot and still clutching his hand. "Jack man, we were just doing what you said. Just getting the fuel." Jack laced his boot into Paul's back once more "Leave him Jack," Johnny whimpered.

He swung around and grabbed Johnny by the throat. Johnny felt his oxygen supply become a privilege not a right. Unable to breathe he became weightless as Jack lifted him inches from the ground and brought him closer to his red, pulsing face. With weak hands Johnny grabbed the arm that supported and it felt like metal – a grip that would release only of its own accord.

"Bother her again and I'll kill you."

"Right, right man... just let me go..." Johnny's voice was forced and pressurised.

"I'm not kidding." He brought him up to his face so that Johnny's limp body dangled in the air like strange fruit. Jack's boiling forehead touched his nose as he spoke.

"Right man, alright," Johnny stuttered as Jack released his grip. He fell to the floor and rasped back sore breaths into his fragile lungs. Jack stared at them and then edged forward, warning of another imminent attack. They got up and fled. He let them go and picked up the discarded lighter fuel.

He placed the tin can gently inside of the door. He wanted to go inside but he knew that it would be wrong. Nathalie would be fine. She'd blame him though. He dug out a five-pound note from his pocket and secured it beneath the weight of the almost empty tin. Shutting the door carefully he stood outside to check that it remained in place. It was as much as he could do to make sure they were safe and he was certain to make sure he did it properly.

From the bottom of the garden, at the foot of Nathalie's

crumbling wall, he grabbed a fragmented brick and threw it as hard as he could through the bedroom window of her next-door neighbour. It shattered and a light turned on. Thin lace curtains blew out into the night and caught on the shards of glass but no figure appeared at the window. For some reason this pleased him.

Chapter Eighteen

"Did you get it?" Jack asked Tommy, who was sitting triumphantly on the roof of his stolen car, a burning cigarette dangled from his smirking lips like some bizarre centrefold cutting. He pulled a hand through his greased hair and tutted.

"'Course I did. There's plenty inside. Couple of that lot's got some as well; reckon they want to join in with the festivities." Jack scanned the group that had assembled beside Tommy's car. They were a sorry bunch. Most of them would have been put down were they born with four legs. He could tell that they had been out for the duration of the riots; tufts of untouched hair sprouted out of their bumpy, scarred heads. Ruffled coats with black smudges and nominal fire damage clung like tar to their nervy frames and stank. Fire damage was a somewhat unappealing quality in a prospective arson partner, Jack noted. But at least they showed willing. And they could take some of the flack if he persuaded them it would further their inclusion.

Two of the group had been Darren's comrades from school. They had been his own obedient posse. The ones whose tablets he used to take in return for his elusive protection from the St Cuthbert's Lads. *"They'll break your legs and leave you for dead,"* Darren had warned them in his spiel. *"You never wondered how Billy ended up with the patch? They'll get you lot too, unless they know you're mates with me – then they'll leave you alone.*" Terrified they would pass him their daily doses, plastic capsules every colour of the rainbow, and breathed a sigh of relief that once more the menaces were to be held at bay by their armoured knight. The majority of Darren's adolescent readies came from flogging the tablets as ecstasy to the younger kids on the estate. The thought of even Darren being able to get one over on them made Jack chuckle to himself. They were easy prey – soft and eager like warm wax, which he could twist into whatever he wanted – and what he needed was someone to take the brunt of the responsibility for his opus.

"Whatever you like." Jack shrugged. "let's just do it."

"Where are we going?" asked one member of the group, sloshing his can of oil nervously by the side of his leg.

"Finish off the community centre," said Jack as Tommy jumped from the roof and got into the car. "Meet us round there." Jack climbed in as Tommy revved the engine, swerving around the gang and darting the short distance to the centre.

The fires had begun to dim to a more tranquil ripple of flames and embers that gnawed through the foundations of the shops and houses. The smoke spun through the streets like a web. It made even breathing seem difficult. Sooty clouds dried their mouths and scratched desperately all the way down their throats and into their lungs like victims dragged through a dark alleyway. Throughout the smashing and the violence people had begun to look even less healthy, bent double like beggars and spluttering through the milieu as they marched on amid the heat. They still broke and smashed wherever possible though; fed the ephemeral flames with wasted fuel as glass bottles and bricks shattered against crumbling surfaces. But they had begun to look tired. Their actions seemed pitiful and grudging as they coughed and shirked through the warmth of the night. They looked like slaves, or soldiers on whom the futility of their mission was finally dawning. Slowly they began trudging towards the community centre.

Towards the front people moved quickly and angrily. Mostly the young and the stupid, those still gilded with the sugar-fix of enthusiasm. At the back though they dragged their heels and hung their heads, their pace and temperament allowing them time to look around for the first time as though vision had been restored. Their own homes were smouldering and rotting. Curtains twitched like nervy ticks and the faint din of crying babies jangled on the wind like chimes. Some even segued into side streets and alleyways as they walked onwards like absorbed minerals disappearing into the ether.

Peter walked through the crowd with his eyes scrunched, trying to blink his way through the stinging fog. He remained somewhere in between the front and back of the crowd. He wanted to seem involved but not eager, and nor did he want to have to talk to the chattering classes dawdling behind. The best lies are the briefest, he had found; the more detail he had to go into the more likely he was to trip himself up and be unmasked before the crowd. This was not a thought he relished and so he gauged his speed, ensuring that he remained perfectly central, suspended and floating with the movement of the group.

"Here bud, do you want something... or something." A boy cut through the crowd to Peter's left and offered him two oil canisters like a hardened souvenir tout.

"No thanks."

"Fiver for the both of them?"

Peter shook his head and moved slightly faster aiming to lose himself among the deluge so he wouldn't be bothered again.

"Here mate..." he heard the boy try again behind him.

Brian, Adam and Glen were already standing outside the community centre when Jack approached. A wave of bodies advanced biblically over the grass verges that led to the large two-story red brick building on the far edge of the estate.

"Where are the others?" Jack asked as he dragged canisters of oil and petrol from the back seats of the car, handing them to those with empty hands.

There was a moment's pause before Glen could no longer stand the silence. "Had to go home. Their Mams wanted them back in before it got too late." He spoke hurriedly like bare feet on hot sand. "We can do it on our own though."

Jack rolled his eyes and took an axe in his spare hand, leading the small troupe to the side of the building. Using just the blunt edge of the axe's head he took out the upper pane of the fire escape window in one swift swing of his arm. Edging through the glittering shards he pulled the metal leaver from inside and opened the door.

"Come on."

They followed him in. Walking through the main hallway they gathered in a circle in the main foyer of the building.

"We'll split up. Everyone go a different way" he instructed them, pointing his bat down the three small corridors that branched from the heart of the centre. "Cover everything – the floors, the walls, the ceilings. Get the oil everywhere then get out – meet out the front when you're done. I'll see to it in here."

They disbanded quickly, running through the corridors, trailing liquid like aeroplane slicks in a clear sky. Glen crashed through the double doors as he dragged a canister along the ground and watched as the marbled drops oozed across the floor. When it became lighter he picked it up and waved it around his head – strategically dribbling down the walls and ceilings until the entire area was damp. Tommy and Brian did the same. Leftover sugar paper wall charts and posters sagged and tumbled to the floor as they soaked in the sweet smelling fuel that tickled when they breathed in.

Adam ran ahead and mounted the small, narrow staircase to the first floor where another reception area led to two rooms that had been used for the adult numeracy classes. He upturned a desk on which scraps of yellowing paper lay discarded before raising the canister carefully above his head and lowering the spout onto where the wall met the ceiling, carefully allowing each drop to slip from the top to the bottom of the room.

In the central hallway Jack placed his can of oil on the ground and swung his bat at the fixtures. They were all that was left – a scattering of seating arrangements, two old computers, some magazines and building blocks that hadn't been packed up before the building became obsolete. He picked chairs from the ground and smashed them against walls. Swinging his axe into the fire alarm a dense chime screamed at him as the sharp head of his axe cut through the red plastic square and bit hard into the wall. He tore it back out and brought it down onto the table by the main seating area. Small toys and torn magazines flew across the room as the table broke in half.

Leaning over the counter he picked the computer up and dragged it across the receptionist's desk, placing it gently onto the floor and turning the monitor on. As it coughed and spat electronic messages on screen – password request, data keys – he swung his oil can around wildly, pooling it in the centre of the room and artistically in arches up the walls.

Peter anxiously watched the building with the crowds. It felt strange to be observing something so still and to know that something so big was about to be brought down to its knees by nothing more than three or four angry young men with too much time and fuel on their hands. There was the sound of glass and the crowd cheered. Then more. From the four side windows two bodies crawled like maggots from a dead animal and blended into the group.

A loud smash sounded and the front door to the building burst open. Out Jack stepped looking poetic and dangerous. Another great cheer. He walked over to the crowd.

"Where's Adam?" asked Tommy.

"Didn't he come out with yous?" Jack said.

"No. I think he went upstairs."

"He'll be down in a bit," said Jack, shoving a piece of cloth into the top of a glass bottle.

Peter moved back through the crowd, pushing against bodies like he was swimming from a predator, eager to keep his presence secret from Jack. He managed to reach the outer layer of revellers where the mass of bodies were dotted throughout the streets and not packed tight and warm like one giant being. It was then that he heard them.

"Armed police put down your weapons!" Five riot vans pulled onto the estate followed by a braying horde of police cars. Behind them regimented troops carrying plastic shields followed determinedly. The van doors swung open and the crowd disintegrated.

"Shit" Jack whispered.

Peter didn't wait long enough to adhere to the etiquette of such situations. He and a small group ran as fast as they could as armoured guards stepped out from the vans. Streams of faceless, black clad warriors poured out carrying long guns and truncheons. Masked like killers they ran towards the remaining crowd who fought and yelled in vain.

Peter didn't fight. He fled. Hard and fast. The background noise dimmed as he flew forwards, running to the furthest point of the Meadow Well before hitting the tall wooden fence.

"You want a leg up?" shouted one lad who had managed to keep up with his desperate pace.

"Yeah." Peter swallowed through the sting of adrenaline and sharply inhaled night air.

The boy cupped his hands and allowed Peter to step up and onto the top of the fence. Bending back down Peter grabbed the boy's arm and dragged him up and over. In the distance he noticed, firstly, how far he had travelled in such a short time. Maybe he was a runner after all. Then he saw the guards. Residents ran from the police who grabbed them and pressed them onto the ground. Some fled in packs, making their capture all the more difficult. Chants of 'Filth' and 'Killers' could be heard over the commotion. Noises that had been so often repeated throughout even Peter's involvement in the riots that they had lost their meanings completely, become dead weights on the tongue.

They grabbed whoever was in reach. Truncheons and guns pressed into delicate areas, handcuffs applied without question regardless of age or potential threat. Peter watched it unfold while gripping the edge of the wall, slowly feeling his body slide uncomfortably towards the other side. Like the black and white films his university friends had been so fond of, he had to occasionally remind himself of who exactly the villains were.

From inside the community centre Adam heard the racket change from a low murmur to a more frenzied din. He stopped kicking the empty filing cabinet and walked over to the window at the front of the room, slipping on a sweet smelling patch of oil as he went. He saw what seemed like a hundred riot police storm through the streets. All of them armed, most carried clear shields that they pushed painfully through denser gangs like a comb through wet hair. He couldn't see Jack or Tommy. A gang of girls ran past and were pushed flat onto their stomachs by men in uniform.

The fumes suddenly began to make Adam feel giddy and warm; like he himself were the petrol, fizzing and sticky and anxious to be lit. But through the fumes a sense of dread crept like damp and took over his thoughts. He pushed himself from the window and ran to the door, ready to flee the building. More crashes emanated from outside and he stopped himself at the top of the stairs.

The stench of the building became overwhelming and washed over his consciousness in waves. He began to feel both heavy and light all at once and a pressing nausea grew in his belly. He wiped the sweat from his upper lip and swallowed hard to stop himself from weeping. Were he to stay in the building then he would risk the highly likely petrol bomb within the non-too distant future. But as the police shrieks began to overtake even those of the rioters outside, the thought of stepping from the final touch to the riots themselves – alone and reeking of fuel – was something he was eager to avoid. He'd be locked up. Double locked. They'd toss the key and let him rot. A quick and painful death or a long and excruciating life seemed in the space of thirty seconds to have become his rock and hard place. He dangled one foot over the lip of the stairs and looked back into the room he had so thoroughly drenched in petrol as he weighed up his dilemma.

From the wall on which he balanced unsteadily Peter saw Jack strike a match and tease a small flame onto the tip of the cloth that dangled from the glass bottle he held.

Jack felt it in his hands. He knew that Adam was still inside, but they were there for a reason, a greater good. He felt it in his hand, and then with one smooth arch through the air it was gone. The bottle flew from his control and smashed through the window of the building's ground floor. There was a stillness as the attention of the remaining mob turned to the centre.

With just a small roar at first it didn't look too different. And then there was a bang – a volcanic projection that swallowed the building whole and turned it into a ripple of white and orange that stung to look at. The momentary stillness was shattered with a great birth of light as the pause button was removed and the police continued against the thunder of the flames. The helicopters trailed random clusters of rioters on foot – the x-ray beam tracing their movement as the police followed them stealthily.

The ground moved beneath his feet and Adam, though physically unharmed by the sensation, fell to the floor. His mind became blank. Jack had done it anyway. And he was going to die if he didn't move. This was all he could think. Despite fleeting notions of a Sunday school afterlife or the concept of a world without him, instinct took over until all he could focus on was the fact that it would hurt like hell.

He stood up and peered down the stairs. The lower floor of the building wailed and groaned and the floor became warm to the touch. The smell increased and black smoke began creeping up the stairwell to the main reception area in which he sat, petrified. Standing up, a door banged open and a tornado of flames swirled angrily around the main frame of the door and teased up the wall as it mounted the lower steps.

Adam crawled along the floor towards the large window behind the waiting area. With a fallen chair he slammed the glass frantically with no rhyme or rhythm to his blows. He pelted the glass as the smell of the flames grew closer and the warmth of the room began to bulge around him like the air was turning solid. He felt his back drip and his legs shook beneath him. Tears blinded him. He screamed loudly and shouted Jack's name as the chair bounced back once more from the reinforced glass and fell to the floor. The smoke danced mockingly through the hallways and shadows began to build on the wall of the staircase as the flames grew nearer and nearer to his floor.

He edged forward towards the fire. The skin of his face began to prickle and dry as he got too close. Breathing hurt. The fire had almost reached the top of the stairs and was only moments from eating into the damp pools he had drawn from the reception area towards the staircase. Panicked and desperate Adam noticed a small window to the far left of the corridor. Only one small pane but perhaps big enough to escape from.

He pulled the chair from the floor and threw it as hard as he could at the window. It shattered almost silently against the backdrop of the fire's roar and without allowing himself time to smile at his victory Adam ran towards it. He didn't notice the jagged beads of glass that punctured his skin, nor the blood that oozed down his arm. Even the scorching warmth at the back of his neck could have been happening to someone else. He felt euphoric with release as the chilly night air filled his lungs and drenched his face.

Pulling himself to the window's ledge and without even checking the safety of his destination Adam threw himself from the first floor. Before he reached the ground a great rush of light filled the sky as the upper floor of the centre erupted.

Peter saw that Jack hadn't moved. A team of three policemen travelled cautiously towards him. Poised with truncheons and shields their masked faces edged forwards like bulls ready to charge. But then they stopped. Jack didn't move. He stood stone still and watched the building rise and fall in the bizarre light. As the boy fell from the side of the building the policemen closest to the centre changed their course and rushed over to the broken pile where he lay beside the rising fire. They dragged Adam away from the flames and lay him on the path in front of the centre. Jack noticed them surrounding his limp body – bloody and awkward and perfectly still – and stirred himself from his daydream.

Peter wanted to stay. He wanted to see what Jack did and to find out whether or not the boy who fell would be alright. He wanted to ask Jack whether he knew someone had been inside when he threw the bomb. There was no way he couldn't have known. He probably even knew the boy's name. Peter wanted to stay and find out whether or not Jack would go any further, but he forced himself away. He ran until his legs stopped dead beneath him.

"Come on," Jack said as two policemen eventually began to move away from Adam and towards him again. He dragged Tommy by the arm towards the side of the burning building.

"Where?"

"Just come on." Jack pulled harder.

They ran to the back of the centre where the car still sat. Jack took the driving seat and Tommy sat beside him on instinct.

"What we going to do?" asked Tommy

"Make it as hard as possible for them."

Jack drove slowly round the building, carefully choreographing the fleeting crowds. Four riot police ran toward the car as Jack reversed in a perfect semi-circle, positioning himself in alignment with the centre of the estate, in front of which a police car had parked. He stared at the car and nodded. Tommy followed his gaze and felt a sharp inevitability tug in the bottom of his stomach.

"You ready?" Jack said, with his eyes fixed on the target.

"Yeah." Tommy nodded. "Got any last words?"

Jack didn't reply. Slowly pressing his foot down the car roared around them for a split second before they began to move forward.

They saw it tear through the mess like a clean blade. It was coming straight for them.

"Get out of the way," Dobson yelled. From the passenger seat she pulled at the steering wheel of the car. Constable Richards, holding tightly on to the wheel in front of him, remained transfixed with the glaring figure behind the wheel of the approaching vehicle. He fixed his stare, certain that he was calling his bluff.

"He won't do it," he said surely.

"He fucking well will." She panicked as the car shot towards them. She placed her hand on the door, contemplating escape. But by then it was too late. It hit them head on. They shot backwards in their seats, heads rolling like they had been freshly severed. Their arms gripped tightly to the steering wheel and dashboard trying to absorb as much of the shock as possible.

Tommy flew forward on impact and felt a crunch inside his head as his nose merged perfectly with the dashboard. Jack shot forward but snapped back like a yo-yo onto the soft headrest. The front of the car was crumpled and smoking. The police car was worse though. Inside they were still. Two vans pulled up either side of the vehicle as police dragged his tender body from behind the wheel.

"Police, get down. Get down now!" They gave him a good kicking as he stumbled to the floor. Behind him the fire burnt angrily and proudly as he stumbled to his feet. Three men surrounded him with cuffs but he didn't go easily. Jack spat in the face of one as the butt of his gun swung into his ribcage. Still kicking they raised him from the ground and smashed him into the floor. Jack knew he was screaming but wasn't sure what. It was as though the sound was not his own. He felt a knee in his back and then a tearing sensation as his arms were prized behind his back and the two flimsy metal bracelets clicked too tightly around the skin of his wrists. It took three of them to carry him into the police car as he flailed and writhed like a fish out of water. He caught one final glimpse of the fire, cut up into flickering shadows by fleeting rioters who were becoming outweighed by the number of policemen, before the doors were slammed shut.

Chapter Eighteen

The interview room was cold and clean with an artificial warmth that you only noticed once you stepped back outside into the real world. No-one was supposed to see him. Jack's behaviour in the back of the riot van had been what the officers on the desk had diplomatically referred to as difficult, the way you tell a parent that you 'met someone' when really you mean 'fucked'. One officer had been kicked where it hurt. Another head butted where it showed. And the female driver was still in tears over the malicious whispers that Jack had uttered throughout the short journey. He was like that, Peter had found. Jack was big and loud but it was his quietness that had the potential to cause the most damage. He could be an avalanche packed in a snowball and you'd only know it once he hit you with his full, murmured force. Jack knew which buttons to press.

But Peter had links. Limited as they were but poignant nonetheless and after half-an-hour of wrangling he had managed to secure ten minutes for both he and Shirley to separately see Jack before he was locked away awaiting trial. Another formality. With Jack's insistence, and his pride, over his guilt there was no question as to his fate.

Shirley hadn't lasted long. She emerged frail and older from the room within her first five minutes and sat down without making eye contact with Peter. They had travelled there in rigid silence. Shirley with her head pressed tightly against the car window and Peter navigating the roads intensely as though on a new and unpredictable route. As they drove the houses and factories blurred with the flush of the streetlamps and became a slumbering orgy of exhausted workers. The riots had already shifted overnight from local crisis to fish and chip wrapping; no morals taught, no lessons learned – yesterday's news.

Along the corridor pre-weekend pissheads and minor dealers screamed their innocence as they were pushed to the ground by uniformed men with angry eyes.

"Nah man, it's for personal use," a colossal man with more tattoos than skin choked into the polish of the floor. "Medicinal, innit? I've got ME... glaucoma... *AAAAH YOU FUCKING PIG!*"

"State of him," Shirley said quietly to Peter. "Looks like the door of a pub bog."

"Get him into the cells, *now!*" shouted the policeman, raising his knee from the base of ink-boy's spine as they dragged him by the ankles to another row of rooms.

"Are you alright?" Peter asked her, resting his hand on hers. Her body temperature dipped as she pulled her hand from his and nodded, turning her head away as the tears emerged.

"I better go in. Wait here. I'll give you a lift home," Peter said.

She nodded again without looking at him.

"How are you Jack?" Peter said after the night officer had left them alone in the room. A tape recorder sat unplugged on the table along with Jack's untouched glass of water. Other than that they were alone. Harsh halogen lights made the room seem odd, too clean and orderly, detached from the chaos outside like they had stepped out of their living room and into the kitchen of another house. The blood on Jack's face – an informal warning from the injured riot police – looked fake and childish like a ketchup prank on Halloween. Jack didn't respond. He looked past Peter towards the door. Peter hesitated for a while before sitting down uninvited, pulling his chair tightly under the table until he was as close to Jack as the policemen had informed him was wise.

"Are you hurt?"

Jack remained silent. He looked at the door. Then the wall. And after rolling his head back on his neck, revealing more bruises to the top of his chest, fixed his stare on Peter and allowed himself one crescent moon of a wry smile. "Just my arm really. From the crash. Take off these cuffs and I'll show you."

"Funny."

"It wasn't a joke."

"It fucking well was," Peter said loudly. Still relatively quietly if compared to most other people's ability for noise, but as loud as Peter was willing or able to go. "What did you think you were doing Jack?"

"Which part?" he said again with a snide enjoyment. He reminded Peter of the cats that play with mice before halving them with a snap of their jaw. Only Jack had no attack left.

"All of it."

Jack's smile dropped as his chest rose; inflated with the assurance of a practiced speech. "It was for Darren and Thomas." He spoke eloquently and bluntly, manufacturing each word with the precision of a blacksmith hammering hot metal into battle weapons. Peter had heard it before though; over and over again until the mantra had become stale. It was all smoke and no more fire.

"No."

"Yes."

"No. It was at first. Like Shirley said. I saw you long after it had stopped being for Darren and Thomas – a crime of passion and all that. It was boredom and anger by the end, the only currency you ever really deal in. You were enjoying it, weren't you?"

"Got to find pleasure in the simpler things in life," Jack said stonily, staring past Peter once more. The only thing he liked less than being questioned was being wrong.

"Is that what you told Shirley?" Jack shifted uncomfortably like his head was being held to a violent image "Or your friend Nathalie, or her baby?" Their names were the flap of the butterfly's wings from which the hurricane develops. Jack's entire demeanour changed in front of Peter as he continued talking. He made himself pulse with anger and fury. It was a thin, flimsy veil though. It was the eyes that gave him away. After decades of avoiding contact through fear of further awkwardness Peter had grown to realise that everything you needed to know could be found in the momentary glance of an initial reaction. Jack's glance lingered; a mourning, sad look that almost said sorry. "Where are their simple pleasures going to come from? *Visiting day?* The bus ride to get a pint of milk because all the shops have been burnt down? Getting to open the curtains every morning onto a bombsite because you couldn't handle –"

Jack shot forward. Still handcuffed he lunged noisily from his chair towards Peter. It stopped Peter suddenly in his speech but this was his only reaction. He remained still and calm. Jack stopped too, bent over and raised from his seat; his face pushed threateningly towards Peter's unflinching gaze. He looked at him and narrowed his eyes.

"Would it really make it any better?" Peter asked. Jack remained frozen and then slowly sat down, staring at the floor. "I brought you this." Peter slid the cracked photograph onto the table. "I'll see you again Jack," he said before standing up and walking towards the door. Jack remained still as Peter banged the door quickly but loudly to alert the guard's attention.

"Come on," he said to Shirley in the corridor. "Let's get you home."

She stood up with her back towards the cell door and walked on slowly with him, heading back to the car. Back to the mess.

Shrieks emanated throughout the wing at night. Innocent pleas whistled past the sealed, barred window of the tiny room. The space was sterilised white with the sort of deathly striplights that make everyone look as though they hadn't seen daylight for weeks. Beneath their glare Jack felt the throb of tiredness build behind his eyes. Sounds ended abruptly but rang in his ears as he tried to blank out his surroundings. He concentrated hard and began to fade away. The room dimmed until there was only a thick, dull darkness in which he didn't have to think. A clean blackboard of a thought where nothing was spoilt and nothing had gone wrong. For a brief moment this made him happy.

A loud crack against the door snapped him back into his own grim reality.

"You need anything else lad?" hollered the watchman from outside the door. Jack didn't respond. He held the scratchy blanket around his body as he sat bolt upright and wished, fleetingly, that he could have changed things. Not stopped them but changed them. The riots didn't seem real anymore. In his mind they had already become that story – the funny recital – '...*remember the time*...?' – in which the teller always declares your attendance despite a certainty that you weren't there.

Muttering outside of the door stopped him from drifting off again. He wouldn't allow himself to sleep. He was too alert, poised like he was ready to strike. He sat at the farthest edge of the hard bench, left of the middle, that would double up as a bed for those inebriated enough to nod off in such circumstances.

The muttering persisted and he found it increasingly irritating like a growing itch that progressed until you were so agitated that you scratched until it bled. He tried to stop his thoughts but the only image his brain would allow him was that of the baby and her mother. Sometimes he would wonder whether or not guilt was a fallacy: an invention that people used to make themselves sound more interesting. It was simply a quality that he did not have. The part that seeped that particular emotion into other people's veins and minds was empty inside of him and nothing he ever did, to him at least, felt like anything but the right decision. Maybe this was it though. As he thought about the pair of them, forgoing pity for his own mother, running to standstill in the aftermath of his own mess, it was this that caused the churning sensation that stuck like glue to his skin and thoughts.

A fly zipped and fizzed at the corner of his head. He didn't look up. The door in front of him scratched and the muttering faded to a halt. He knew they'd raised the spy hole. They were watching him and he didn't know why. Didn't care either.

The fly spun in a halo above his head before falling gently down and landing on the exposed skin of his hand – teetering for a while before settling weightlessly onto the stretch between his thumb and wrist. He watched it twitch, hesitant in its new surroundings. It walked fussily around on the unfeeling surface of his skin before settling gloomily back on the patch at which it began. He wanted to kill it. Just one quick slap and it would be all over. It would have been the kindest option. A quick sting and it would be gone. The alternative was worse. A night with Jack in the windowless room, stagnating and rotting until boredom and dud air slowly suffocated it and it felt itself die. He should have killed it but didn't. Slowly he raised his head and locked his stare on the tiny glass circle of the heavy door, narrowing his eyes fractionally. He was still for a moment before he heard more muttering and the scratch of the peephole locking in place. He heard their footsteps begin and fade.

"Lights out," a voice shouted from the furthest end of the corridor. There was a mechanical buzzing noise that bounced off the hard walls of the cells and a stirring of anxious guests who threw themselves excitedly at the doors and walls of their temporary purgatories at the suggestion of the first change in circumstance in hours. There was the sound of something hard hitting a metal gate three times that seemed to hold a strange significance. At its wordless request inmates quietened and settled to a low fuzz of noise and movement. Jack stayed still and listened to them settle. He closed his eyes to try and rest. And then it was dark.

Shirley said goodbye to Bob and reminded him of their meeting at The Comet later that evening. As she put down the phone she felt a chill and pulled her cardigan tighter around her shoulders until the fabric began to stretch out of shape. On the mantelpiece stood an excitedly torn envelope containing the official details of Jack's day in court. Beneath that sat an old money box of his that he had never found adequate use for. He hadn't been granted bail, which suited her down to the ground. The sentence wouldn't be that long. And as much as she missed him she felt it was too soon. She wanted it to be tidier for when he got back. She wanted the streets to be cleaner and safer. No trace of his damage left. Anthony's return from work would provide him with further enthusiasm. She hadn't told Jack this over the phone the night before as she wanted to see the reaction on his face when she told him in person. Her second Visiting Order was due in two day's time.

The weather outside was brighter than it had been. Still cold, but the autumn rays had become intense over the past fortnight since the riots ended and the whole mess was illuminated in a bright glow like a spotlight shining on evidence.

The detritus was now a mark of shame, something already seldom commented upon. Those involved who hadn't been arrested walked with their heads down through the rubble, increasing their pace and avoiding eye contact. No real attempts had been made to neaten the streets. Immediate patches outside of other people's houses or the few remaining functioning shops had been nominally swept but on the whole the estate lay broken and withered.

Staring out of the window she saw them walking together closely and smiling. Nicole sat upright watching the pavement disappear beneath her feet. Anthony pushed the pram in which she sat and Nathalie held tightly to his arm as though he would float away if ever she let go. They saw Shirley at the window and waved on their way past. They would be gone within the month. Shirley smiled as she saw Nathalie sneak her hand into Anthony's back pocket and grope him sharply. He jumped in shock and laughed, kissing her neck as they mounted the pram onto the step leading to their front garden.

Humming a nonsensical tune out loud Shirley strolled through the living room and tried to keep warm, planning in her head the outfit she would wear for her meeting with Bob that evening and wondering whether buying a new pair of court shoes would be a good investment or an ominous jinx on Jack's future dealings. As she turned on the radio the hiss of dead air from the broken aerial was louder than the music itself but through the din she could just about make out the song playing. Pulling her cardigan tighter around her body she felt a hard, flat round shape in the pocket with a hole in it. Inside she found a tarnished fifty pence piece that she couldn't remember having lost in the first place.

She passed it backwards using her thumb and forefinger as chance spun awkwardly like a square wheel – heads, tails, heads, tails, heads, tails. It moved jauntily to the rhythm of her chilled, hard hands and with every flip of its face it answered a different question she had posed in her head. Each time it provided the correct answer. The one that comforted her the most.

Three sharp pops sounded at the furthest edge of the living room as the opening drops of a storm spat against the window. Dispelling her own concerns for the cost with a shake of her head Shirley clicked the fire twice before she felt the bars ignite and ward off the chill of the rain before it had a chance to develop. With a sigh she dropped the coin into the money box. It clicked on impact and slid to the bottom of the growing yet meagre pile of copper that she had been saving since his first day in custody. She sat down heavily in her seat and closed her eyes, unable to suppress a dim smile at the thought of Jack's return.

Book Group Questions

At Legend Press, we only publish books that are well worth talking about, that will generatate conversation, as well as being written by some of the world's top writers and being fantastic reads. After all, the reactions and conversations they generate are what makes books so unique, thought-provoking and so amazing.

A vital part of book conversations are book groups and to be of assistance we've listed a few questions in no particular order that may be worth considering. Whether you take them into account or not, we expect this book to generate debate and please feel free to send us any comments:

info@legend-paperbooks.co.uk

1. How did you feel about the Meadow Well Estate setting?

2. What are your thoughts on the character of Jack, from his introduction at the start of the novel through the narrative development to the end?

3. Did you have have any thoughts on the relationship between Jack and his mother?

4. What was your instinctive reaction to the actions of Darren and Thomas?

5. How do you feel towards life portrayed within the estate and that outside of its walls? Are the two kept completely separate?

6. What was your understanding of the relationship between Jack and Nathalie?

7. How do believe the character of Peter developed through the novel and what did you make of his relationship with Jack?

8. What was your overall reaction to the actions taken by those on the estate following the accident?

9. What was your reaction to the end of *Ashes*? Did it have any effect on your perceptions up until that point?

10. Matthew Crow is one of the UK's top young writing talents. What did you make of his style and what comments do you have on him as a writer?

I hope you enjoyed this fantastic novel. Please come and visit us to learn more about Matthew Crow and also other amazing books at Legend Press: **www.legendpress.co.uk**

Matthew Crow was born in North Shields in 1987. At the age of 16 he moved in with family in Darlington to complete his A-Levels at Sixth Form College. During his teens Matthew freelanced for several online magazines writing pop reviews, which led him to move to London to work freelance. Matthew quickly secured a literary agent and is one of the most exciting young writers of his generation.